'I don't give a damn about compromising you!

It's your feelings I'm not sure of.'

Araminta laughed unsteadily. She stretched out her hand to his sleeve in a gesture of appeal that spoke louder than words. 'My feelings are perfectly simple,' she said. 'I love you, Jack.'

He swept her to him then with all the force and vigour he had until this moment kept in check. Araminta's breath was crushed out of her body in his embrace and she welcomed it, responding with a fire and passion that she had barely suspected she possessed.

It was Jack who broke across her newly aroused and still unfettered instincts. His whispered, 'Are you sure?' shattered the mood.

'I'm sure I love you,' she said, but there was melancholy in her voice where there should have been triumph.

Jack looked down at her, his body tense as if at last something he had waited for would happen, but only if his luck held. 'What's the matter?' he asked.

'Nothing,' she said and then, since that was patently untrue, she added, 'Nothing we can do anything about,'

He kissed the curls nestling against his shoulder. 'Tell me,' he suggested.

Janet Edmonds was born in Portsmouth and educated at Portsmouth High School. She now lives in the Cotswolds, where she taught English and History in a large comprehensive school before deciding that writing was more fun. A breeder, exhibitor and judge of dogs, her house is run for the benefit of the Alaskan Malamutes and German Spitz that are her speciality. She has one son and three cats and avoids any form of domestic activity if she possibly can.

Previous Titles

A CIVIL MARRIAGE
SCARLET WOMAN
WOLF GIRL

HIGHWAYMAN BRIDE

Janet Edmonds

M I L L S & B O O N L I M I T E D
ETON HOUSE 18-24 PARADISE ROAD
RICHMOND SURREY TW9 1SR

*First published in Great Britain 1990
by Mills & Boon Limited*

© *Janet Edmonds 1990*

*Australian copyright 1990
Philippine copyright 1990
This edition 1990*

ISBN 0 263 76795 7

*Set in Times Roman 10 on 11¼ pt.
04-9004-79406 C*

Made and printed in Great Britain

HISTORICAL NOTE

BOTH the Red Lion Inn and the Flying Bull at Rake actually existed—and still do, though only the latter is still a hostelry. The Red Lion was notorious for its involvement with smugglers in the eighteenth century and the then current landlord was implicated in the singularly unpleasant disposal of two Revenue men in 1747—around the time my heroine was born.

The Saracen's Head in Winchester is fictitious but the Black Swan is not. The City Fathers seem to have been rather keen on building gaols: from the sixteenth to the nineteenth centuries, they appear to have had a debtor's prison—the Westgate, now a museum—a Marshalsea, a House of Correction, a Bridewell and a County Gaol, in addition to today's prison. Of the earlier ones, only the Westgate still exists. I have taken a chronological liberty in using the Bridewell: it was built about twenty years after my story but, although no trace of it is left, its site on the older site of Hyde Abbey is known. I have been unable to discover where its predecessor, the House of Correction, stood, nor could I find pictures of either institution, so my Bridewell is entirely imaginary in every sense except the fact and place of its existence.

Few of the great town palaces of the eighteenth century aristocracy remain today. Burlington House is perhaps the most notable of that sort of private dwelling and is the one upon which I have very loosely based Cosenham House. Copenore is the derelict Cams Hall, near Fareham. It was built later than my story, but to so typical a mid-eighteenth-century pattern that it fits very

5

well. It is a house that has fascinated me since childhood but it was requisitioned by the Army in World War II and never recovered. It had sunk beyond repair when I last went over it, some thirty years ago, an eloquent and poignant testimony to the military talent only to destroy.

Cosenham and Copenore are the Domesday names for Cosham and Copnor, the former now a suburb and the latter a district of Portsmouth.

Janet Edmonds.

CHAPTER ONE

LADY ARAMINTA WAREHAM stood to one side of the schoolroom window and looked down on the drive. A groom was walking Thomas Kineton's horse up and down and had been since the visitor's arrival. The fact that no message had been sent to take the animal round to the stables was a clear indication that Lord Cassington did not expect the interview with their neighbours' son to be a long one. Araminta sighed. It was not a felicitous sign. A voice from behind echoed her thoughts.

'Is the horse still there?' The enquirer was Lady Georgiana, at fourteen the youngest of the Earl's four daughters.

'Yes, he is.' Araminta, at twenty, was the eldest.

'That means that Papa intends to say no,' her sister remarked in satisfied tones.

It did, but Araminta did not like the smugness in her sister's voice.

'I shouldn't sound so pleased about it, if I were you,' Araminta told her. 'After all, you're at the bottom of the line, and if the rest of us don't get married first you may well be doomed to become Mama's spinster companion.'

'I don't think things will come to quite such a desperate pass as that.' Georgiana was unmoved by the prospect of the fate just described. 'If I don't receive an offer, or if Papa refuses his permission, I shall just run away.'

'And what will you do then, miss?' Araminta cast a glance at her sister's sampler. 'You certainly won't make a living as a seamstress.'

'I shan't try. I hate sewing. I shall think of something—after all, there's plenty of time yet. Besides, I should quite enjoy being Mama's companion. Mama is very good fun—in a quiet sort of way.'

Araminta could find no fault with this, since Lady Cassington was good-natured and as easygoing as controlling four headstrong daughters allowed her to be, but it would never do for Georgiana to win an argument, and she searched for the appropriately cutting rejoinder. Before one sprang to her lips, however, the need was anticipated by the third occupant of the room.

'I don't suppose she will be when she's eighty,' Lady Florentina interjected. 'Old ladies get very crotchety. Haven't you noticed? Think of old Lady Combe.'

Georgiana did, and was silenced.

No one spoke after that until the unmistakable sound of the front door opening and closing, followed by that of booted feet running down stone steps, rose to the window above the porch.

Georgiana's needle and Florentina's pencil both stopped in mid-air.

'Is that him?'

'Has he gone?' they asked simultaneously.

Araminta watched Thomas's slight form mount his horse, and noted the dejected line of his shoulders as he took up the reins and turned the very useful hunter down the drive. Not once did he glance up at the schoolroom window where he knew the sisters sat, though the elder two were too old for further formal instruction.

'Yes, he's gone,' she confirmed. 'It looks as if Georgie's supposition was correct. He doesn't have the bearing of a man in raptures with the world.'

'I expect he'll soon fix his interest somewhere else instead,' commented the worldly-wise Georgiana. 'I once overheard Lady Combe telling Mama that all this talk of love was nonsense. It was all right for dairymaids and gardeners, she said, but it had no place in the lives of ladies and gentlemen. "Our sort", she called them, and Mama agreed. At least,' she amended honestly, 'she didn't *disagree*.'

'No one ever does—not with Lady Combe,' Florentina pointed out. 'She doesn't go on and on about whatever it is for half so long if she thinks you share her views.'

'In this instance, I think you'll find most people do agree with her,' Araminta said, and added, as she heard feet running up the stairs, 'Oh, dear. This must be Izzy.'

Lady Isabella was the second of Lord Cassington's daughters. At eighteen, she fitted neatly into Lady Cassington's pattern of having a child every other year until her doctor's advice to have no more, despite the absence of an heir, had to be faithfully adhered to. Araminta had often wondered whether this very precise spacing of her offspring had been a matter of pure chance, of discussion and agreement between both parents, or the result of clandestine planning by one or other of them. It was not the sort of question one could ask one's mother, but she thought it might account for the fact that her mother, not having been burdened with the chore of producing a child every year, looked both younger and fitter than any of her contemporaries.

Isabella, like Georgiana, had her mother's golden hair and pale complexion, unlike her sisters, who favoured Lord Cassington's side of the family, with dark hair and an ivory skin that was all too easily spoiled by the sunshine. Neither the Earl nor the Countess could possibly have planned that the colouring of their children would neatly alternate so perhaps the spacing, too, had been pure coincidence. The thought crossed Araminta's mind as she stepped forward, her hands outstretched, to comfort her clearly distraught sister.

Isabella shook off the proffered comfort. 'Go away, Minty. It's all your fault. Oh, how I hate you! I never thought to hear myself say so, but it's true. I do.' As she finished speaking, the tears which she had been holding back burst forth but, despite her stated loathing for her sister, she made no further attempt to shake off the comforting arm round her shoulders that led her to the sofa beside the empty grate.

'So Thomas was unable to persuade Papa to consent to your marriage,' Araminta said. She already knew the answer, and not only from her sister's demeanour. Thomas Kineton was a pleasant, sensible young man, the only son of fond but not doting parents. He was a perfectly respectable catch, though Isabella, who was the beauty of the family, could expect to do better. She had, however, fallen in love with Thomas, and Araminta believed that he, in his prosaic way, loved Isabella. What he certainly lacked was the intellectual ability to convince Lord Cassington by dint of trenchant argument.

Isabella spoke with difficulty between sobs. 'Of course he was! Papa told him he wasn't the least opposed to the match in principle, but that he couldn't possibly allow me to be married before you because to do so would be to condemn you to the shelf——'

'So *you* could be Mama's companion,' Georgiana interrupted gleefully.

Her sisters ignored the comment. 'Papa said that as soon as you find a husband he'll be happy to consent to my marrying Thomas,' Isabella went on. 'He told Thomas it would be a good test of his devotion.' And her tears burst forth with renewed vigour.

'I don't think anyone doubts Thomas's devotion,' Araminta assured her.

'That's just as well, isn't it?' Georgiana butted in. 'It could be severely tested. After all, Minty is twenty and no one has offered for her so far, even though she was presented for two Seasons at enormous expense. How on earth she's going to find a husband down here in the depths of the country where we know there are no suitable candidates for her hand, when she didn't succeed in London which must be full of them, is a mystery to me!'

Araminta sighed with exasperation. 'Will you please hold your tongue, Georgie? What you say may very well be true, but it doesn't comfort Izzy, does it?'

Isabella sniffed. 'That's just what's so lowering,' she said. 'Georgie's right. I don't mean to be unkind, Minty, but the fact remains that, if we have to wait till you get married, it could mean waiting forever and I don't think I *could*.'

'I don't think the position is quite as hopeless as that,' Araminta said. 'I think Papa will give up all hope for me after a few more years. Then he'll let you marry Thomas.'

'A few more years! I don't think I could wait that long.' Isabella looked at her sister curiously. 'Minty, don't you *want* to get married?'

'Of course I do! At least, I very much want to be mistress of my own household, which is what marriage amounts to. The trouble is, I've never met anyone I had the slightest desire to hold house for, and even when I met someone who wasn't positively repugnant they didn't seem to be very appreciative of my tendency—which I really did try to curb—of saying exactly what I thought. Papa said most men simply don't want to know what a woman thinks.'

Florentina looked up, surprised. 'Papa does. He and Mama discuss all sorts of things—and he's always willing to explain almost anything to us, if we ask.'

'I think Papa is rather unusual in that respect,' Araminta told her. 'He was explaining the Treaty of Paris to me when the vicar called, and when the vicar discovered what we had been discussing he told Papa it was scarcely a suitable subject for ladies. He said it jocularly, but he was really quite shocked.'

'And what did Papa say?' Florentina asked with interest.

'He said he was no admirer of ignorance in either sex and that sensible questions merited sensible answers.'

Florentina considered this answer. 'I don't suppose Mr Wootton liked that.'

'He didn't. There was a distinct chill in the atmosphere for the rest of his visit. Papa's right, though— about most men, I mean. If one makes an intelligent comment, they look incredulous, and if one attempts to discuss something at any length their eyes glaze over and then, under the pretext of fetching lemonade, they disappear.'

Georgiana stared at her eldest sister open-mouthed and then shouted with laughter. 'Is that how you frightened all your suitors away? I wondered at your total lack of success, and when I asked Mama she just said, "Hush, dear, that's Minty's business, not yours," so I hushed, but I still wondered. It sounds quite foolproof. I shall bear it in mind when my turn comes.'

Isabella sniffed. 'I do wish you'd been a little less nice in your taste, Minty,' she said reproachfully. 'I'm sure you could have dealt with *one* of them, and then there would have been no obstacle between Thomas and me.'

Araminta laughed ruefully. 'Indeed, I wasn't unduly nice, Izzy. The truth is that none of the eligible men was seriously interested in acquiring a wife with a very limited dowry and three sisters to whose own portions he was likely to be expected to contribute. That was a far greater handicap, I assure you. If I had had eighty thousand in the funds, I fancy my unfeminine opinions would have been regarded with the indulgence of minor eccentricities. Would you like me to speak to Papa on your behalf? I'm quite willing to assure him that I don't mind your being married first. I'll take my chances afterwards, but it would never do to risk losing yours.'

Isabella was unsure whether to be grateful for the offer or offended at the implicit suggestion that Thomas might not wait and that, if he did not, she might not easily find another suitor. She reminded herself that Araminta was not unkind and had not intended anything more to be read into her offer than a willingness to stand aside for her younger sister. 'I don't think it would do any good,' she said doubtfully. 'He didn't speak as if he thought there was any doubt about your *eventually* finding a husband, and I don't think he will let me stand in your way—which is what I should be doing if I married first.' She sighed an uneven, sob-laden sigh. 'I just don't know what I'm going to do if he goes on withholding his permission.'

'You'll have to run away with him to Scotland,' Georgiana suggested helpfully.

'Georgie!' Araminta exclaimed, shocked at such a suggestion from one so young. 'You're not supposed to know about such things!'

'I don't see why not,' Florentina remarked. 'After all, you know about the Treaty of Paris and that isn't even useful.'

'The two issues are not comparable,' Araminta said crossly. 'No lady should even consider elopement, and I'm quite sure Izzy is as conscious of that fact as anyone else.'

Georgiana was not so easily silenced. 'Then she'll just have to wait until Thomas runs out of patience and marries some farmer's widow with buck teeth. Then she can hide her breaking heart by running away to sea or becoming a highwayman or a soldier.'

'Don't be silly,' Araminta said.

'She can't. They're all men,' Florentina pointed out.

'She'd just have to wear breeches.' Georgiana had no intention of letting go of a perfectly good scheme while there was still life in it. 'Of course, sailors get very sick and soldiers get hit by musket-balls, so if the choice were mine I'd take to the high road.'

'They hang,' Florentina told her.

'Not always.' Georgiana's tone was defiant.

'Always,' Florentina said with finality, and then amended it. 'Well, more often than sailors are sick or soldiers hit by musket-balls.'

'That's enough,' Araminta said firmly. 'I've heard you two indulge in silly arguments before, but this is beyond anything. Besides, can you see Izzy doing any of those things?'

The two youngest sisters looked the tearful subject of their discussion up and down in a frank and appraising manner, and agreed that the image conjured up was not one in which it was easy to believe. Florentina went further. 'In fact, I can't quite imagine Izzy climbing out of her bedroom in the dead of night and escaping down a ladder, can you?'

Georgiana agreed, and even Araminta, much as she deplored this conversation and felt for Isabella, was obliged to admit to herself that her heartbroken sister was the least likely of any of them to take such drastic steps. Isabella would weep, but she would obey her father and, however willing Thomas Kineton might be to wait for her, sooner or later his parents would start introducing him to other eligible young women and encouraging him to think of marriage with one of them. They would be failing in their parental duty if they didn't. So far this grim probability hadn't occurred to any of the other sisters and, since it could only serve to depress Izzy's spirits further, Araminta had no intention of bringing it up. First of all she would speak to their father.

She persuaded Isabella to lie down in the privacy of her own bed-chamber, away from the idle chatter of schoolgirls, and led her there herself, drawing the curtains and thoughtfully placing some freshly laundered handkerchiefs on the bedside table. Then she ran downstairs and sought out her father who had, as she suspected, retreated to the solitude of his study after his interview with Thomas Kineton and a more distressing one with his second daughter.

The Earl looked up as his eldest daughter came in, and put his quill aside. 'Is Izzy a little more calm now?' he asked.

'No, Papa, she's not. I've persuaded her to lie down. In the quiet of her own room she can cry herself out, and certainly Georgie and Flossie weren't helping her with their somewhat childish suggestions. Did you really tell Thomas they must wait until I'm married? They are truly attached, you know, and, although no one could call him a brilliant match, it's as good a one as any of us can hope for, bearing in mind the fact that none of us will have anything more than a modest portion. Besides, it could be a very long wait—and Sir John and Lady Kineton are going to want to see their son married, if not to Izzy, then to someone else. Might it not be wise to see at least one of us comfortably settled as soon as may be?'

The Earl sighed. 'I'm trying to consider the interests of both my daughters,' he said. 'You're a sensible girl, Minty, so I don't have to beat about the bush. You're twenty, and your chances of finding a suitable husband diminish by the month. I had hoped that two London Seasons would solve that problem, but it was not to be. All the same, if Izzy is seen to marry first, everyone will assume you prefer spinsterhood and there will be even less chance of a suitable offer being made. For that reason, I told young Thomas they would have to wait. However, I have to be realistic and—as you so sensibly point out—he can't be expected to wait forever, and I have no desire to see him slip through our fingers. Quite apart from the improbability of someone equally suitable offering for Izzy's hand, she doesn't have your down-to-earth temperament and would, I know, take it hard. I've told Thomas—and I shall write to his parents to this effect—that if, at the end of a year from now, you are still unattached, I will raise no further objections. I think, even at their relatively tender age, their love should survive a year, don't you? It's not as if I'm forbidding them to see each other. They will be able to go on much as they have in the past.'

Araminta nodded. 'Izzy didn't mention that. Perhaps she was too distraught to comprehend fully what you had said. It seems a very reasonable arrangement, but I don't expect Izzy will consider it so, not for the time being, at least.' She paused. 'So I have a year to find a husband. Does that mean the expense of yet another London Season?'

'That is something I shall discuss with your mother. I feel bound to say that, if the first two were unproductive, I'm not very hopeful about a third, especially not at your age—it rather smacks of desperation.'

'With good cause.'

'Indeed. On the other hand, if we brought Izzy out—something which, if she agreed to it, would at least take her mind off her temporarily breaking heart—there would be no harm in your being with her.'

Araminta wrinkled her nose. 'I'm not sure which would do the worst for my chances: to stay at home while a younger—and more beautiful—sister comes out, or to be the shadow to her sun.'

'You do yourself less than justice, Minty. Izzy is undoubtedly a beauty, but there is nothing remotely shadowy about you. In any case, I suspect Izzy will reject the opportunity. She has little interest in frivolity—far less than you have—and will be afraid that I'm trying to find a better catch for her than young Kineton. What about you? Do you think you can turn another Season to your advantage?'

Araminta threw her arms wide in a gesture of mock despair. 'Oh, Papa, how can I answer that? I failed to "take" before and I haven't changed since then. I suppose I could pretend to have done so, but that would be dishonest. I might catch a husband, but it would hardly be the basis for a satisfactory partnership, would it? I can only suggest you have a word with the Bishop. Perhaps he knows an eligible curate. My chances are at least as good in that direction as at Court!'

Lord Cassington smiled perfunctorily. 'You're a good girl, Minty, but it really is a matter of some seriousness and, to tell the truth, I haven't the slightest idea what's to be done for the best. Perhaps your mother will have some ideas. Perhaps if the two of you put your heads together, some solution will present itself.'

'Perhaps it will,' Araminta agreed, though privately she doubted it. The Earl and the Countess must have discussed it many times before and it was hard to believe it might be more successful now. There was nothing to be gained by expressing this opinion, however, so she took her leave and, after a brief hesitation, sought out her mother.

Lady Cassington was seated by the window of the sitting-room attached to her bed-chamber. The clear northern light fell on her embroidery frame, enabling her to match silks and set stitches with the precision necessary to produce the exquisite work for which she was noted. She was, Araminta thought, simply an older, fuller version of Isabella, with the same pale gold hair and blue eyes. She was dressed, as always, with taste and care, never in the forefront of fashion, but never trailing behind like any provincial squire's wife. The Earldom of Cassington was far from being one of the country's wealthiest estates, but neither was it poverty-stricken, save by the most demanding of standards, and, although Araminta had been aware that the expense of her two London Seasons—and particularly of the second—had been an unwelcome burden on the family's finances, she knew too that it had not been crippling. Some retrenchment had been necessary. The installation of drainage systems in several fields was delayed, as was the addition of a library wing to Cassington Hall, one of the Earl's most cherished schemes and one which was unlikely to proceed until all his daughters were satisfactorily established. But nothing had been stinted to make Araminta's debut into society a success, and she remembered in particular the splendour of the hugely hooped gown Lady Cassington had worn when she had accompanied her daughter to her presentation to the young King George III and his wife, Queen Charlotte Sophia. Araminta's failure to attract an offer could not be laid at her parents' door.

The Countess glanced up briefly as her daughter came in, and then completed the stitch she was setting before speaking. 'I imagine you've come to plead Izzy's case,' she said.

'I've come to discuss what's to be done for the best,' Araminta replied. 'It's not as if you and Papa regard Thomas as quite ineligible. Papa says they will have to wait a year and, if I am still not spoken for by that time, he'll give his consent.'

'Does that seem unreasonable?'

'Not at all. Lowering to one's self-esteem, perhaps, to learn that in twelve months one will be regarded as beyond hope, but not unreasonable.'

'You speak as if a husband is out of the question.'

Araminta sat down on a little gilt chair whose seat bore witness to her mother's skill with the needle. 'Have you a candidate in mind?' she asked.

'Your father and I have been expecting Thomas's visit any time these last eight or nine weeks. Do you think we haven't racked our brains to think of someone of our acquaintance who might be eligible or have a son or cousin or nephew who is? The problem is, Minty, that younger men require a more substantial dowry than we can provide, and older men are inclined to prefer a wife who is more——' she searched for the right word '—more *biddable* than you are inclined to be.'

'Perhaps—if I did have another Season—I could make a very great effort and restrict myself to conversational commonplaces and to fluttering my eyelashes over my fan,' Araminta suggested.

'The effort would kill you,' her mother said, without rancour. 'Besides, it would hardly be honest. Think of the shock the poor man would get once you were married.'

Araminta giggled. 'He would, wouldn't he? It would be almost worthwhile, just to see how the poor creature dealt with it! Still, we mustn't forget the other side of the coin: such a man would drive me to distraction, and I think I should almost certainly have poisoned him by the end of the first month. Of course,' she added reflectively, 'that would make me a *very* wealthy widow, so perhaps it's not such a bad scheme after all.'

'Such talk is most unbecoming,' Lady Cassington told her daughter, but in a voice which indicated that the reprimand was a token one, for form's sake. There was nothing in her expression or demeanour to suggest that she was either surprised or shocked that it had been forthcoming. She paused briefly and gazed vacantly out of the window. 'Such a pity Mr Wootton is unsuitable,' she said.

'Mama, quite apart from his being unsuitable, he also has a wife, five children and another on the way. That surely must render him ineligible, as well!'

'It's called clutching at straws,' Lady Cassington told her, unmoved.

'I don't think a married man, however tedious he may be, constitutes a straw. I did suggest to Papa that he write to the Bishop and ask what he could offer in the way of a curate,' she added helpfully.

Her mother looked doubtful. 'Curates do vary, of course. When one considers that there are some quite remarkable clergymen about, it's reasonable to assume that they must have been remarkable curates at some stage in their careers. It's just that I can't recall ever having *met* a remarkable curate. In any case, I can't quite see you as a clergyman's wife. By the time you had taken the Bishop aside and told him just how to run his diocese, your poor husband could wave goodbye to any hope of preferment.'

'It seems we're agreed I'm a hopeless case,' Araminta said. 'We might as well accept that fact and let Izzy's betrothal go ahead.'

'It will do neither of them any harm to wait a few months, and who knows? Something may turn up. I suppose you could do the Paris Season,' the Countess added doubtfully.

'No, Mama. I have no desire to marry a Frenchman, and any Englishmen I met there would be likely to be the scaff and raff of this country packed off by their devoted families to get into trouble elsewhere. No, thank you. I prefer to remain unwed.'

'Words easily spoken,' Lady Cassington remarked. 'It may not seem so dreadful a fate from the viewpoint of twenty years of age. I fancy it might look very different from forty, or fifty, or sixty.'

'Then I shall have to have recourse to Georgie's solution,' Araminta said lightly.

'And what was her solution, may I ask?' The Countess made no attempt to hide her misgivings.

'To put on breeches and join the navy.'

'Preposterous—but how very typical. If that young lady ever transforms her hoydenish ideas into action, the whole family will have to take refuge in the colonies!'

Araminta laughed and took her leave. She hesitated at the schoolroom door and then, instead, went to her own room at the back of the house and stood looking out over the garden below. A formal parterre of the old-fashioned sort lay immediately beneath her, and was likely to remain because the Earl loved it, but beyond lay the Countess's extensions and improvements, separated from the parterre by a ha-ha and formed—because the Cassingtons could not afford to indulge themselves in the luxury of a gardener to uproot everything—by a careful adaptation of the trees and pasture already there. Immediately around Araminta's window were the gnarled and twisted stems of a fig-tree which had, her father told her, been there even before the parterre. Only Isabella, the least adventurous of the sisters, had never used it as a short cut into and out of the house.

Araminta's heart went out to Isabella. She had never been in love herself and her observations suggested that it was hardly worth all the torment. But Isabella was in love, and with a young man who was entirely suitable, which was not always the case. Lord Cassington would have given his consent immediately had he not still had Araminta on his hands, and she therefore felt guiltily stricken that her sister's happiness should be risked for her sake. Araminta was not hoping to find a man with whom she would fall in love. She would be entirely content with one whom she could like and respect. That, it seemed to her, was the recipe for a contented union. Love would follow, though not, perhaps, the tempestuous, disturbing passion that seemed to have overtaken her sister—and for the pleasant, unexciting Thomas Kineton, of all people. For her part, Araminta would be very happy to settle for the sort of relationship that appeared to exist between her parents.

It was all very well to have these theories. Putting them into practice was quite another matter. In the first place, there was the small difficulty of finding a man who fitted her two fundamental criteria. She had met several men whom she liked to a greater or lesser degree, but none for whom she had felt any lasting respect. Perhaps she was a great deal too nice in her requirements. Perhaps she should lower her sights and persuade herself to be satisfied with less. Looking back on the couples she had met during her two Seasons in the capital, she could only conclude that most women were considerably less demanding.

She sighed, and the fingers of her left hand played with the mourning-ring she invariably wore on her right; a panel of ivory set in gold, it bore a silhouette portrait of her grandmother. Araminta had been very close to the Dowager Lady Cassington who, for her part, had been particularly fond of her eldest grandchild and had ordered the ring to be made before her death. It was, she had told her son, the only way she could be sure her wishes were carried out. Araminta had been touched by the particularity of the bequest and had continued to wear it even in London, despite her maid's assurance that rings were not at all the thing. Her family regarded it as a useful touchstone of Minty's feelings; it was soon noticed that, in circumstances in which most people could

be expected to lose their temper or sink into a black melancholy, Araminta played with her ring.

She knew there was no realistic prospect of finding a
husband from among their acquaintance in the country,
and doubted very much whether yet another London
Season would be any more successful than the others.
Perhaps she should ask her father's permission to move
into the Dower House, empty since Grandmama's death,
and set up her own establishment there. She smiled to
herself. It would be preferable to a life at sea. Even as
the idea occurred to her, she knew her father would not
agree to it. In ten years' time he might be only too pleased
to see his eldest daughter set up with some small degree
of independence, but not yet—not at twenty.

Araminta turned away from the window and threw
herself down on the bed where she lay with her hands
behind her head, staring up at the ceiling. The others
would wonder why she hadn't rejoined them, and how
could she explain that she couldn't bear to witness Izzy's
brave attempts *not* to blame her for her present unhappiness? No, she would stay here for the time being, ideally
until either Izzy had come to terms with her father's decision or Araminta had devised a solution to their dilemma. It was difficult to decide which might happen
first.

CHAPTER TWO

HIGH drama could not be sustained forever, and within a few days life at Cassington Hall slipped back into its usual leisurely style, with only the occasional sigh from Isabella to indicate to everyone else that she still suffered. Since the Earl had imposed no restrictions beyond those of good manners on Thomas Kineton's visits, she saw as much of him as she had ever done, and Araminta began to lose patience with her sister's soulful gazing into the middle distance whenever she had nothing more pressing to do. She held her tongue, however, reminding herself that, if anyone was to blame for Isabella's low spirits, it was she and, since there was nothing she could do to put matters right, at least she need not make them worse.

There was a noticeable increase about this time in Lord Cassington's correspondence with his man of business, and about two weeks after dashing Isabella's hopes he was obliged to go to London for an indefinite period. This was an unusual occurrence, the Earl being a man who liked to have everything neatly planned, and Araminta wondered whether something was amiss. Lady Cassington seemed entirely unperturbed by her husband's absence and the uncertainty surrounding his return, and Araminta concluded that, since it was none of her business, she had best take her tone from her mother and depress the more fantastic speculations of her two youngest sisters.

Lord Cassington was gone for the better part of a month, and when he returned he had had the fore-

thought to equip himself with presents for his family.
Happily for his daughters, he was not a man who thought
in terms of improving books, so there were no collec-
tions of sermons in his saddle-bags. For Araminta there
was a lawn kerchief edged with a broad band of the finest
French lace, for Isabella he brought a dainty Chinese
fan with a blue border that exactly matched her eyes.
He brought Florentina some white silk stockings which
made her feel, she said, entirely grown up, and Georgiana
was delighted to have a silver-mounted riding-whip with
her own initials engraved on its butt. Lady Cassington
was no less pleased with several ells of taffeta which her
husband had been assured were the very latest thing, a
verdict with which she entirely concurred.

'And was your visit a success?' she asked, when
everyone had done admiring the others' gifts.

'I achieved my objective, certainly,' her husband told
her. 'I'm far from sanguine about the final outcome. It
will require care.'

'Best left a day or two, then.'

He kissed her affectionately. 'I don't enjoy London
at the best of times. Country air and country smells and
a few good nights' sleep are all I need to restore body
and soul.'

It was an exchange which the two youngest girls did
not even notice. Isabella noticed it, but it meant nothing
to her so she dismissed it from her mind. Araminta was
puzzled by it but, since her parents seemed perfectly
happy, she saw no reason to be concerned.

She rode next morning and, when she returned to the
stables, the lad who took Halcyon's head while his rider
dismounted told her that His Lordship wished to see her.
She slid down into the supporting hold of her accompanying groom.

'I'll leave you to see to Halcyon, Ditchling,' she said.
'I'll be back to see him settled when I've spoken to Papa.'

She turned to the lad. 'Did Lord Cassington say where he would be?'

'He said his study, m'lady.'

Araminta thanked him and went in by the kitchen door, the shortest route to the main body of the house. She opened the study door and put her head round it.

'How urgently do you wish to speak to me, Papa? Do I have time to get out of all my dirt?'

'There's no immediate urgency but, since you're here, you may as well come in. I dare say I shall survive the sight of you with a bit of mud on your skirts.'

He privately thought that his eldest daughter looked to best advantage in the rather mannish severity of her riding-dress. It was bottle-green with gold-embroidered facings in the manner of hunt livery. She wore a cravat tied in a broad bow at her throat, but he had persuaded her to abandon the fashionable jockey cap in favour of a broad-brimmed black beaver trimmed with egret plumes, feeling that such a hat would protect her complexion to a greater degree. Araminta enjoyed riding and excelled at it. It was unfortunate that she had the colouring that quickly became an unbecoming shade of brown. Lord Cassington hoped the broader brim would minimise the effects of the sun's rays.

'Come in and sit down,' he said, indicating the chair facing him across his writing-table.

Araminta closed the door and did as she was bid, disguising a slight feeling of apprehension. Perhaps it was her imagination, but she rather thought her father's words, unexceptionable as they were, hinted unconsciously at a desire to get an unpleasant task over and done with as soon as possible.

'You will recall the occasion of young Thomas Kineton's offer for Isabella's hand and the conversation we had immediately afterwards,' he began, and Araminta nodded. 'As you may imagine, your mama and I also discussed what was to be done for the best—and not for the first time, although on previous occasions there had been no sense of urgency.'

'And suddenly there is?'

'A year passes very quickly. Your mama said that you had no useful thoughts on the subject yourself and were not enamoured of her suggestion of a Paris Season—a view we share, and not only for reasons of expense, but it was a possible solution.'

'I hadn't thought her to be serious!' Araminta exclaimed. 'I'd have given it deeper consideration had I realised.'

'It doesn't matter; your immediate reaction was a truer indication of your feelings than would have emerged had your thoughts had an opportunity to be influenced by considerations of duty. However, there's no escaping the fact that something has to be done and, frankly, both in your mother's opinion and mine, you are not cut out for a life of spinsterhood. I've therefore—somewhat reluctantly, I must confess—been playing the old-fashioned father and setting in train enquiries which will, I hope, result in a marriage for you being arranged.'

He paused and Araminta stared at him in silence for a few moments.

'Papa, how very Gothic!'

'Very possibly, my dear, but somebody has to do something. It doesn't seem very likely that some eminently desirable suitor is going to come galloping up the drive with an offer for your hand, does it? So it behoves your parents to make some positive moves in the matter.'

Araminta looked at him steadily. 'I infer, from the fact that you sent for me, that your enquiries have proved successful.'

'I should prefer to say "productive". I shan't consider them successful until you are married.'

'I'm intrigued to learn just how Gothic you intend to be, Papa. Shall I have an opportunity of meeting your selection before the wedding, or does he burst upon me as a surprise, pleasant or otherwise, in the church?'

'Of course you will meet him first.'

'And if I don't like him? If I find him positively repugnant? Shall I be permitted to turn him down?'

'Now you're being as foolish as Georgiana,' her father said, in the voice of a man striving hard to be patient. 'There can be no question of your being forced to marry anyone against your will. You will naturally be free to say no. That would go without saying.'

'I'm relieved to hear it,' Araminta told him with some asperity. 'It was, however, a reasonable query when one considers that the enquiries you have been making were done without any prior reference to their subject.'

'There seemed little point in raising your hopes or expectations until there was something to raise them for, and I would strongly advise you to practise curbing your tongue. Such sharpness is unpleasantly close to impertinence and unlikely to be appreciated by any husband.'

Araminta was immediately abashed. 'I'm sorry, Papa. I didn't intend to be disrespectful, but you will admit I have reason to be surprised.'

Lord Cassington's voice softened. 'Indeed, and I acknowledge that you are in a very difficult position. We must hope that it can be resolved as soon as may be.'

'Then may I know to whom I'm to have the honour of being allied? I can only assume it isn't anyone to whom I was introduced in London.'

Lord Cassington seemed hesitant. 'On the contrary, I'm assured you did meet him, but I don't imagine you would have regarded him as a possible future husband.'

'How ominous! That must mean that he is either very old or very young—or perhaps, to look for a brighter possibility, he was married and is now widowed and I shall become stepmama to seven or eight hopeful children.'

'He is neither young nor old and I'm assured has never married.'

'Then how can it have come about that I overlooked him before?'

'Perhaps because you never set your sights on becoming a duchess.'

'A duchess?' Araminta cast her mind over the small array of dukes of her acquaintance and could think of none old enough to be at Court who were not securely married. 'Which one? I can't recall any who were eligible.'

Lord Cassington smiled briefly. 'You display too much haste, my dear. You'll have to wait a while before you become Your Grace. Until your father-in-law dies, as a matter of fact, and I feel bound to point out that, although the Duke of Droxford is in his sixties, he is rather more hale and hearty than most men ten years his junior.'

Araminta frowned. 'Droxford?' she queried. 'Then obviously you are referring to his eldest son—whose name escapes me.'

'Justinian Fencott, Marquess of Cosenham.'

'I've heard the name, I think. I must have done.' She paused, turning over in her mind such men of her London acquaintance as she had *not* considered matrimonial prospects. It was a depressing cavalcade. 'How old is Lord Cosenham?' she asked. Such information might narrow the field.

'Thirty-two.'

Araminta wrinkled her nose. It was older than she would have preferred, but beggars, she reminded herself, could not be choosers. Nevertheless, the question had certainly narrowed the field. 'Do you mean the Macaroni?' she asked suspiciously.

Her father coloured faintly but perceptibly. 'I believe the Marquess does move in the forefront of fashion,' he admitted.

'The forefront of fashion!' Araminta exclaimed. 'Oh, Papa! If he's the man I think he is, he is the very antithesis of everything you admire!'

'What I admire is irrelevant, Minty. It's you who will be his wife—if you are agreeable, of course.'

'You surely realise that my taste has been largely formed by the example set me by you and Mama,' Araminta pointed out. 'You must have some reason for even being prepared to countenance a marriage to a man for whom I cannot believe you have any great admiration.'

'One does not have to admire a man to consider him a suitable husband for one's daughter,' the Earl reminded her. 'Young Kineton, for example, is a pleasant, harmless young man who will suit Isabella very well, but I wouldn't describe my feelings for him as admiration.'

'Lord Cosenham is a very different kettle of fish. As you say, Thomas is pleasant enough and harmless. Would you apply either word to the Marquess?'

Her father picked his words with care and with the scrupulous honesty on which he prided himself. 'As to his being pleasant, I'm not qualified to comment, being only very superficially acquainted with him and, while one cannot admire his fashionable foibles, he undoubtedly has the income to indulge them and I can't see that they do much harm. One might have expected him to have grown out of them by now, of course, and the fact that he hasn't may well indicate rather less common sense than one would like.'

'Not to mention intelligence,' Araminta murmured.

The Earl chose to ignore the interruption. 'But common sense is your strong suit, Minty, and the Duke and I are agreed that it might be just the thing his son needs.'

'So the arrangement is between you and Droxford,' Araminta commented. 'What was Cosenham's re-action? Or has he yet to be told?'

'I understand he has expressed himself perfectly willing to fall in with his father's plans—which suggests he may have a conveniently malleable nature, a factor which I'm sure you will be able to turn to your advantage.'

'He grows more attractive by the minute,' Araminta remarked. 'What are his other recommendations? I feel sure you have discovered something more than a malleable nature.'

'They're mostly of a practical nature, but not to be despised on that account. As a marchioness—and later, a duchess—you will have a very enviable position in society. You will receive a generous—a very generous—allowance and will be able to command a way of life far beyond anything Cassington Hall has ever seen. Furthermore, the Duke is prepared to settle substantial portions on your sisters so that they may have every expectation of being able to choose between the most eligible of candidates.'

'But Izzy would still marry Thomas? You wouldn't expect her to hold out for a better bargain?' Araminta asked anxiously.

'A vulgar way of expressing it and your fear is unfounded. Of course she marries Thomas. They had my word on that.'

Araminta sat back in the chair and gazed thoughtfully at the table before her. 'The Duke seems desperately anxious to see his son married,' she remarked. 'If he's such a catch, why has no one landed him before?'

'I understand the Marquess has steered very clear of any of the previous young women his father has put before him for consideration.'

'Then why has he apparently changed his mind this time?'

The Earl shrugged. 'Who can say for sure? He doesn't get any younger of course, and must be aware of the necessity of providing the Duke with a grandson. You are suitable from every point of view: quite apart from your pedigree, you're a good-looking woman, you dress well and you know how to go on. Furthermore, you're young enough to provide several grandchildren and old enough to see that they are brought up sensibly.'

'Thus repairing His Grace's mistakes with the previous generation. Papa, it isn't a very romantic prospect.'

'Romantic!' the Earl exclaimed, surprised. 'Since when has that been one of your prerequisites? I don't recall your ever having mentioned such an element before.'

'I don't mean it in the sense that Izzy might. I hope I have more common sense than that. But it does seem that there is quite simply something missing from this arrangement and I can't think what else it might be.'

'The Duke and I hope that you and Justinian will be able to deal together tolerably well and we feel that, with a little give and take on both sides, that is entirely possible. However, if it should not turn out to be the case—and provided you have done your duty to the succession—Droxford assures me there would be no objection if you both maintained separate establishments.'

'Truly a prospect to look forward to,' Araminta said with heavy irony. 'You did say I should have the opportunity of meeting this enthusiastic suitor before I gave my decision—and you did say I would not be forced to accept. What arrangements have been made for the meeting to take place?'

Lord Cassington perceptibly brightened. 'At least you're not turning him down out of hand. I told your mama you were too sensible for that,' he said. 'The Marquess will shortly be visiting friends in Oxford. He is invited to break his journey here for one night. To be sure, Newbury will be a little out of his way if he adheres to his plan of travelling by barge, but he could very easily travel by road instead these days.' He looked at her anxiously. 'Minty, I would not wish to give the Marquess a false impression of you and he will only be here for a very short time. I do feel the importance of letting him see your—your *softer* side.'

'In other words, you don't want him to take a dislike to me,' Araminta said bluntly. 'I will do my best, Papa. You must hope the Marquess doesn't provoke me into showing the sharper side of my tongue. I do think, however, that a word with Flossie and Georgie wouldn't come amiss. If Lord Cosenham travels in anything resembling the attire he wears socially, it will be their tongues that let the family down, not mine.'

'I don't think they need know the purpose of his visit,' Lord Cassington said, acknowledging the justice of his daughter's suggestion. 'He will just be the son of an old friend of mine, travelling this way for the first time. I think that will suit, don't you?'

'For about two minutes, I should think,' his daughter laughed. 'You can't keep anything hidden from those two for long, you know. Quite apart from their natural acuity, they listen unashamedly to kitchen gossip, and if the kitchen isn't already speculating on the purpose of your recent visit to the capital I shall be very surprised.'

Araminta's two-minute estimate proved to be hopelessly generous. No sooner had Lady Cassington given warning to her household to anticipate a visitor who could be expected to arrive with a full complement of grooms, valets and even—or so it was rumoured—a cook, than the speculation in the kitchen reached the schoolroom, where it became an undisputed fact.

'Will you really become a marchioness?' Georgiana asked her, and continued without waiting for an answer, 'How very grand! Does that mean Mama will have to curtsy to you?'

'Don't be silly, Georgie,' Araminta said crossly. 'No one expects their mama to curtsy to them.'

'The King does,' Florentina interposed.

'What would you know about it, miss?' Georgiana asked sharply.

'It's a well-known fact,' Florentina said, unmoved. 'Everyone curtsies—or bows, of course—to the King. Except his father. But then, he's always dead, so he can't.'

Isabella's demeanour brightened considerably when the speculation reached her ears. Her eyes shone again and her cheeks became quite flushed. She took her sister aside. 'Is it true, Minty?' she asked. 'Are you going to marry Cosenham? Everyone seems to think it a settled thing.'

Araminta was moved by her sister's obvious happiness at the thought that her own marriage would be able to proceed more quickly than she had anticipated and she was reluctant to dash the hopes that had been raised.

'The possibility is there,' she said gently. 'A formal offer hasn't been made and cannot be until we have met and, even if Lord Cosenham decides to make such an offer, I'm not obliged to accept it. Don't look so cast down, Izzy, but I have to warn you it is by no means certain that there will be a marriage, and I would be doing you no good turn by letting you think it was.'

'I thought it was too good to be true,' Isabella said dejectedly. 'You won't mind if I keep my fingers crossed?'

Araminta kissed her and assured her that she hadn't the slightest objection to Izzy's doing anything at all that

might encourage the future happiness of both of them,
but her face grew serious when the younger girl had left
the room and she realised she had not been giving full
weight to the dependence her sister had been placing
upon this marriage's taking place. The decision to marry
should be a simple one, determined only by one's own
expectation of happiness, but Araminta had other considerations to take into account. Isabella's happiness, too,
depended to some extent upon her elder sister's decision
and so—although they themselves were unaware of it—
did that of the two younger girls. If Araminta accepted
an offer from the Marquess—always assuming he made
one, which, she reminded herself, was by no means
certain—Flossie and Georgie would be sufficiently well-
dowered to find husbands without much difficulty. Not
only that but, with a sister placed at the very top of the
social tree, they could expect to come out under her aegis,
thereby both enhancing their prospects and easing the
financial burden on Lord and Lady Cassington. The
awesomeness of her situation and, in particular, the far-
reaching consequences of declining any offer Lord
Cosenham might choose to make, bore down upon
Araminta's spirits, and she began to wonder whether she
really had any choice in the matter at all.

The younger girls might be unaware that their own
futures were shortly to be determined, but they were very
much alive to a deterioration in their eldest sister's customary good humour and missed very few opportunities
for telling her so.

'Thomas offers for Izzy and *she* goes about with a
face like a funeral, and no sooner are *you* told to expect
an offer than you snap heads off at the least provocation,' Georgiana told her indignantly.

'And sometimes at no provocation,' Florentina added,
without lifting her eyes from the book she was supposed
to be reading.

Araminta opened her mouth to prove them right and shut it again. There was more than a grain of justice in what they said and she'd rather prove them wrong, so she whisked up her skirt and left the schoolroom, though not without closing the door behind her with a snap that caused the two occupants to exchange knowing glances.

The Cassingtons' household never went about its tasks negligently, but the news that Lady Araminta might receive an offer from the anticipated visitor had the effect of ensuring a deeper sheen on the furniture and a warmer glow on the copper jugs that lined the corridor into the kitchen. The Marquess would naturally not visit the kitchens—though presumably his cook would, and might well report back to his master on how he found things there—but if His Lordship chose to have a bath, these were the jugs which would carry the hot water from the kitchen cauldrons to his bed-chamber. The Warehams might not be able to boast the enormous wealth of the Fencotts, but no Fencott would find the household wanting.

The Marquess decided to travel by road and his host's household was suitably impressed, though his host's wife's heart sank at the size of his entourage. First to spring into view round a bend in the drive were two armed outriders. Between and slightly behind them came the Marquess's post-chaise, a vehicle in the French style, heavily ornamented and drawn by a beautifully matched pair of blacks. Two footmen sat behind the body of the vehicle in the same brown and gold livery of the postilion and the outriders. Behind the post-chaise came a more humble carriage bearing His Lordship's valet, his cook, and a secretary. Behind that, and also accompanied by two armed outriders, came the baggage-wagon, and bringing up the rear were four liveried grooms, each leading a horse on either side of his mount, clearly replacements for the carriage horses, apart from one large black animal that appeared to be a saddle-horse.

Watching with her sisters from the schoolroom over the porch, Araminta was obliged to concede that her suitor's taste in horseflesh was flawless.

'Goodness!' Georgiana exclaimed. 'How very grand! How will he go on in our household? We're not half so grand as that!'

'I'm sure Lord Cosenham will be too much the gentleman to make us aware that he notices any difference,' Araminta said repressively.

'You'll just *have* to marry him,' Florentina commented. 'Then you can invite me to stay and I can go about the countryside in that sort of pomp. I shall enjoy that.'

Any retort hovering on Araminta's lips was cut short by the opening of the carriage door, the letting down of the step and the emergence of its passenger.

He was observed from above in a stunned silence that lasted several minutes and was broken, to no one's surprise, by Georgiana.

'Good gracious!' she said. 'What an amazing sight! It would be difficult to miss him in a crush, wouldn't it?'

'Not amazing,' Florentina corrected. 'Extraordinary. Minty, he can't possibly be ten feet tall!'

'I believe—my recollection is that he is quite a tall man. You see, he wears high heels, and that very tall wig adds to the illusion. Without it, I don't think he would be any taller than the ordinary.'

'I don't think "ordinary" is a word that could ever be applied to that man,' Florentina remarked, and Araminta had to admit to herself that her sister was probably right.

Isabella looked anxiously from the vision below to her elder sister. 'He certainly seems...remarkable,' she commented, choosing a word which she hoped did not sound too excessive.

He did indeed. It was difficult to identify the fabric his coat and breeches were made from, so heavily were they embroidered with gold thread, but it appeared to be brown, an opulent echo of his servants' livery. Despite the fact that he had been travelling, he wore gold silk stockings and high-heeled shoes ornamented with a huge bow instead of the boots that might have been expected. His wig, which did so much to exaggerate his height, was tall and sloped back as it rose from his face. Two long, horizontal curls covered each ear and the back of the wig hung in a long and ornately curled pigtail, the whole being powdered white. More startlingly to the girls in the schoolroom, the Marquess's face was also white. Any hint of his natural colouring had been hidden under a maquillage which gave his face a vacant, characterless expression, relieved only by the darker recesses of his eyes and a black patch on his cheek. He held a gold-topped ebony walking-cane elegantly in one hand and a fan in the other, while a quizzing-glass hung round his neck. As he stepped out of his carriage, he allowed the fan to hang from the ribbon which attached it to his wrist and lifted the quizzing-glass, which sparkled as if it were set with diamonds, to his eye and surveyed the house before him.

Araminta immediately stepped back. It would never do for him to see her gawping at him as if he were a freak at Mop Fair, though, if he lost his fortune, he could probably replace it by setting himself up as exactly that, she reflected cynically. The younger girls had no such inhibitions, and when Georgiana drew back it was in indignation.

'I do believe he looked at the house and *sighed*,' she declared.

'I wonder who he's staying with in Oxford?' Florentina speculated. 'If they're friends of his, they must be either very grand or very silly.'

Which, Araminta thought, summed it up rather well, though it would never do to let Flossie know that.

Lady Cassington took one look at her guest and then, as soon as he had been shown to his room to recover from what he described as the ravages of his journey—though the Countess later confided to her husband that she had seldom seen anyone less ravaged—she made her way post-haste to the schoolroom to alter certain arrangements.

'Naturally, Flossie, you and Georgie will be introduced to the Marquess. It would look most singular if you weren't. However, you will both hold your tongues and murmur nothing but the sort of shy pleasantries two young misses from the schoolroom might be expected to murmur. You will not now put in an appearance in the drawing-room. You are both of you very inclined to let your tongues run away with you, and I'm not inclined to place too much dependence upon Lord Cosenham's failing to understand at least some of your probable comments.'

'He is a figure of fun, isn't he?' Florentina remarked.

'No one,' Lady Cassington said firmly, 'with the wealth of a Fencott can possibly be a figure of fun.' She had thought the Marquess's vacuous manner had been belied by a certain sharpness she fancied she had caught in his eye. Consequently, and despite the brevity of their acquaintance, she found him rather sinister, but that was not something she intended to impart to her offspring. In any case, it was probably her imagination, a trick of the light.

If Lord Cosenham had, indeed, sighed at the sight of Cassington Hall, it was his only deviation from impeccable courtesy. Not even when advised that they kept country hours and dined early did he betray by so much as a flicker of an eyelash that the news was unwelcome, though his cook was rather less restrained, casting his eyes up to heaven and imploring the Almighty to succour him. The Cassington's cook, a female with the backside of a hunter and an exceptionally light hand with pastry, was not impressed.

'It's not the Almighty that succours anyone in this kitchen. It's me and I'll thank you to remember it. And we'll get one thing quite clear. This is my kitchen and we does things my way, whether or no they fits your fancy foreign ideas. Now, if you likes to advise me of anything His Lordship is partial to or has a disgust for, I'll undertake to do what I can to cater for his taste, but it's me that's cooking in this kitchen, not you, and we'll have no misunderstanding about that.'

The Marquess's cook, who said his name was Gaston, though Mrs Liss noticed that there were times when his accent was closer to Shoreditch than Paris, assured her that there would be no problem. He was there in a purely supervisory capacity to see that things were done the way His Lordship liked them.

'Are you, indeed?' Mrs Liss replied in ominous tones. 'Well, if you start telling me how to cook, young man, you'll be out of that door with a rolling-pin bent round your neck before you've even caught your breath. And don't you stand there sniggering,' she went on, rounding on the kitchen-maid. 'It's one thing for two cooks to have words. It's not for the likes of you to express an opinion.'

Araminta had retired to her room with a sinking heart to change for supper. Lord Cosenham was even worse than she had remembered him. Of course, they had never spoken—he had been pointed out to her as one of the sights of the season—and she must hope that his converse had more depth than his appearance suggested.

Clutching at that straw, she took particular pains with her appearance and, when she entered the drawing-room to be introduced for the first time to the man who might possibly become her husband, she knew she looked to advantage.

She maintained the country practice of neither powdering her hair nor wearing a wig. Instead, her maid had dressed it high and smooth at the front with a soft knot on the top while below the ears softly rolled curls framed her face, and at the nape a broader curl was turned under and held in place with a soft, lemon-yellow ribbon which exactly matched her silk gown. Both the skirt and the quilted petticoat were of the same material, the cut and the lines being of greater simplicity than was often seen, to allow the beauty of the fabric to be appreciated. There was no lace on the skirt at all, but ruffs of fine Honiton lace edged the sleeves and bordered the kerchief that, shawl-like, covered her shoulders and lent modesty to the low-cut bodice. A long, lace-edged apron concealed the top half of the petticoat, leaving the bottom to show beneath the open skirt. Araminta had decided against any jewellery other than her memorial ring, but she tied a ribbon in a flat band around her throat.

Her father led her forward. 'You will wish to meet Lord Cosenham, my dear,' he said. 'My lord, permit me to introduce my daughter, Araminta.'

The Marquess swept her an exaggerated bow and then reached for her fingers and kissed them briefly. 'A delight, my lady,' he said, and his voice was not quite what Araminta had expected, though she would have been hard put to it to explain what it was about it that somehow did not quite fit. The Marquess affected the currently fashionable drawl, but there was nothing odd about that. It lay more in the almost sibilant softness of his voice, which was also higher than one would have thought, and the sounds seemed to escape with difficulty almost, she thought suddenly, as if he were half strangled. His eyes, which glittered almost black in his white face, took in her appearance in one efficient glance. 'I observe with pleasure so propitious an omen, madam,' he added.

Araminta had not the slightest idea what he meant and she knew her face had gone completely blank. 'You do, my lord?' she said. 'Pray share it with us; propitious omens are not lightly to be disregarded.'

He turned his head to the right and raised his right arm to the side, the palm upturned in a graceful gesture. 'Why, we match, my lady. We match.'

They did, indeed. The Marquess had exchanged his opulent traveling costume for an even more striking one of damask silk woven in broad stripes of blue and lemon, the weave intermingling at the edges of the stripes so that there was a faint green haze blurring the dividing line. The effect was positively dazzling, and gold lace at wrist and neck and gold braid edging the coat, together with buttons set with what Araminta suspected were diamonds rather than paste, only served to increase the effect. She rather thought his wig was higher and more elaborate than it had been before, but that seemed an unimportant excess when viewed against his overall splendour.

There was nothing forced about her smile. 'So we do, my lord,' she agreed, and dropped her eyes demurely, afraid to meet those of either Izzy or her parents.

As the evening progressed, Araminta had to give Lord Cosenham his due. She found the situation a little awkward and was therefore uncharacteristically tongue-tied, contributing little to the conversation except when directly addressed. The Marquess was clearly under no such restraint. He was a master of inconsequential, shallow social chatter, and if ever a topic seemed to be deepening he quickly guided it back into the shallows again before introducing another. He gave his listeners no inkling at all of his true feelings on anything, and it was difficult to determine whether, in fact, he had any feelings deeper than those he expressed. Even on the subject of horses, of which his own animals indicated he was no mean judge, he had nothing serious to say.

'Colour is everything,' he said. 'One must be so careful that one's horse sets off one's apparel. I favour blacks. One can rarely go wrong with a black. But a dun! I don't think I would care to be seen on a dun. What would one wear?'

'Then it's fortunate that bloodstock is very rarely dun,' Lord Cassington remarked drily.

'Fortunate? My lord, you cannot conceive how often I have sent up a small—but very sincere—prayer of gratitude for that very fact!'

When the ladies withdrew, Isabella confessed that she found the Marquess very hard to like. 'He's not in the least like Thomas,' she concluded.

'I think we may all agree on that,' Lady Cassington told her, 'but it would be a mistake to assume that Araminta would be best suited by a replica of your own dear Thomas.'

Isabella looked doubtful. 'But he is so *very* different.'

'Then it's just as well he's not here as a possible suitor for you, isn't it?' Araminta said lightly. Another Thomas Kineton certainly would not suit her, but the Marquess of Cosenham seemed to be from the opposite end of the spectrum.

When the gentlemen rejoined the ladies, there was nothing in Lord Cassington's manner or his face to indicate how he had found his guest when they had been in a situation likely to provoke more profound discourse. In the drawing-room, Lord Cosenham's converse was of the same style as it had been at table, and

Araminta said goodnight to the family with no clearer idea of his character than she had had when he arrived.

Isabella, who naturally retired at the same time as her sister, was keen to discuss the Marquess in the solitude of one or other of their bed-chambers, but Araminta declined.

'To what purpose, Izzy?' she said. 'The man that suits you wouldn't suit me, and I have a strong suspicion we have seen all there is to see of Lord Cosenham.' The truth was, she didn't want to discuss him. She had known him to be a fop. She had discovered him to be shallow. The question she had to ask herself was whether those were characteristics she could live with for the rest of her life, even if it were for the sake of her family duty.

She supposed the foppishness might wear off as fashion changed, but shallowness of mind was unlikely to change. To what extent would enormous wealth and a title—to say nothing of a sense of having done what was expected of her—compensate for an incompatible partner? Less and less as the years went by, she suspected. Had it not been for the thought of Izzy's future happiness and the prospects that would open up for the younger girls, Araminta would have sought out her father forthwith and instructed him to decline any offer. As it was, she supposed it was a pity propriety prevented her and her suitor having any time for private converse—though, casting her mind back over the evening, Araminta doubted whether there would have been much point.

She had always been an early riser, and the following day was no exception. The presence of a guest in the house meant that it would be discourteous to go for her usual morning ride, but it was a fine day and there was no reason why she shouldn't take a turn in the garden. She dressed with care; sooner or later Lord Cosenham would get up, and would eventually leave to continue his journey to Oxford. No purpose would be served by his taking his leave of someone who looked as if she had thrown her clothes together without a passing thought. Nor had she any desire to incur Lady Cassington's displeasure, so she took care to tie a broad-brimmed chip-straw hat over her cap to protect her complexion.

Araminta strolled at a leisurely pace along the gravelled paths between the little box hedges that bordered each of the beds of the parterre. She seemed to be deep in thought, and in a way she was, though she would have been hard put to it to clarify what those thoughts had been or where they were leading. She was roused from her contemplations by the sound of brisk footsteps behind her, and turned to see Lord Cosenham striding towards her in a manner very different from his usual mincing gait. It looked odd when contrasted with his travelling clothes, his wig and his heavily painted face and, as if conscious of this, his gait reverted to its customary style as soon as he realised she had seen him. Araminta waited for him to draw level.

He bowed profusely when he had done so. 'A pleasure, my lady,' he said.

Araminta curtsied. 'Not a delight, my lord?' she murmured, and caught the flash of a suddenly sharpened eye, a flash which was gone almost before she was quite sure she had noticed it.

He wagged an admonishing finger at her. 'You tease me, madam. Something I suppose I must accustom myself to if our fathers' plans go ahead.'

'Forgive me, my lord. I must learn to mend my tongue.'

'Not at all,' Lord Cosenham said politely. 'I am unlikely to change my ways to any significant degree. Why, therefore, should I expect you to?'

Araminta opened her eyes wide and looked at him in surprise. 'You're very generous, sir. Most men would not, I think, hold so eminently reasonable a view.'

'Ah, but then, I am not like other men. You may have observed,' he drawled with an affected modesty that provoked a sharp glance from Araminta in her turn. His face told her nothing. The thick maquillage covered any expression there might have been.

'I have, my lord,' she said demurely.

'So you have a taste to be a duchess,' he said, changing the subject without warning and taking her off guard. It was the first time she had known him to come to the point.

'Don't you mean a marchioness?' she replied. 'I understand your father still lives and enjoys particularly good health.'

'Very true, but you could expect ultimately to take the higher rank.'

'Assuming that I didn't die in childbirth—which I understand would be one of my duties—and that my husband didn't meet with a fatal accident during his father's lifetime.'

'Dear me, what a pessimistic view of life! Do I look like the sort of man who takes unnecessary risks?'

'No, you don't,' Araminta said bluntly. 'In fact, you don't look like the sort of man who takes any risks at all, but I saw your horse and he didn't look to me to be the sort of animal chosen by a man who prefers to play safe.'

He made a deprecating gesture. 'Can I persuade you that he is nothing more than an affectation? That I like him to be seen in my stables, but never ride him?'

'No. It would be a waste of a good horse, and I don't believe anyone with the eye to buy such an animal in the first place would let it go unridden.'

'But I *never* take him out of a trot,' he assured her seriously.

Araminta stared at him and then burst out laughing. 'Oh, forgive me, my lord. I mean no disrespect, but really, I've never heard anything so ridiculous in my life.'

His eyes narrowed and Araminta wished she could read their expression, and then changed her mind and decided it was probably better that she couldn't. When he spoke, his voice was softer, its sibilance more noticeable, though his tone was perfectly affable. 'Shall we keep that as our little secret?' he suggested. 'If it got about, others might concur. One wouldn't wish to be generally regarded as a figure of fun.'

'You need not doubt my discretion,' Araminta assured him.

'It was more your lack of it that concerned me,' he said softly. 'Dear me, the sun becomes unpleasantly warm. You won't wish to risk your complexion, I dare say. Allow me to escort you back into the civilised world.'

Araminta held a totally opposite opinion of the sun's warmth, but, realising he was doing nothing more than curtailing the conversation, she acceded to his suggestion. Once indoors, he parted from her with another of his hyperbolic flourishes and she returned to the privacy of her own room. She stood by the window, leaning her head against the shutters which had been folded back against the sides of the embrasure, and absent-mindedly turned her ring.

She had no idea what to make of Lord Cosenham. He was an affected, mincing fop who adopted fashions no sensible man would give more than a passing thought to. His converse yesterday evening had been bland and inoffensive, as befitted a social occasion, though it was not calculated to lead to a better understanding between two people between whom a marriage had been proposed. This morning she had seen a glimpse of some-

thing more. The man looked a fool and sounded like a
fool, but the morning's brief encounter had seemed to
hint that there was a sharper mind behind his vacuity
than he chose to exhibit. Araminta was not at all sure
it was a sharpness she wanted to pursue. Nor could she
make up her mind whether she wanted to marry him if
he did decide to make an offer.

Of course, the decision might be taken out of her
hands if he decided she was not to his taste—something
she thought very probable. If that happened, Izzy would
be very disappointed, but she couldn't blame Araminta
quite so directly as she would be able to if it were her
sister who cried off.

And what if Lord Cosenham did make an offer?
Would she accept it? She didn't know. It was hard to
decide which aspect of him appealed to her least: the
effeminate, inconsequential, drawling fop that was his
public face, or the sharper, shrewder, almost sinister facet
she felt she had glimpsed beneath the surface. Yet always
she must offset against her personal feelings her
awareness of the importance of her decision to her
family. Still, the offer had yet to be made. Perhaps the
choice might never arise. She determined to put it from
her mind until such time as she had no option but to
consider it.

She was recalled to the present by a tap on the door
from a maid with the message that His Lordship was
leaving now, and His Lordship—by which she meant the
Earl—would like his daughters to take their leave of him.
Accordingly, Araminta smoothed her skirts and checked
her cap in the glass before joining the others in the hall.

The door was open when she got there and the
Marquess's carriage was standing outside, its door open,
the step down and the two attendant footmen waiting
to hand their master in. The rest of the Marquess's
entourage was assembled in due order behind the car-

riage and round the neatly scythed turnaround in front
of the house.

The Marquess took an effusive leave of the Earl and
Countess, and a more subdued one of their daughters,
particularly the younger two. Araminta was the only one
to be accorded the honour of having her hand delicately
lifted and brushed with painted lips. He bowed to her
and made a double obeisance with his right arm.

'A pleasure *and* a delight,' he told her in his peculiar
voice.

Araminta curtsied. 'You're too kind, my lord,' she
murmured.

'Oh, I don't think so. I don't think so at all,' he replied
and then, bowing once more to his host and hostess, he
swept out of the door and allowed his footmen to hand
him into his carriage. A gracious inclination of his head
at the window as the carriage moved off was the splendid
last glimpse the Warehams had of him on that occasion.

As they turned to go indoors, the Earl guided his wife
towards his study but turned his head towards his eldest
daughter. 'Don't go far, Minty,' he said. 'I shall want
to have a word with you shortly.'

'I shall be in my room, Papa,' Araminta told him,
unable to read into either his face or his voice any indication as to whether she was going to have to make a
decision.

Isabella's face was apprehensive. 'Oh, Minty, I do so
hope he has made an offer for your hand. I'm sure you
didn't say or do anything to cause him to take you into
dislike—and his parting words were most promising, I
thought.'

Araminta, who knew that promise had nothing to do
with their utterance, smiled doubtfully but said nothing.

Georgiana felt that Isabella was overlooking an important factor. 'Minty's under no obligation to accept
him even if he has,' she pointed out, 'and *I* think she's

got too much sense to want to marry such a popinjay as that, even if it would mean she became a duchess.'

Isabella paled. 'Oh, Minty, you don't mean to turn him down, do you?'

Araminta smiled perfunctorily and put her arm round her sister's shoulder. 'Let's wait until we know whether I have the choice, shall we?' she suggested. 'You two can get back to your books,' she added, looking at the younger pair, 'and, Izzy, I'm sure you can find something with which to occupy yourself. I should rather like to be left alone for the present.'

'Of course, how selfish of me. You will want to consider what's best for you,' Isabella said guiltily. 'You will forgive my putting my own interest first and having spoken without considering that yours might not coincide?'

'There's nothing to forgive,' Araminta said warmly, and then hurried up the stairs before her face should betray the dismay she felt at Isabella's obvious dependence, not only on the Marquess's making an offer, but on Araminta's accepting it.

The imminence of the probable need to make a decision effectively banished any ability Araminta had to think about it clearly, and coherent thought deserted her as she paced up and down her room, unconsciously turning her ring back and forth. She told herself to be sensible, to sit down and read, but the words blurred, and when she had read a passage three times and still had no idea what it was about she laid the book aside. Her work-basket was no more efficacious a panacea for a troubled spirit and, since she seemed to have lost the ability to guide the needle away from her finger, and blood was not the decoration she really wanted on her handkerchiefs, she abandoned sewing as well. Nevertheless, the abortive attempts to calm her mind did at least occupy time and, although it seemed an age before her father sent for her, it was actually no more than three quarters of an hour.

The Countess left the Earl's study as her daughter arrived, and stood aside to let her pass, according her an encouraging smile as she did so. The encouragement was obvious. Araminta was unsure whether it was to enable her to brace herself against disappointment or to urge her to make a wise decision.

'You sent for me, Papa,' Araminta said as she closed the study door behind her.

Her father smiled. 'I wish I could believe it was filial duty rather than curiosity that induced such prompt obedience.'

'You will at least own that I've every justification for exhibiting curiosity,' Araminta pointed out.

'Sit down,' he said, and when she had done so he followed suit, rearranging some papers on his table before he continued, as if he were uneasy about what he had to say. 'You will, I hope, be pleased to learn that the Marquess of Cosenham was gracious enough, before he left this morning, to make a most flattering offer for your hand, and the onus is now on you to decide whether you wish to accept it. I feel bound to point out that the terms of the contract agreed between the Duke and myself are extremely generous in your favour and, frankly, even if the Marquess were a royal Duke, they couldn't be better. As a matter of fact,' he went on honestly, 'if he were a Brunswick, they'd be a great deal worse. I can go into the detail if you wish, but it is a complex document.' His hand indicated the sheaf of closely written parchments on the table. 'I think it only fair, however, that you should know the general provisions it makes. You will have a very generous allowance—very generous indeed—which will continue until you die, when it will transfer to your daughters. It can only be discontinued if you choose to set up separate establishments before you have provided an heir and while you are still of child-bearing age.'

'Which means that if I have ten daughters but no sons, I have to go on trying,' Araminta interpreted.

'There has to be at least the outward appearance of that,' her father amended.

'Go on.'

'There are some detailed arrangements concerning the Droxford jewels, but they are only what one would expect. In addition, the Duke will make very generous provision for your two youngest sisters, and is even prepared to settle a considerable sum on Izzy at the time of her marriage.'

'His Grace is very anxious to see his son settled,' Araminta commented.

'He's very anxious to secure an heir,' Lord Cassington corrected her. 'I understand Lord Cosenham has been disinclined to pursue a connection with any lady of his own class, though as a young man his association with those of another sort altogether gave his father some cause for concern—though that is to be expected of any young man, of course,' he added hastily.

'Of course,' Araminta murmured.

'I gather the Marquess spends a great deal of time in Paris,' her father went on. 'The family has connections there, so you could expect to move in Society there as well as in London.'

'A considerable inducement,' Araminta commented. She had little regard for Society, infinitely preferring country life, and her father knew it. 'Tell me, Papa, if Lord Cosenham has shown so little interest in securing the family's future before this, why has he suddenly decided to do so?'

'I imagine his father has succeeded in imbuing his son with a sense of urgency in the matter.'

'Is that a tactful way of saying that the Duke told him to get married or have his funds cut off?'

'I very much doubt whether the Duke gave him an ultimatum as crude as that, but I understand it did require a certain amount of pressure to make the Marquess agree in principle.'

'And was Lady Araminta Wareham the Duke's idea or the Marquess's?'

'I understand the Marquess told his father that if he could find a suitable candidate, he—the Marquess— would view her favourably. It seemed to me that, although there were aspects to the case about which I had reservations, I should nevertheless be failing in my duty to both my daughters if I didn't look into it.'

'Were you acquainted with the Duke?' Araminta asked.

'We had, naturally, met, but I can claim no closer acquaintance than that of exchanging bows once or twice a year. We do have friends in common, however, and it was through one of them that I moved.'

'And you feel that I should accept this offer?'

'You'd be a fool not to consider it,' Lord Cassington said bluntly. 'I can't pretend to like Lord Cosenham, and I don't imagine he fulfils any young girl's picture of her dream husband—apart, perhaps, from his rank and wealth. The decision is yours, Minty. I have no desire to influence you in any way. I can see all the arguments for and against, and if you decide to decline there will be no recriminations from me. I only ask that you don't take too long.'

Araminta returned to her room in thoughtful mood. It wasn't recriminations from her father that she dreaded; it was the reproachful glances Izzy would involuntarily cast her way from time to time, and she had to remind herself that she should not decide her own future on the basis of what was best for Izzy. It was very unlikely that Thomas would start looking elsewhere for a wife in the coming year—a year which was already a quarter of the way through its course—and that meant that he and Izzy could have every expectation of marriage regardless of Araminta's decision. Nevertheless, it was Izzy's reproachful glances that flashed across her inner eye, and with them came the prospect of future reproaches when Flossie and Georgie discovered—as discover they inevitably would—that she had also thrown away their chances of making a worthwhile match or—worse, perhaps—that they might have to reject a suitor they loved because neither he nor they could support the married state.

Such considerations seemed even more important than the very fundamental question of whether she could bear to live with Lord Cosenham.

He had given a small indication that he possessed a dry sense of humour and an acid tongue, facets of his personality which, while their very unexpectedness rendered them more than a little intimidating, Araminta found a great deal more attractive than the bland contents of his converse and his affected mannerisms. She could imagine quite easily, and with remarkably little repugnance, a life in which they sat opposite each other at table or strolled in the garden—if his lordship could bear the sun—or attended together a Drawing-Room or a ball, but she found it quite impossible to imagine them sharing the more intimate aspects of marriage.

Araminta was a practical countrywoman and knew she was not at all missish. She had a very clear idea of what the duties of marriage entailed, and no particular apprehensions about them, but she could not, even for a passing moment, imagine Lord Cosenham as a partner, either with her or with any other woman.

The advantages of the match were concrete and obvious. She would have a financial independence undreamed of. She would have title, status and expectations—things she might not set any very great store by, but that other people did. She would live in inconceivable luxury and she would be able to travel—something which she had always longed to do but had never mentioned because of the enormous expense. It was costly enough to send a young man on the Grand Tour, but any lady attempting anything similar needed more than a tutor and a courier—a chaperon, armed guards and a string of carriage horses in addition to a maid and a major domo to oversee arrangements. These were all beyond Lord Cassington's reach and he had never learned of his daughter's aspirations to see the world beyond Berkshire and London. Now those aspirations could be realised.

But, above all, she could never overlook the effect her decision would have on her sisters. It was true that Thomas's fondness for Izzy was unlikely to wane in the next few months, but if Araminta chose not to marry Lord Cosenham, they would be deprived of the additional dowry the Duke was going to make available. As for the other two girls, the provision that would be made for them would affect both the quality of the husband they could attract and the speed with which he might be attracted. There would be no need for two London Seasons for either of them when their time came, and they would hardly thank Araminta for depriving them of their chances.

The inconceivability of a physical partnership with Lord Cosenham was undoubtedly likely to prove a barrier to a harmonious marriage but, as Araminta weighed up the various arguments, its importance seemed to recede when considered against the very real and material advantages of the match. For one thing, it seemed from the terms of the Duke's marriage contract that physical union was not expected to be required of her with any great frequency, a consideration that had also, no doubt, weighed strongly with the Marquess. She turned all the arguments over in her mind a second time, and then a third, and then she sought out her father.

He was in his study and, although Araminta knew she had been in her room for the better part of two hours, he did not appear to have moved from the position in which she had left him. He looked up as she came in.

'So soon?' he asked. 'Have you come to a decision so quickly?'

'You asked me not to take too long,' Araminta reminded him. 'I would be grateful if you would tell Lord Cosenham that I accept his offer.'

'Are you sure about this? Quite sure?'

'Yes, Papa. It seems the best thing to do from every point of view.'

'And not just for your sisters' sakes?'

She hesitated almost imperceptibly. 'No, Papa,' she said firmly.

Lord Cassington noticed the brief hesitation, but he, too, was the subject of conflicting opinions, and he was too relieved at the words and the determined tone in which they were uttered to want to enquire too deeply into the reasons behind that hesitation. 'I'm glad you've come to that decision, Minty,' he said. 'I can't pretend that the Marquess would have been my first choice for you, but I think you will find there are considerable compensations for his—his lack of intellect.'

Araminta looked at him, surprised. 'I don't think he lacks intellect, Papa. I think he simply disguises it very well.'

'Yes, well, it's very commendable that you should seek to find virtues in your future husband. He has given me his direction in Oxford so I shall waste no time in apprising him of his good fortune—and his father as well, of course. The contracts have only to be signed and then the marriage can go ahead.'

'I think I should prefer to be married as soon as possible,' Araminta told him. 'Now that I've made up my mind, there seems little point in delaying.' She hoped it sounded plausible, but the truth was she had a suspicion that the longer she waited, the less inclined she would be to go through with it.

Lord Cassington gave her a shrewd glance which, had she noticed it, would have told her he quite understood her reasoning. 'Droxford and I had discussed this,' he said. 'The banns can be called as soon as the contracts are signed, which means that, unless there are any unexpected hitches, you could be the Marchioness of Cosenham in a month. I ventured to suggest to His Grace that you might prefer to be married from your village church and he was quite agreeable, but if you would prefer a more grand affair in London he will be equally happy.'

'What would Lord Cosenham's preference be?' Araminta asked doubtfully.

'He will concur with his father. I did raise the matter with him, just to be sure, you understand, because he is of an age to have very decided views on such matters and he doesn't move much in country society, but he said your wishes must be paramount. He indicated, however, that, if you shouldn't be averse to it, a wedding-journey to Italy might be appropriate.'

For the first time since Lord Cosenham's visit had been mooted, Araminta's face lit up. 'To Italy? Why, I should like it above all things!'

Lord Cassington was a little taken aback at her vehemence. 'Well, that's an auspicious beginning, I must say. I understand the Marquess has a yacht at Portsmouth, which is but two days' journey from Newbury, given Lord Cosenham's style of travelling.'

'A wedding from here would suit me very well,' Araminta told him, 'and you may tell Lord Cosenham when you write that I am delighted at his suggestion of Italy.'

'I shall do so. There is one other thing, Minty. I know your time will be very much occupied in the preparations for this marriage, but you will have to find time somehow to visit your great-aunt Sybil. She will want to see you, and can hardly be expected to travel from Abingdon to Newbury at her age and in her state of health. She was a great friend of your future father-in-law in his youth, and I'm sure she will welcome this match. Indeed, I fancy she would be happy to meet the Marquess as well. Would you have any objection if I advised him of your projected visit and suggested he might like to ride over? Abingdon is not so very far from Oxford.'

Araminta looked doubtful. 'Of course I've no objection, Papa, but do you think it altogether wise? Great-Aunt Sybil is not noted for her tolerance of what she calls "fashionable foibles" and you can't deny Lord Cosenham does rather carry them to excess.'

'I don't suppose it will do him any harm to be given a dressing down for once,' her father replied drily, 'and your great-aunt will derive a great deal of pleasure from administering it. In any case, I don't feel such considerations should outweigh those of duty, do you?'

'No, Papa,' Araminta said, a gleeful glint in her eye which should certainly not have been there when the subject was her future husband's possible discomfiture.

CHAPTER THREE

SINCE it would be some days before Lady Cassington's urgent demands for samples from certain silk warehouses could be productive, Araminta's visit to her great-aunt was fixed to take place the day after a letter to that effect, sent by the hand of one of the Cassington grooms, would have arrived. The Dowager Lady Nettlebed was a formidable old lady, but she held house generously and was particularly fond of her great-nieces, despite the scathing aspersions she frequently cast upon her nephew's inability to produce male heirs. She was always perfectly happy to accommodate any member of her extensive family upon receipt of twenty-four hours' notice of their intention to visit and, since she hadn't left the Dower House for so much as one night in the last twenty years, it was inconceivable that she might be absent on this occasion. Nor was she.

She greeted Araminta with an affectionate kiss and an instruction not to mind the fact that, once carried downstairs to her couch she didn't rise from it until she was carried up to bed. 'One of the disadvantages of getting old is that one becomes considerably less agile,' she confided to her visitor. 'I don't let it inconvenience me, however, nor shall I until it affects my brain, and when *that* starts to deteriorate Derby has strict instructions to smother me.'

Araminta cast an involuntary, startled glance at her great-aunt's maid, but that lady, almost as old as her mistress, gazed back impassively, giving no indication as to whether this was an order she would obey or ignore and, since Derby's reputation in the family was of being at least as independently minded as her mistress, Araminta would not dare to guess what she would do if the situation arose.

'I hope Derby will do no such thing,' she said bluntly. 'Indeed, it isn't something one should ask of a servant.'

'It's certainly not something one can ask of anyone else,' Lady Nettlebed retorted. 'When you reach my age—*if* you reach my age, which I take leave to doubt— you will view it differently.'

This pronouncement was made with such positiveness that Araminta felt it wiser to change the subject. 'And why should I not outlive you, Great-Aunt? We are, after all, a long-lived family.'

'Not on your mother's side. I can't think of one of them who has lived beyond sixty,' Lady Nettlebed told her, choosing to disregard the inconvenient handful who had.

'I take after Papa in most respects,' Araminta reminded her. 'I see no reason why I shouldn't prove to be a true Wareham in this, too. In fact, I think I shall take very good care to outlive you, on a matter of principle.'

Lady Nettlebed snorted. 'You can hardly fail to do *that*, given your tender age, even if we take into account the hazards of childbirth. Let's hope your Wareham ancestry will hold you in good stead in that respect, too.'

'What an extremely depressing conversationalist you are, Great-Aunt!' Araminta said cheerfully. 'That sort of talk could put some girls off marriage altogether.'

Her great-aunt considered the possibility dispassionately. 'I doubt it very much,' she concluded. 'I've never heard of anyone's being deterred by the prospect of an early death. Most young girls can't wait to leap into matrimony. You, for instance.'

'Now that's hardly fair!' Araminta exclaimed. 'After all, I had two London Seasons and didn't leap.'

'Only because no one offered,' Lady Nettlebed reminded her ruthlessly but without rancour. 'What on earth has induced you to accept Cosenham?'

'Perhaps because no one else offered,' Araminta said tartly. 'It is a very good match, you know, Great-Aunt, especially when one considers that Papa has four daughters to settle respectably.'

'Balderdash! Oh, it's good enough from any practical point of view, I suppose, but what Droxford's been about to let the boy get out of hand, I can't imagine.'

'Cosenham isn't exactly a boy any longer, Great-Aunt,' Araminta reminded her.

'Which makes it all the worse. I haven't see him for— oh, nearly fifteen years, but he was always a bright boy. Unusually bright, as a matter of fact. Adventurous, too: always getting into mischief of one sort or another. Then Droxford packed him off to stay with relatives in Paris— to give him some style, he said, though I never thought style was what Justinian lacked—and from there he did the Grand Tour and came back a changed man, or so they tell me.'

'He is certainly at the forefront of fashion,' Araminta said doubtfully, trying to equate this picture of the youthful Justinian Fencott with the man she had agreed to marry, and finding the only hint of similarity lay in her great-aunt's assessment of his intelligence. 'Papa did suggest to him that he might like to join us here; he's staying with friends in Oxford and could quite easily ride over and drink tea with us.'

'Your father was good enough to tell me he had invited him. He won't come.'

'I don't see why he shouldn't. You are, after all, an important member of the family and, although you don't go about now, there's not much that goes on that you don't know about. In any case, you're an old friend of the Duke's, so what could be more natural than that he should visit?'

'Because when I received your father's warning I wrote to Cosenham and told him he was welcome to come, but that the house was closed to popinjays and macaronis, so if he did visit he'd better do so in the guise of a reasonable human being.'

Araminta stared at her aghast. 'Great-Aunt! How could you? That was quite extraordinarily rude!'

'Yes, wasn't it?' the Dowager said with satisfaction. 'One of the great advantages of extreme age is that one can be as rude as one likes to one's juniors and there's not a thing they can do about it. It makes up for all the times one's elders were rude to one in one's youth.'

Araminta tried to repress a smile, and failed. 'I'll try to bear that in mind for the future,' she said, and turned the conversation into less hazardous paths.

Araminta enjoyed her brief visit because she enjoyed her great-aunt's astringent tongue and the fact that that lady was perfectly happy to be answered in kind. The forthcoming marriage was not alluded to again until Araminta took her leave of her great-aunt.

The old lady kissed her warmly. 'I hope everything goes off well,' she said. 'I don't anticipate anything else, of course; your mama may not have produced sons, but she has always been an extremely efficient organiser. As to the marriage itself—well, I hope you don't regret your decision. I have to confess that, had I been consulted, I should have advised against it. Still, it's done now. I'm sure I don't have to remind you that, having made your bed, you have no choice but to lie in it.'

'I know that, Great-Aunt, and I promise you I did not make the decision lightly.'

'I'm sure you didn't, just as I'm sure that Cosenham will have no reason to blame you for any shortcomings the marriage may prove to have. Safe journey, my dear. My prayers go with you.'

With such a valediction, it was hardly surprising that Araminta climbed into her carriage with somewhat dampened spirits and an uncomfortable realisation that she didn't actually want to go home. It was as if her short stay in Abingdon had somehow held the forthcoming marriage at bay and her return would hasten its taking place. Her maid sensed her mood and the carriage bowled along at a steady mile-consuming trot without a word's being exchanged between its occupants.

There was no need to spring the horses. Two hours at this pace on a relatively good road should see them in Newbury with the horses barely breaking sweat. Only when they came to Gadd Hill did the coachman slow them to a walk and, although there were trees near the top of it that were both too thick and too close for any conscientious coachman's comfort, it was broad and sunny daylight and it didn't even cross the coachman's mind to warn the armed footman beside him to be on his guard.

So it was that the sudden appearance before them of a black-cloaked man on a black horse and pointing a pistol in an unwavering manner directly at the footman took everyone by surprise.

'Drop it,' he commanded as the footman fiddled with the cocking mechanism of his gun and, since the rider's pistol was clearly already cocked and pointing straight at the footman's head, he did so. 'Stay there and don't move, and nothing will happen to you,' the rider went on. 'Move and I'll shoot.'

The coachman and footman exchanged glances and then nodded. Lord Cassington's displeasure would not be something to look forward to, but it was preferable to a premature grave.

By this time Araminta had let down the window. The sight of the musket on the ground and the pistol in the stranger's hand was enough to tell her what was going on, and her immediate feeling was one of annoyance rather than fear. 'Are we being delayed because some half-witted nincompoop thinks we're worth robbing?'

The rider tapped his tricorne with the barrel of his pistol in salute and Araminta noticed with some surprise that he was not masked. 'Are you telling me you're not, my lady?' he asked.

His voice was light and pleasant and—surprisingly, that of a gentleman. Perhaps he could be reasoned with. All the same, Araminta was very glad she had not taken so much as a string of pearls with her, having contented herself with a plain velvet band at her throat. Her only jewel was her mourning-ring and that was happily hidden by a glove.

'We have neither jewellery nor coin,' she asserted.

'Indeed? How, then, does the coachman pay for the change?'

'We travel only between Abingdon and Newbury,' Araminta told him. 'No change of horses will be needed.'

'Ah, that would explain it,' he said, accepting her word without quibbling.

Araminta looked at him curiously. It seemed odd for a highwayman to be so easily satisfied, but then, it was odd—surely?—for a highwayman to be unmasked. Not that she could make out a great deal; his hat was tipped well forward and threw a dark shadow over the face beneath. The sun was behind him and shining directly into Araminta's eyes, and she could make out very little except that it was long and lean, and she had an uncomfortable feeling that he was laughing at her.

He pressed his horse forward and opened the carriage door. 'Step down,' he commanded.

'No, thank you,' Araminta replied, aware of the incongruity of such politeness in the circumstances. 'I feel safer in here.'

'You can be shot just as easily inside the coach as out,' he pointed out reasonably, diverting the pistol barrel briefly from its target on the box.

Araminta hesitated briefly but took his point, and, pushing the step down in front of her, did as she was told. He swung himself down to join her with a warning glance at the two men on the box. 'Don't be foolish,' he admonished them. 'It won't be you that gets shot if you are. It will be your mistress.' He turned back to Araminta. 'So you've nothing to steal?'

'Nothing at all.'

He put his head on one side and looked at her speculatively. 'Not even a silk kerchief?'

Araminta opened her reticule and drew one out. She handed it to him. 'Is this enough reward for the risk you take? Aren't you afraid another traveller will come by?'

He turned the kerchief over in his gloved hand. 'It's a poor reward, as you say,' he commented. 'As for passers-by—no, why should I fear them? All they will see is this,' and he swept her into his arms, his cloak enveloping her while his mouth sought hers in a kiss the like of which Araminta had neither experienced nor imagined.

Her initial shock was supplanted by a sense of outrage but, as his mouth moved on hers and his arms pressed her body ever closer to his own, the outrage subsided and was replaced by a feeling of incomparable longing of a sort she had never imagined and only partly understood. Her body and her lips softened against his and then, as if this was what he had been waiting for, he raised his head and slackened his hold.

'No mask, you see,' he continued as if the interlude had not taken place. 'Just a pair of star-crossed lovers snatching a clandestine tryst.'

'On the main post-road to the south?' Araminta said dubiously, wondering why she felt a sudden disappointment.

'One must snatch one's opportunities where one may,' he replied.

'And with a loaded and cocked pistol in your hand?'

'Trickier, that. Your father entirely disapproves of the liaison and has given his servants instructions to horse-whip me if I show my face. The pistol is my deterrent.'

'I should think any father who disapproves of a liaison with you would be entirely justified,' Araminta retorted. 'So far as mine is concerned, I rather think he would be more likely to seek you out and horsewhip you himself—as he may very well do, when he hears.'

He held her at arm's length and looked at her ap-praisingly. His angle to the sun had slightly changed, giving her an opportunity to see him more clearly. She would not describe him as handsome, precisely—his face was a shade too long for that, and his mouth too thin—but it was a strong face, a face she would be inclined to trust, and in a strange, indefinable way, an oddly fam-iliar one. He was undoubtedly a gentleman, even if his present behaviour belied it, and she cast her mind back to her two London Seasons to see whether he fitted anyone she might have met there, however briefly, but, sadly, no bells rang. 'Will you let me go?' she concluded.

He shook his head. 'I don't think so. Not yet. I'm inclined to take a chance on no one passing for the time being.'

His arms enfolded her once more and Araminta was startled by her own readiness to respond to his embrace, subtly different this time in that it seemed less urgent, as if he had made his point and sought only to reinforce it. Her arms crept up round his neck, almost without her being aware that they were doing so, and her heart seemed to achieve a contradictory feat in that it both beat harder yet simultaneously felt as if it were dissolving into the all-consuming yearning to be part of this man's body.

He released the tension between them gradually with a succession of smaller, less intense kisses, until he sensed her heart was back in its normal place and functioning in a somewhat less extraordinary manner. Then he stood back, retaining only one of her gloved hands.

He raised it to his lips and kissed the fingers and Araminta knew as he did so that he must have felt her ring under the leather. Her eyes flew to his face in alarm, but he made no reference to her small deception, handing her back into her carriage instead, before folding up the step and closing the door. He picked up the guard's musket and swung himself into the saddle with it. 'I'll leave this halfway down the hill,' he told the guard. He uncocked his own gun and tucked it into his belt under the cloak. Then he touched his hat in a brief gesture of salute to Araminta. 'Your servant, my lady,' he said, putting his heels to his horse's sides almost before he had finished speaking and, before Araminta could reply, he had disappeared over the crown of the hill.

It was several minutes before the group at the carriage had gathered its wits together and it was Araminta who gave them some purpose.

'For goodness' sake, don't let us just sit here like cabbages,' she told the coachman. 'Collect your horses and get us back to Cassington Hall as fast as may be.'

The maid was fanning herself with her hand. 'Oh, my lady, what shall we tell Lord Cassington? And how you can sit there so calm and all after an experience like that, I really do marvel, my lady!'

'We shall tell Lord Cassington exactly what happened,' Araminta told her tartly. 'As to my being calm, I'm not at all sure that I am, but somebody has to decide what to do and it doesn't look as if any of you are capable of it.'

The footman kept his eyes open as they descended the hill, and was relieved to find his musket exactly as the highwayman had said he would. He heaved a sigh of relief. Lord Cassington was going to be angry enough at what had happened and would be sure to blame the footman's lack of attention. His anger would know no bounds if he also mislaid his firing-piece. The coachman pulled up to allow him to fetch it, and the footman returned to the carriage cradling it in his arms.

'You know what I reckon, my lady?' he said, stopping by the door. 'I reckon that there were Jack Ranton. That's what I reckon.'

'Who is Jack Ranton?' Araminta asked, mystified.

'He's a bridle-cull—a highwayman, beggin' your ladyship's pardon,' the coachman called down, 'with a reputation of never disguising his face yet never bein' recognised. That's who Jack Ranton is. But it's the first time I ever heard of him operating in this neck of the woods. Hampshire's his territory, and they do say he's been as far as Dorset and Sussex, though it's my belief they get him confused with smugglers. At all events, Oxfordshire and Berkshire he leaves alone, or so I've always heard.'

'No reason why he shouldn't move on,' the footman argued defensively, unwilling to let go of an appealing theory.

'And no reason why we shouldn't move on, either,' Araminta said. 'Or were you planning to stay here until another . . . bridle-cull . . . comes along?'

The coachman gathered up his reins again. 'I'd be obliged, my lady, if you'd not use that word—leastways, not in front of His Lordship. I didn't ought to have let it slip out, and that's a fact.'

Araminta chuckled. 'Don't worry, Letchworth, it won't soil my lips in polite company—and the quicker we get home, the quicker I shall forget I ever heard it.'

Letchworth knew a hint when he heard one and wasted no more time. Araminta cast a final disgusted glance at her maid, who was still behaving as it had been she who had been violated rather than her mistress, and decided to ignore her continued 'Oh, lordy me's and 'Whatever is the world a-coming to's in favour of her own confused thoughts.

Quite suddenly the universe had changed, the world had turned upside-down and, thanks to a common criminal, nothing could ever be the same again. Were these the feelings Thomas Kineton aroused in Isabella? Araminta thought of dull, nice, respectable Thomas and her quiet sister and found the idea inconceivable, but was it really any more inconceivable than that Lady Araminta Wareham could be reduced to a quivering jelly—or at least, she amended hastily, to a palpitating milksop—by a...a *bridle-cull* —she preferred that word; it lacked the misleading romantic overtones of 'highwayman'—whose only assets were a pleasant voice, a beguiling manner and a rather striking height, not one of which had any bearing at all on his character, his intelligence or his moral standing. Indeed, she reminded herself, his undoubted lack in the first and the last areas named suggested that he was not someone with whom any right-thinking individual would wish to be associated.

The undoubted accuracy of this reflection did nothing to alleviate her intense and growing desire to see him ride out of the trees once more—only this time he would take her with him when he left.

Her parents attributed her low spirits to the extremely unpleasant ordeal to which she had been submitted and were most understanding. Lord Cassington, a magistrate, expressed the opinion that, despite similarities, the highwayman was almost certainly not the Jack Ranton who had become something of a legend in Hampshire. The Earl did not altogether believe in the existence of the alleged Ranton, having always been of the opinion that the name had been used to cover an amalgam of criminals of the lower sort who took to highway robbery as a quick means of putting together a pound or two. The dressing down he gave the footman was enough to make that young man count himself fortunate to retain his position at all.

Lady Cassington hoped that the excitement of preparing for so very grand a wedding would be enough to take her daughter's mind off what had transpired and thus raise her spirits to the level expected of a bride, and Araminta, who had reasons of her own for wanting to be diverted from her thoughts, threw herself into the preparations with enough apparent enthusiasm to satisfy even the most anxious parent.

CHAPTER FOUR

IT CROSSED Araminta's mind that her betrothed might wish to pay his affianced wife another visit on his return to London from Oxford, and she braced herself to receive him, but it appeared he was content to leave everything to their respective fathers and the lawyers to settle. Lord Cassington wrote to him from time to time about one detail or another, but always received the same reply: 'Whatever best suits Lady Araminta will be perfectly acceptable.'

Lady Cassington read the third of these replies, which concerned the domestic arrangements for the wedding-night, and remarked to her daughter, 'If he proves one half as compliant as this when you're married, my dear, you will have made a very good choice.'

Araminta would naturally not receive her splendid allowance until after the wedding, but her parents were determined that no expense should be spared to make the ceremony one appropriate to the standing of the groom and his father, and certainly a more splendid affair than the village church had seen for a very long time. When the guests returned to Cassington Hall for the wedding breakfast, a veritable feast would be set out for them, and a hardly less generous one for everyone on the estate, which was to be held in a tented pavilion set up in the park at the front of the house.

Araminta's wedding-gown was of heavy slipper satin in a delicate shade of pink. The heavy overskirt was worn over a dome-hoop, which Araminta said she preferred to huge panniers, and was open at the front to reveal

72

the petticoat consisting entirely of flounce upon flounce of silver lace. The hem and edges of the skirt were embroidered with silver braid in a pattern of lilies of the valley and a similar theme, though smaller in scale, carried the embroidery up the bodice to edge the low, square neck. An echelle stomacher of the same satin and embellished with a silver bow, the centre of which was a stylised rose, completed the bodice, and generously pleated lace cuffs covered her arms from the elbow almost to the wrist, surmounted in their turn with wide bows of silver lace. She was to wear her hair powdered; a magnificent diamond necklace, the most valuable of the Wareham treasures, encircled her neck, and tear-shaped baroque pearls hung from diamond studs at her ears. When Araminta looked in the glass, she had no reason to feel dissatisfied.

'I almost wish I'd decided to be married in London,' she said. 'I may even outshine Lord Cosenham.'

'He will certainly have no grounds for complaint,' her mother agreed.

The groom had, in fact, made a discreet enquiry as to the colour of his bride's gown and had expressed thanks for the sample of fabric Lady Cassington had sent him. The Countess had made no mention of this to her daughter, but owned herself intrigued to see what her future son-in-law should wear. Both the Duke and his son had declined an invitation to stay at Cassington Hall for the period of their stay in Berkshire, the Marquess declaring it to be unlucky to meet the bride before the ceremony, and his father saying that it was better if at least one of the parents-in-law was off the premises for the wedding-night, though he was happy to accept an invitation to dine and meet his future daughter-in-law the day before the ceremony. The couple would leave for Portsmouth at mid-morning on the day after the wedding, and two adjoining rooms had been made ready for the bridal-night amid much sly nudging and giggling from those members of the household given the task of preparing them.

The Duke of Droxford, unlike his son, did not go out much in Society, preferring his books to idle chatter, and Araminta had therefore not seen him during either of her visits to the capital. He had the reputation of being austere and unapproachable, and she viewed his impending visit with some apprehension. She was both relieved and surprised to find she liked him.

He was tall, and that seemed to be the full extent of any similarity between him and his son. He dressed soberly but not unfashionably, except for his wig: he favoured the Campaign wig, a style that had not been worn in fashionable circles for some ten years. Although he had turned to his books when his wife had died some twenty years before, he had certainly not lost the knack of social conversation, and Araminta could not help contrasting his pleasant, easy style that subtly drew out his companions with that of his son, which was designed to show himself to advantage rather than to give his audience the chance to shine.

After dinner, the Earl and Countess tactfully withdrew, taking their younger daughters with them, to give their guest a chance to get to know their daughter a little better.

'I see you maintain an old-fashioned garden,' he remarked. 'Shall we take a turn about it?'

Araminta immediately fetched her chip bonnet and they stepped out on to the terrace that led down to the parterre.

'I find such geometric symmetry immensely satisfying,' he remarked. 'Justinian, on the other hand, favours the new style.'

'As does Mama,' Araminta told him, indicating the new garden beyond the ha-ha. 'I should have thought

Lord Cosenham would have appreciated the more man-nered formality of the old style.'

'I suspect he is torn between his natural inclination and the current fashion,' the Duke said drily. 'Where does your preference lie?'

'I have to plead indecision, Your Grace. I like them both, according to my mood, and I really believe Cassington Hall has the perfect solution: the formal garden close to the house and the informal at a distance.'

They walked on in silence for a while and it was the Duke who next spoke.

'You will not necessarily find marriage to my son easy,' he said.

'I don't imagine I shall,' Araminta agreed. 'I have a suspicion that no marriage is entirely smooth.'

'An intelligent approach,' he remarked. 'I should be inclined to keep it in mind, if I were you.' He paused as if there were much more he needed to say. 'I'm sure you can depend upon your parents' support,' he went on. 'May I assure you that you may equally well depend upon mine? I know my son very well—better, I think, than he suspects—if you remember that, you may find it easier in the future to talk to me. I assure you, you will always be very welcome.'

'Thank you,' Araminta said. She was not at all clear quite what underlay his remarks, and didn't know him well enough to ask, but with every word he spoke any faint similarity between the Duke and his heir receded still further and she found herself almost wishing it had been the Duke who had sought a wife.

Good manners required Araminta to remain with the company until the Duke took his leave towards mid-afternoon, but as soon as he had gone she sought her room, ostensibly to rest.

Her mother applauded the idea. 'Very sensible, my dear,' she said. 'Tomorrow will be a strenuous day for you, and the day after won't be much better. Get what rest you can. I'll make sure no one disturbs you.'

Araminta knew that rest was one thing she need not expect. There was too much else to think about. She knew her parents had reservations about this forth-coming marriage despite its obvious advantages. The Duke's generous provision could be interpreted as meaning that he, too, was more than ordinarily pleased it was to take place. His words had been kindness itself, but what had prompted them? At the very least, they appeared to imply that he did not anticipate a particu-larly harmonious union, and it was very clear his sym-pathies would be with the daughter-in-law rather than the son. Araminta wondered what he and her parents knew that she did not, and then she rebuked herself for such uncharitable thoughts: the Duke might well keep pertinent information from her if it suited his purpose, but her parents would never conceal something if they thought it might materially affect her happiness. She cast her mind back over her extremely limited acquaintance with the Marquess, but could find no clue there; nothing struck her that she had overlooked before. She could not respect a man who put fashionable affectations before everything else and she didn't much like him, either, which was probably, she thought suddenly, far more important, but she could think of nothing more specific to account for what she saw as the excessively considerate treatment she was being accorded.

Her thoughts were inconclusive, leaving her with the uneasy feeling—one which her recent encounter had done nothing to mitigate—that perhaps this marriage was going to prove a mistake. There was nothing she could do about that: marriage contracts were a serious business, although she had no doubt that if she could go to her father and say, 'I've just discovered so-and-so,' and mention something heinous that could be laid at

Cosenham's door, the Earl would arrange for the betrothal to be terminated. But she couldn't, and at this late stage it would need something more positive than an uneasy feeling and a chance encounter with a highwayman. Probably no one would take her seriously; they would tell her it was just nervousness and was entirely understandable in any well-brought-up young woman. She could imagine all too clearly Izzy's stricken face when she learnt that her own betrothal was once more in doubt. Isabella had had the air of someone walking on clouds of euphoria these last few weeks, and it would be an act of the most heartless cruelty to dash her hopes once more. A little voice deep inside her suggested that perhaps her own happiness was a high price to pay to ensure Izzy's, but Araminta suppressed it. It wasn't as if she was being forced into this alliance against her wishes. She had accepted Lord Cosenham of her own free will, and she could just as easily learn to love him as Izzy had learned to love Thomas. Well, perhaps not *just* as easily, but, if she failed, it wouldn't be for want of trying.

The wedding might be taking place in a country church, but there was nothing countrified about the arrangements. Both sides of the church were full, and at the back were as many of the Wareham tenants and retainers as could squeeze into the space. A great many of the groom's fashionable friends seemed to have been only too happy to stay with friends and relatives in Oxford and Abingdon, Highclere and Andover, in order to be able to ride or drive over to see their friend lose his freedom, as one of them jocularly put it.

The groom had excelled himself. A new wig had reached new heights and had thereby, many confidently predicted, set a new fashion. His coat was of a deep pink velvet, a fabric which increased the illusion of depth.

The breeches and the long-fronted waistcoat were of a matching heavy satin. Coat and waistcoat were heavily ornamented with silver braid which, on the coat, took the form of acanthus leaves with a lighter, more stylised version of the same design edging the waistcoat. The cuffs were turned back and heavily frogged in the military style, and the profuse lace at wrist and neck was cunningly embroidered with silver thread so that it glinted whenever it caught the light. Those who counted the Marquess a friend doubted whether the bride could be anything more than a pale shadow by comparison.

They had reckoned without Lady Cassington's unerring taste and sound instincts, and many cast a speculative eye over the younger Wareham girls. Who would have guessed that the family was so far removed from the provincial gentry they had been taken to be?

The Marquess inclined his head towards his bride as he stepped into the aisle to take her hand. 'Once again we match,' he murmured. 'How propitious!'

Araminta made no reply and suppressed a little smile, correctly guessing that chance had had nothing to do with the perfect harmony of their apparel.

Because of the circumstances of their betrothal, no betrothal ring had been given when the contracts were signed, and it was used, instead, to seal this, the final element of the contract. The Marquess's responses were made in the unemotional drawl he habitually used, so that anyone who didn't know him might have been excused for thinking he was uncertain whether to make them or not. Araminta's responses, on the other hand, were uttered quietly but firmly, as if she were convincing herself that she had no qualms.

When the formalities were over and the couple made their way back down the aisle, the bride's modestly downcast eyes met with approval in some quarters, though others said afterwards that a smile, preferably radiant, might have been more suitable. It was noticed that the groom didn't smile, either, but that was probably because he was loath to crack his carefully applied maquillage.

A whole ox and two sheep were roasting on spits over fires in the park where kegs of ale and a barrel of wine, together with bread, cakes and sweetmeats, had been set out for the tenants and estate workers. At the Hall itself, nothing had been stinted to ensure that the wedding breakfast was of a style and substance commensurate with the standing of the groom and his family. Georgiana and Florentina had never seen such splendid abundance in their lives, but had more sense than to say so until all the guests had gone. Georgiana made quite sure she sampled every single dish, even if good manners decreed that she should only take a small portion.

'After all,' she confided to her sister afterwards, 'who knows when we may expect a similar opportunity? It won't be for Izzy's wedding—Thomas's father is only a knight. I think you and I had better set our sights on another duke's son.'

'They're not all that plentiful,' Florentina told her, 'and if they all look like Cosenham, that's probably just as well. In any case, I'd not let Mama hear you talking like that, if I were you. She'd say it was vulgar.'

The newly married couple circulated among their guests, thanking each one for their good wishes and the gifts that had been received, but when everyone had been spoken to the Marquess was separated from his bride by some of his friends, and Araminta took the opportunity to converse more fully with some of hers. When she looked round for him, he was nowhere to be seen, and her puzzled frown brought the Duke to her side.

'I believe Justinian will be found in one of the side-rooms,' he told her. 'He is inordinately fond of cards. Would you like me to invite him to return?'

Araminta smiled. 'Invite, Your Grace? I think better not. We don't leave for Portsmouth until tomorrow. There will be time enough to become better acquainted. It is probably easier for both of us to take advantage of the presence of our own friends for the time being.'

The Duke bowed his acquiescence. 'As you wish, my dear. So long as you don't feel slighted.'

'I don't, and, if I don't appear concerned, the concern of others will soon dissipate, don't you think?'

The Duke did, and privately congratulated himself on the calm good sense of his daughter-in-law, unaware of her dismay at learning that her husband had so little taste for her company that he was not even prepared to maintain the pretence on his wedding-day.

Nor, as the time passed, was there any sign of the Marquess's tearing himself away from his card game to fulfil his marital obligations. It was customary, when a couple did not leave for their wedding-journey or their home on the day of the wedding, for guests to remain at the wedding breakfast until they had retired to bed. In earlier centuries guests did not leave until the news was brought them that the marriage had been consummated, but that custom had largely been discontinued, except in some bucolic circles. Therefore, since guests often had long journeys in front of them and travelling after dark could be a perilous undertaking, it was customary for the bridal pair to retire at an hour early enough to enable their guests to leave when it suited their convenience to do so. The Marquess seemed unaware of the predicament in which he was placing his guests.

Araminta caught the occasional anxious glance through the window, the surreptitious consulting of watches, and took her mother aside.

'Is there a tactful way of drawing Cosenham's attention to his obligations?' she asked.

'I fancy it would best be done by his father.'

A few minutes later she saw the Countess's head and the Duke's together in brief but earnest consultation, and then the Duke slipped unobtrusively out of the room. When he returned he was tight-lipped and very angry.

'I apologise for my son,' he said to Araminta and her mother. 'He suggests that you retire, my dear, and he will follow when he has finished his game.'

'It will look most particular,' Lady Cassington objected.

'It will, indeed. He has, however, agreed to stay where he is until those guests who have a long way to go shall have left. If Lady Cosenham is agreeable, I suggest she slips quietly away upstairs and we can then let it be known that the couple—overcome with shyness, you understand,' he added drily, 'have already retired, leaving their guests free to go.'

'Won't it look odd when those who stay see him emerge from the card-room?' Araminta asked.

'They won't,' the Duke said grimly. 'I've told him to leave by the window and come in by the kitchen and the back stairs. And, to make doubly certain, I've locked the door,' and he turned to Lady Cassington and handed her the key with a small but triumphant flourish.

'A man of initiative, I see,' she said. 'Will he do as he's told?'

'He will.' Neither the Countess nor her daughter knew how he could be so sure, but his tone was positive enough.

Lady Cassington turned to her daughter. 'Araminta?'

'His Grace has found the only solution. I'll slip away now.' She held her hand out to her father-in-law. 'Thank you, sir—and goodnight.'

'Goodnight, my dear. I look forward to meeting you again when you return from Italy.'

'And I you.'

Knowing that her husband had no intention of joining her for some time, Araminta went to her own bed-chamber where her maid, sent for by Lady Cassington, soon joined her.

'You shouldn't be here, my lady,' she scolded. 'This isn't the place to get ready for bed.'

'I know, but I feel more comfortable here. Just help me out of this gown, undo my hair and take the jewels back to Papa and then you can return to the cel-ebrations. I'll return to the other room presently. There is a robe in the chest, I presume?'

'Oh, yes, my lady. I didn't pack the green one—but there's a rose-pink one in the bridal-room—far more fitting.'

'I'll put it on when I get there,' Araminta promised.

When the girl had gone, Araminta put a cloth round her shoulders and began brushing the powder out of her hair. The window was unshuttered and partly open, and she could hear the bustle of leave-taking below and, from outside, the sound of carriages being brought round. Those guests of a nervous disposition or who had trav-elled a long way were losing no time. A long lull fol-lowed and Araminta knew she should make her way to the rooms that had been prepared for them, but she was loath to leave the comforting familiarity of the room that had been her own sanctuary for so many years.

After the lull, there was another bustle as the nearer friends and neighbours took their leave, and as that began to die down there was a tap on the door. Araminta's stomach gave a lurch and she felt sick. She shouldn't still be here, and hoped Cosenham wouldn't be too displeased that he had had to come searching for her.

'Come in,' she called, mustering a confidence she lacked.

It was Lady Cassington. 'Most of our guests have gone,' she said. 'All save the Marquess's card-playing cronies. The Duke left with the first wave—he said it would look strange if he stayed, which is true, but, without him, I'm not at all sure how to dislodge his son from his cards.'

'Why bother, Mama? Even his friends will have to leave some time, and I really cannot believe that an hour here or there is going to make much difference in a lifetime of marriage.'

'Bravely said, but one's wedding-night is not the same as the rest of one's married life,' the Countess said tartly. 'Your Papa is very displeased and I'm not at all sure he shouldn't put a halt to Cosenham's inconsiderate behaviour.'

'No, Mama. Let it be. I suspect my lord is merely demonstrating that, while he dances to his father's tune eventually, it needs more than a click of the fingers to bring him to heel.'

'At thirty-two!'

'Mama, we're discussing the rest of my life. Let it be my decision. Ask Papa to leave it be.'

'Very well, if that's your wish,' the Countess said doubtfully. 'It would be better if you were waiting for him,' she added.

'I know. I shan't stay here much longer.'

When her mother had gone, Araminta turned over in her mind what had transpired. It wasn't so much what her mother had said, but her own reaction when she had thought the tap at the door had been her husband. The next time she heard that tap, it really would be he, and Araminta knew now with an awful certainty that all her feelings of unease about this marriage had crystallised into a quite simple and straightforward physical distaste. It was 'Jack Ranton' whose arms she longed to feel round her once more; it was 'Jack Ranton's' kisses she longed to return; it was 'Jack Ranton' she wanted in her bed and it was 'Jack Ranton' she yearned to feel move within her. The thought of the Marquess touching her at all, much less lying with her, made her shudder with revulsion but, since her primary duty had been very clearly defined as being to provide heirs, lie with him she would have to.

She sank into a chair by the window and buried her face in her hands. What had she done? Had she really been so seduced by the thought of title and wealth that she hadn't looked beyond them? No. She knew those had not been the prime inducements. Izzy's happiness had played a larger part and she supposed, if she were absolutely honest, there must have been at the back of her mind the feeling that it would be satisfying to confound all those who had come to regard Lady Araminta Wareham as being on the shelf. That was before that fateful visit to her great-aunt. When she had made her decision, her heart had not been touched. Now that she had discovered the spark that could fly between two people, she realised that the price demanded by her previous decision was going to be a heavy one. Too heavy, perhaps. Certainly too heavy to pay willingly. She raised her head and leant back in the chair and, as she did so, a branch of the old fig-tree shifted in the night air and tapped on the pane. It had probably done so many times in the course of the evening, but this was the first time she had noticed it. She smiled in spite of herself. When she was young it had always seemed to be beckoning, offering illicit egress unless by some mischance she had been spotted from the house as she ran across the garden, in which case she was unceremoniously hauled back. But her parents, however displeased they might have been, had never chopped the tree down or even pruned away those branches closest to hand, nor had they fastened her window to prevent her repeating the exercise.

Looking back, she realised they had been remarkable parents.

Suddenly the lethargy of despair left her and she sat bolt upright, her mind racing. She glanced at the ornate blue-enamelled clock on the mantelshelf. Then she stripped the coverlet from the bed and threw it on the floor. The blanket beneath she folded neatly into four, breadthways. She opened the press and selected the darkest of her habits, the green one with gold frogging. She flung off her robe, tightened the drawstring at the neck of the shift beneath and climbed into the habit. She pulled on stockings and boots and found a three-cornered beaver which she clapped on her head after tying her hair loosely back.

She scooped up brushes and combs from the dressing-table and wrapped them in a clean shift from the chest at the foot of the bed, and then placed them carefully on the folded blanket. They were followed by a handful of stockings and another clean shift and then, after deciding that a second habit would be too much, she rolled the blanket up, carefully folding the edges in over the contents to prevent their falling out. She found a belt to strap round one end of the finished bundle and a broad ribbon to secure the other. She found a warm, heavy cloak and hesitated. It would be heavy to carry down the fig-tree and, if she wore it, it would get in the way. Still, it would be very necessary. She wrapped it round the bundle and then slid the window up and peered out. No one stirred, and only cracks of light appeared on the terrace, which meant that the internal shutters had been closed across the windows of those rooms which were occupied. She picked up the bundle and dropped it out of the window, giving it as she did so a small shove to take it beyond the hampering branches of the tree. She heard it thud gently on the terrace and then listened in case anyone else had heard it and came to investigate.

There were no new sounds. Only one thing remained to be done: she removed her betrothal ring and placed it on the dressing-table where it would be found in the morning, if not before.

Checking that her hat was firmly on her head, Araminta clambered on to the sill and reached across to the branch. It was many years since she had made use of its services, but she had done it so often in the past that her old skills returned very quickly and, despite the encumbrance of her skirts, she was soon standing on the terrace. She stood for a few moments to let her eyes become accustomed to the dark, and at the same time to listen for any indication that her progress down the tree had attracted attention. There was none.

She could see sufficiently well now to locate the bundle, and she made her way as stealthily as possible along the terrace, down the steps and on to the grass path leading to the front of the house, where, by remaining on the grass, she could slip along to the stable block.

Because the card-players had not yet left, the massive gates to the yard had been left open. One lantern hung in the stables where the visitors' mounts had been saddled up in readiness for their owners' departure. This was not customary practice, but the Earl, annoyed by the lack of consideration of his new son-in-law's friends, had told his grooms to tack up the horses and go to bed.

Araminta took down the lantern and carried it to the far side of the stable, where Halcyon in his box recognised her step and whickered. She hushed him and lifted the saddle down from its iron tree on the wall opposite, sending up a prayer of thanks for a father who insisted that, daughters or not, any child of his could both saddle up a riding-horse and harness up a driving one. She had strapped the bundle on to the back of the saddle and was about to lead Halcyon out when she thought of something else. She knotted the reins quickly over his neck and tiptoed as fast as she dared along to the tack-room. To her relief it was both unlocked and empty. The moon was shining in now, and she had no difficulty finding what she had come for. On a peg under one set of carriage harness hung a wide, holstered belt. This housed a brace of flintlock pistols which the coachman or, if the vehicle was a post-chaise, the postilion was supposed to wear in case they were waylaid, though Araminta had never quite worked out how the men were supposed to control the horses at the same time as firing the gun. A powder-horn hung with it and she took that, too, slinging it across one shoulder to hang at the opposite side.

When she got back to Halcyon, she hung the holsters over the saddle, attaching them to the pommel-horn, and then, having thrown her cloak round her shoulders, she led Halcyon to the mounting-block and settled herself in the saddle, pausing only to check that the small purse of money she always wore round her waist under the skirt of her habit was still there. Lord Cassington rested easier in his mind for knowing that, if anything happened to his daughters in the hunting-field, they would always have the means to get home either by hiring a farmer's gig or by sending a messenger to fetch help.

That done, she collected Halcyon and rode him across the yard and through the gate. If luck was on her side, anyone who heard his hoofs would assume it was another of the guests leaving, but Araminta was disinclined to press her luck and, as soon as grass offered, she put him on to that.

It was not very long before she was well away from the house and into the woods that fringed the Countess's new garden at the back of the house. Here Araminta drew rein briefly and looked across at Cassington Hall. The house loomed grey in the moonlight and, although its mass could be clearly discerned, no detail could be made out except that from only one window—that of Araminta's bed-chamber—was there a light. She could only assume that the card-party still continued. Long may it do so, she thought, for the longer the Marquess sat over his cards, the longer it would be before he realised his wife was missing.

She took a last, sad look at the house where she had been so happy and then collected Halcyon once more and turned him into the seclusion of the trees.

CHAPTER FIVE

ARAMINTA dared not ride fast. Quite apart from the
danger of the horse's stumbling in a rabbit hole in the
dark, she must husband his strength. She needed to put
as much distance as possible between her and Cassington
Hall before dawn, when her father might reasonably be
expected to send out search parties, but there was no
point in pushing the horse so hard that she was obliged
to stop for several hours for him to rest. If she could
resist the temptation to take him out of a walk, he could
probably go for the rest of the night with only the occasional stop. By dawn they might, with care, be twenty
miles away, perhaps more. For a few days it would be
to her advantage to travel by night and rest by day,
though finding a suitable resting place would not be easy;
if she went to a cottage or an inn, word would soon get
back to her family. No, she would have to find a cave
big enough to hide both herself and Halcyon.

Her choice of direction had been arbitrary, determined more by the shortest route away from anyone
looking out of Cassington Hall than by any rational decision as to where she was going or what she was going
to do when she got there. She was travelling in a broadly
south-easterly direction and, although there was plenty
of sheltering forest, the Hampshire Downs were not
noted for their caves. When dawn came, she watered
both Halcyon and herself at a stream and looked around
her for somewhere to pass the daylight hours.

She began to despair until a small clearing where
already the undergrowth was beginning to re-establish

itself opened up quite unexpectedly before her. Here were the remains of a charcoal-burners' camp. The strange buildings, like thatched roofs set down on the ground without walls, were in various stages of disrepair, but one of them was large enough for both travellers. It was hardly weatherproof, but fortunately there had been no rain for some time so the ground was at least dry.

Araminta dismounted and unsaddled Halcyon, then, despite her exhaustion, she kept watch for intruders while he grazed on the rejuvenated grasses of the forest floor. After what she judged to be an hour or so, when his hunger was clearly blunted, she led him into the primitive structure, tied him to one of the stronger of the supporting poles and then, using the saddle as a pillow and wrapping herself in her cloak, she lay down at the other end of the building. Sleep, deep and uninterrupted, came swiftly, and she didn't wake up until the sun had worked its way round and sent a shaft through one hole right on to her face beneath. She sat up instantly and knew at once from the light that evening would soon be upon them. She knew from her stomach that she was ravenous.

Feeding Halcyon presented no problems, but there was nothing with which to assuage her own hunger. They would ride through the coming night and then she must buy food somewhere the following day, even at the risk of its leading her father to discovering her whereabouts. She calculated that, if she had covered twenty miles last night and were to cover the same distance tonight, she would be sufficiently far to be out of his reach. She guessed that no one would have expected her to ride right through the night, and would probably start looking for her in out-of-the-way villages and inns where the Warehams would not be recognised. When she added to that probability the fact that they would have no idea in which direction to start looking, she felt that by to-

morrow morning the risk entailed in buying food somewhere would not be too great.

The card party broke up within a very short time of
Araminta's taking a final look at Cassington Hall and,
when the last guest had left, Lord Cosenham bade his
exhausted parents-in-law goodnight and asked them to
direct him to the bridal-suite. He was a little surprised
to find it in darkness, but soon lit the candles in the
dressing-room and then, after only a brief hesitation,
opened the door that connected the dressing-room with
the main bedroom beyond. Presumably his bride had
tired of waiting and was sound asleep.

There was no sign of Araminta.

The bed-covers had been turned back, but the bed had
very clearly not been disturbed in any way and the
candles beside it had burned themselves out. He frowned.
Perhaps the Earl or his wife could throw some light on
what had happened.

He found the Earl's room by the simple expedient of
listening outside doors until he heard the murmur of
voices. His tap provoked a surprised 'Come in' but the
Marquess, realising his host must think it a servant who
knocked, ignored the request.

'It's Cosenham, my lord,' he called softly. 'May we
speak?'

There was a further murmur of voices before the door
opened and the Earl, wearing a nightcap, a dressing-gown
and a none-too-pleased expression came out. 'Yes?' he
said. His tone was neither conciliatory nor particularly
interested.

His son-in-law was all contrition. 'My most sincere
apologies for this intrusion,' he began. 'There seems,
however, to be a small...impediment to which I feel I
should draw your attention.'

'Indeed?' The Earl's tone was glacial.

'Lady Cosenham does not appear to be there.'

The Earl's interest sharpened. 'Not there? Are you sure? Have you looked?'

The Marquess's tone was apologetic. 'Oddly enough, I did. That's to say, I looked in the bed—which appeared not to have been touched—and around both the bed-chamber and the dressing-room. I have to confess that I didn't look *under* the bed or rifle through cupboards or closets. Or drawers,' he added helpfully.

'But she must be there!'

'One would have thought so.' The sibilance of his voice had acquired a hard edge which the Earl in his bewilderment failed to notice.

'One moment,' the Earl said. 'My wife may be able to explain.' He disappeared into his room and Justinian heard him open what he assumed to be an adjoining door. When he reappeared he was accompanied by his wife, who had thrown on a silk undress-gown of a singularly becoming shade of blue which Lord Cosenham was in no mood to appreciate.

She smiled at her son-in-law encouragingly. 'I'm so sorry, my lord, but I think I know what has happened. I expect she's still in her old room.'

'Why should she be there? It can hardly have escaped her notice that a bridal-chamber had been prepared.'

'No, indeed, my lord, and I'm afraid you will have to accept some blunt speaking. Minty put a brave face on your shutting yourself off to play cards—which, I take leave to tell you to your face, was not at all the thing—but she was very upset. I found her in her old room and I did remind her that she should be elsewhere. She assured me that she would go there shortly. Since she appears not to have done so, I imagine she must have fallen asleep there. It has been a very exhausting day for her—a fact which you, my lord, would do well to bear in mind.'

The Marquess inclined his head. 'Then perhaps you would be kind enough to direct me to her old room,' he suggested.

'Don't you think it would be wiser to leave her to sleep?' Lady Cassington asked.

'If she proves to be asleep, you have my undertaking that she shall remain so. I should, however, like to find out for myself.'

Lady Cassington led the way to Araminta's room and stood outside, her head close to the door. After a few seconds during which no sound at all filtered through its panels, she tapped, gently at first, and then a little harder. There was no response.

Lady Cassington unceremoniously removed the branch of candles from her son-in-law's hand and gently opened the door, but as she stepped into the room, holding the candles aloft, a gust of air from the open window blew them out. The Earl cursed quietly and stepped across to close it, then he relit the candles from the tinder at the bedside and, as he did so, it became perfectly plain that Araminta wasn't in this bed, either.

A quick glance round the room revealed the discarded coverlet, and evidence that both the press and clothes-chest had been rifled. The Countess handed the candles back to her son-in-law and opened the press. She flicked quickly through the clothes hanging there.

'So far as I can tell, her heavy winter cloak is missing and so is the green habit. There seems to be a tricorne missing, too, but I can't be sure of that. Her maid will be able to confirm it. She'll be better able than I to tell us what's missing from the chest. I thought there was another blanket on the bed, too, but I may be wrong.' She went across to the dressing-table. 'There's a brush and comb missing,' she added, and then bent over to look more closely. 'There's this instead,' she said, and held Araminta's betrothal-ring up to the light.

Lord Cosenham took it from her and examined it as if doubting its authenticity. 'Then where is Lady Cosenham?' he asked, all sibilance gone and in a voice hard with anger.

'I can't believe my daughter would have run away,' the Earl said defensively. 'To be sure, that's the first explanation that springs to mind, but there must be another.'

Lord Cosenham strode across to the window, threw it up and looked out. 'This fig seems sturdy enough to support someone's weight,' he remarked.

The Earl coloured. 'It is. All the girls—except Isabella,' he amended in the interest of fairness, 'have used it at some time or another.'

'And the window was open when we came in,' the Marquess insisted, while Lady Cassington relit the candles which had again blown out. 'What other explanation can there be?'

His parents-in-law had no suggestions to offer.

'Tell me,' the Marquess went on. 'To what extent had your daughter felt obliged to marry me?'

'None, I hope,' Lord Cassington said stiffly. 'I made it perfectly clear that she was free to say no.'

'Do I assume a previous attachment proved more compelling?'

'Certainly not,' Lady Cassington interjected. 'Araminta had never formed any attachment. She met no one in London for whom she felt even a passing regard, and there has never been anyone in this neighbourhood to attract her softer feelings. Not even,' she added, forestalling Lord Cosenham's next most likely suggestion, 'someone quite unsuitable.'

'Would you have known if she had formed an unsuitable attachment?'

'Quite possibly not, but my other daughters would have rooted it out and, while Isabella would have been loyal to Minty and Florentina would probably have kept her own counsel, Georgiana would never have been able to keep it to herself. I might not have been told about it. That doesn't mean I shouldn't have known eventually.'

She could hardly have been more candid, and Lord Cosenham accepted her word without further question. His bride had not left him for a previous lover.

'So Lady Cosenham has run away for completely incomprehensible reasons—and on her wedding-night. What do we do now?'

'There's only one thing we can do before morning,' the Earl told him. 'I suggest we check the stables. Any horse or gig could have left here this evening without arousing any attention because there were so many visitors. If nothing's missing, we know she's on foot and cannot go far. If she's taken a gig, she will have travelled further but must have kept to the roads. If a saddle-horse has gone, she will be under no such restraints.'

'Could she saddle or harness a horse on her own?' the Marquess asked, surprised.

'All my daughters can,' the Earl told him shortly, wondering for the first time if it had been such a good idea, after all.

It took the two men very little time to discover that Halcyon and all his tack had gone, though the loss of the pistols was not to be discovered for several days, and as soon as they had ascertained that flight, for whatever reason, really was the only possible explanation for Araminta's disappearance, the two men returned to the house and the Earl's study, where Lady Cassington joined them.

'There's nothing more to be done tonight,' the Earl said. 'Search parties will go out tomorrow.'

The Marquess frowned. 'They must, of course, but how much discretion can your people exercise?'

'My daughter needs to be found. Too much "discretion" would hinder that.'

'With respect, my lord, your daughter is my wife and a husband's authority overrides a father's. Do you imagine I wish it put about that my wife fled before the wedding-night——?'

'You forget, my lord,' Lady Cassington broke in. 'We told everyone that the two of you had stolen away without a formal leave-taking. No one will think she fled before the wedding-night.'

A brief, sardonic smile crossed the Marquess's enamelled face. 'I'm no more enthusiastic at the thought of its being put about that she fled as a result of the wedding-night.'

'We can hardly start searching for someone without admitting they're missing,' the Earl pointed out.

'Let us understand one another,' the Marquess said, and the Countess noticed that his voice had reverted to its normal affected and sibilant drawl, as if he were once more in command, not only of himself, but also of the situation. 'This marriage has not been consummated, and consequently, as you must be very well aware, it can be set aside with little legal difficulty but a great deal of scandal. I have no desire to become a figure of public ridicule—as I will if I have the marriage annulled. No one will care whether my wife fled before or after the wedding-night, or for the fact that no man can consummate a marriage in the absence of his wife. Whichever version they choose to believe, I shall be made to look ridiculous. Your family will face social ruin. Lady Cosenham—Lady Araminta Wareham, as she will become once more—will be quite unmarriageable, and your other daughters scarcely more so. I don't imagine that would suit you very well.'

'It wouldn't suit me at all,' the Earl admitted frankly. 'My daughter's safety is of more concern to me, however, and that is of more pressing importance than what people say—or what you decide to do. First she must be found.'

'I agree, and I have a suggestion. We were due to leave at midday for Italy. I shall change my plans and leave earlier. Much earlier. Dawn, in fact. That would enable us to reach Portsmouth by evening and sail on the evening tide, don't you think? My coach will be ordered and we may even get it ready and away before any of your people notice anything is amiss. Lady Cosenham's maid—who was to have travelled with us anyway—will have to be let into the scheme. She will have to dress as my wife and be seen to leave here in the carriage. She will, of course, be far too upset at leaving her family home to take the normal leave of your household that would otherwise have been expected.'

The Countess was listening to him with interest, and the Earl with incredulity. Lord Cosenham was revealing an unexpected ability to scheme, and at very short notice.

'Go on,' the Earl said.

'I shall leave—apparently for Portsmouth—but I shall actually go to Copenore and there I shall lie low, living the life of a very quiet country gentleman until I hear from you. So far as the rest of the world is concerned, I shall be in Italy with my wife. If I'm unfortunate enough to have visitors, she will be indisposed. Meanwhile you and your people will be searching, not for your daughter, but for her horse, which has vanished from its stable. Only if the horse is found without my wife will there be any necessity for revealing more of the story to the searchers, and that bridge will have to be crossed only if we come to it. Do you wish to comment?'

The Earl did. He was sure there must be some snag to this glib and rapidly constructed scheme, but he couldn't think what it was, so he shook his head.

'Very well. Lady Cassington, would you be kind enough to wake up Lady Cosenham's maid and explain the situation? My lord, if you will but conduct me to my man's room, I undertake to organise my departure with the least possible commotion.'

It was naturally impossible for an entourage consisting of two carriages, a baggage coach, horses, servants and outriders to be assembled in silence without attracting attention, but the Marquess's people seemed to be quite used to obeying extraordinary instructions and clearly thought nothing of so sudden a change in plan, and when a bleary-eyed Cassington groom asked what was going on the Marquess's coachman told him to go back to bed and thank his lucky stars he worked for a reasonable man. This was said with such feeling that the groom did precisely that, and the carriages rolled out having alerted nothing much more than a few curious stares from attic windows. The watchers were able to observe the Earl and Countess taking leave of the occupants of the carriage, and, since the Countess was clearly in tears, they guessed that Lady Araminta was leaving earlier than had been planned, regretted it, wished her happy, and returned to their beds.

Araminta's second night in the saddle was a great deal less fun than the first. For one thing, she was extremely hungry, a circumstance calculated to lower anyone's enjoyment. For another, the sense of urgency had dissipated now that she must be a long way from Cassington Hall, and with it, the sense of adventure. There was also the sense of desolation: for the first time in her life, Araminta had spent twenty-four hours without even seeing another human being, let alone speaking with one. She felt lonely and vulnerable, and a dark forest was not the best place to lift the spirit.

She maintained as well as she could her south-easterly direction, recalling, every time she tried to verify her bearings when the forest canopy thinned enough to enable her to see the stars, stories of people who had simply travelled round and round in a circle, and she decided that the worst thing that could happen would be to stumble again upon the same charcoal-burners' camp. Now she began to question her whole action in running away, and to consider for the first time the possible consequences, not just to her, but to her family.

The only possible good that might ensue was that her disappearance on her wedding-night would enable Lord Cosenham to have the marriage dissolved. However, that could not be achieved without a great deal of gossip and scandal, neither of which Lord Cosenham would relish and both of which would cause her own family much pain. As a consequence of the dissolution, Droxford's sponsorship of her sisters would be lost and their position would, because of the scandal, be worse than it had been before. What would happen to her own reputation was something that didn't bear thinking about.

Her parents would be both upset and worried by her disappearance. Lord Cosenham would, she suspected, be very angry—and who could blame him? A search would certainly be mounted, and Araminta was by no means quite so sure as she had been that she hoped it would be unsuccessful. There was something infinitely alluring in the thought of Cassington Hall and her own comfortable bed-chamber. Except that Cassington Hall was no longer where she lived. There was Cosenham House in London and Copenore, the Marquess's country estate in Hampshire, though he was supposed not to spend much time there. He had an hôtel in Paris, and during their travels in Italy they would have spent some time at a *palazzo* he owned in Venice. None of these was such an inviting prospect as her own room at home.

Not that there was any guarantee he would want to have her back even if she returned now; he must have been humiliated by her disappearance and, slight though her acquaintance with him was, he hadn't struck her as a man to whom humiliation would come easily. Furthermore, she had been away all night, an event sufficient on its own to ruin any woman. The fact that she had been entirely alone all the time she had been absent was immaterial, and not only because it was impossible to prove. No, there was a very good chance that Cosenham wouldn't want her back anyway, and that, she reminded herself, was exactly what she wanted, a useful precursor to the dissolution of the marriage.

Her return home, attractive as it was beginning to look, would bring nothing but shame upon her family. Many parents might refuse to have their daughter back. Araminta didn't think her own parents would come into that category. They would accept her back, glad that she was unharmed, and suffer the shame that ensued. Unfortunately, that shame would reflect upon her sisters and would be recalled when the two younger ones were of marriageable age—which in Florentina's case was only a year or so away. It might even result in Sir John's and Lady Kineton's insisting their son cry off from any arrangement he might have with Izzy and, since no formal betrothal had as yet been entered into, that would be easily enough done. No, it would be better all round if she were never seen again.

Exactly what she proposed doing, Araminta hadn't the slightest idea. She rode well and was perfectly capable of looking after horses, but who had ever heard of a female groom or ostler? Her sewing was competent, but no more, and she doubted very much her ability to teach drawing or music, even though she had a reasonable facility at both. In any case, what parent would employ an governess who could produce no character?

At this stage in her contemplations, she was brought back very sharply to the dangers of night-riding by her horse. Halcyon stopped suddenly, his front legs braced wide apart, ready for flight. He threw his head up and blew short puffs of air down his flared nostrils, a sure signal of alarm.

Obedient to his warning, Araminta reined him in and strained her eyes and her ears through the dark. She saw nothing untoward, but at some distance to the left she could hear a spasmodic whimpering, which every so often was interspersed with a small yelp. Neither sound was what one would expect to hear in a forest in the dead of night, but the only thing it resembled was a dog—and a dog in distress. Araminta told herself that no dog could present a threat to her, and turned Halcyon's head towards the sound, at the same time encouraging him forward. He stepped two paces and stopped again, and this time she could not persuade him to go on.

She hesitated and looked about her. Fortunately the trees were thinner here and the moonlight filtered through. There were signs of recent coppicing, which meant there was very little impeding undergrowth in the direction from which the whimpers came. Araminta hesitated briefly, and then dismounted and tied Halcyon's reins to a convenient branch. She moved cautiously towards the sound. It was impossible to judge how far the coppicing extended, and the shadows cast on the ground made it sometimes difficult to detect obstacles. When she finally stopped—because the whimpering was close at hand now, and intensified—she looked back over her shoulder and was surprised still to be able to make out the deeper black of Halcyon's bulk by the tree. The distance had in fact been slight.

It took her several minutes to locate the source of the noise and she was startled to find that, while her guess that it was a dog had been correct, her assumption, based on the nature of the noise, that it was a small one was very wrong. In this light she could only tell that it was dark-coloured. It lay with one hind leg uncomfortably stretched out to one side. Obviously a large dog, it had pendulous jowls and ears to match, and when Araminta approached it seemed uncertain whether to welcome her as a friend or to send her packing. It was when it struggled defensively to its feet that she realised that the leg that had been arranged at such an uncomfortable angle was held fast in an iron trap.

Or had been. As she fondled the dog's head to distract it from her attempts to look closer at the leg, she realised that it was only held by a part of one toe. Both the foot and the trap were liberally covered with something that gleamed dully and which she took to be blood, and this made it difficult to estimate more precisely just what the situation was. The Earl allowed no traps on his land. He maintained that the loss of rabbits and even the occasional deer was far more easily borne than the mutilation of horse or hound, but many of his neighbours did, and Araminta knew how they worked. She should have no difficulty freeing this dog—if only the dog would let her get near enough to its damaged leg to try.

First she hunted around for a sound piece of wood with which to wedge the teeth of the trap apart. Rotten wood, which broke when she snapped it across her knee, there was in abundance, but finally she found what she sought and, murmuring soothingly to the dog as she did so, she managed to force the mouth open and wedge it with the wood. No sooner was the pressure relieved than the dog pulled its paw free and sat down to clean it up.

'Let me look,' Araminta said. The dog growled when it realised her intent, but she kept up a murmur of inconsequential words and was able to see that it was in a bad way, two of the toes being severed and a third presumably the one that had still been in the trap—almost as bad.

What did she do now? The dog had almost certainly strayed, though it wasn't the sort one saw on farms or in cottages. It was in no condition to find its way home and, if it tried, would be unable to hunt for food; on the other hand, if it didn't try to get home, it would almost certainly be shot by the keeper who had set the trap, which was far too large to have been laid by a poacher. She glanced up at where Halcyon's form could still be made out, and judged the distance. It wasn't far, but it was too far to carry a heavy dog and, although this dog was lean to the point of thin, he was still going to be heavy.

Araminta untied the ribbon that had so hastily been used to hold back her hair and knotted it round his neck so that an end remained, leash-like. Holding this, she encouraged the dog to stagger three-legged over towards Halcyon. He was willing enough to oblige her, but in too much pain to make anything but heavy weather of the short walk. The only way to get the dog out of here so that his foot could be attended to properly would be to carry him in front of her on the saddle. How she was to get him up there—always assuming he allowed her to try—was something of a problem, and it was not going to be made any easier by Halcyon's obvious dislike of their new companion.

She dealt with Halcyon by tying him close and covering his head with her cloak so that he could see nothing of what she was doing and, she hoped, be less able to smell the blood which was probably what was upsetting him. Then she coaxed the dog to his feet again and, recalling the way she had seen men carry calves, she wrapped her arms round each end and found he lifted surprisingly easy, though he complicated the exercise at first by struggling. Once he had stopped resisting, she managed to heave him inelegantly across her saddle. It seemed at first as if he would hurl himself off again, but Araminta, who needed to get her breath back, had rested with her hand on his ribs and was able to calm him. All it now needed was for her to mount and they could be on their way.

It was more easily thought than done. She couldn't push the dog forward and over the horn, to lie across Halcyon's neck, because of the height of the horn, and she had little enthusiasm for the prospect of riding behind the saddle. It was true there was a pad in the shape of her clothes-bundle, but the stirrup would be too far forward and she would have to ride astride. Not only would this be indelicate but also dangerous; she had never ridden astride in her life and had no expertise in the technique, quite apart from the fact that Halcyon was, and had always been, a lady's horse. He had never, so far as Araminta was aware, borne a cross-saddle in his life. In fact, it would be easier to walk and lead the horse.

She dismissed this thought almost as soon as it occurred to her; she had no idea how far she would have to walk and riding-boots were not suited to that form of exercise. Besides, she was trying to get as far away from home as she could. With a sigh, she removed her cloak and steadied the horse before untying him. It wasn't easy to mount with her only aid, the stirrup, at such an unaccustomed angle to where she would be sitting, and Araminta was very glad Halcyon was no taller, but she was up at last, though she felt insecure perched behind the saddle with no stirrup and nothing firm to grip with her knees, as she had seen farm-boys do when they rode home without a saddle. It was, she decided, a good job she had no intention of going out of a walk.

It now became imperative to find somewhere to stop, so the next time a track wider than a path crossed their route she turned on to it in the expectation that it would lead to a hamlet or village or, failing that, to an isolated farmhouse. In fact, it was almost dawn before it arrived anywhere, and Araminta was not encouraged by what she saw.

Three cottages that were little more than thatched hovels clustered together with their outbuildings round an ancient dew-pond. To one side and a little apart was a somewhat larger building, its thatch in better repair, its walls between the timbers of brick instead of wattle and daub. Only its chimney told Araminta that this was the dwelling, and not the almost equally large one behind, which she took to be the stable, though how such an impoverished little settlement could possibly need so substantial a stable she couldn't imagine. Then she noticed that a besom, its bristles upturned, was fastened to the front of the house. She had heard tell of such things but had not seen one, never having ventured into quite such remote parts before. This was no house but a hostelry of some kind, though whether ale-house or inn remained to be seen. Nowadays, with so many travellers upon the roads, and inns vying for their custom, the old medieval brush had been more often replaced with a pictorial sign so that travellers might distinguish between one inn and another, and recommend the Blue Boar as being better than the White Hart or vice versa.

There was an air about this desolate little settlement that made Araminta disinclined to dismount until she had had the opportunity to form an opinion of its inhabitants. They might well be poor, but honest. They might equally well be otherwise. Fortunately the tavern's door opened directly on to the track, so it was a simple matter to knock with the butt of her whip.

Araminta did not expect an immediate response at so early an hour, and was therefore all the more surprised when that was what she got. Her whip was already raised for a second tattoo when the door opened and a burly, unshaven individual, his shirt only partially tucked into his breeches, peered round it.

'Yes?' The inflexion was deeply suspicious.

Araminta smiled with more confidence than she felt. 'Can you help me?' she asked.

The door opened a little wider and the man looked her up and down and then, with far greater interest, scrutinised the landscape beyond and around. 'Why?' he said at last.

'I need a meal and a bed and so does my horse, and I've a dog here that probably needs both, but first his foot needs attention,' and she lifted the edge of her cloak with which the dog had been covered.

The man stepped back involuntarily when he saw the dog. 'Where did you find that? You'll not be telling me it's yours.'

'No, it's not. Do you know where he belongs? Perhaps we could send a message to them. He's quite badly hurt.'

'Pity he ain't dead, if you asks me. No, I don't know where he belongs—not round hereabouts, though, that I do know.'

'Yet you seem to know him,' Araminta persisted.

'I've heard tell. If he's the one I think he is—and he certainly looks like it—every landowner between Andover and Guildford and points south has put traps on his land to catch him. It's so bad that honest men going about their lawful business can't step out at night for fear of stepping into one.'

'I shouldn't have thought many honest men had lawful business at night—at least, not in other men's woodland,' Araminta remarked. 'One of the traps was successful, however, and he has lost a part of one hind foot. Do you have tar in the stable?'

A mixture of curiosity and incredulity began to replace his suspicion. He ignored her question. 'And what are you doing, looking for a bed at dawn? 'Tis at dusk honest folk seeks their bed.'

'Apart from those honest folk who are wandering in other men's woodland, I take it,' Araminta said pleasantly. 'It's a long story and I'm far too tired and hungry to go into it now, but I can pay for anything we eat, if that consoles you at all.'

'Ah, well, I'd probably not believe you, anyway,' he said. 'Money you say? How much?'

'Enough, I should imagine.'

'You don't expect me to get that thing down off your horse, I hope. I was born with ten fingers, you see, and I'd like to die with them, too.'

Araminta chose to ignore the heavy humour. 'I got him up there. I dare say I shall be able to get him down again. I'll take them both round to the stable, and while I'm settling them down you can fetch food for the dog and a bowl for some water. And what about tar?' Tar was the standard treatment for damaged hoofs and Araminta knew no efficient stable would be without it. She had grave doubts about the efficiency of this man's stable.

'There's some on the shelf, but I'll have to charge you for it.'

'Naturally.' Araminta turned Halcyon towards the other building. 'I'll eat when I've seen to these,' she said.

The man made a mock bow. 'And what would my lady like? A game pie, some slivers of ham? Devilled kidneys?'

The use of her customary title startled Araminta. Could word have reached here? Had he realised who she must be? Then she realised he was being ironic. She smiled affably. 'How kind! But quite unnecessary. Bread and cheese will do very well, and something to wash it down. Ale, I suppose,' she said doubtfully, 'though, to be truthful, mulled wine would be more welcome.'

The interior of the stable was a welcome surprise. It was in good order and much bigger than Araminta would have expected a tavern in such an out-of-the-way spot to need. There were eight stalls, all of them empty. A ladder at one end led up to a hay-loft which extended along the length of the building and across about two thirds of its width, which meant that hay and straw could be thrown down directly into the space in front of the stalls without the need to bring it in from outside, as was more usually the custom. Despite the fact that the stable was empty, every hay-rack was full; straw covered the floor, not only of each stall, but also of the passageway in front of them. Two bins at one end proved to contain oats and there was, as the landlord had promised, a pot of Stockholm Tar. Beside the corn-bins stood eight leather buckets, all of them full of water.

One of these Araminta took back to Halcyon, whom she unsaddled and unbridled, using the headstall provided. The stable really was remarkably well equipped. When the horse had drunk as much as she thought advisable, she turned her attention to the dog which still lay where she had put him. It had been much easier to get him off the horse than it had been to lift him up, and now she was able to look more closely at his foot. It was not a pretty sight. A quick search for clean rags on the shelf above the corn-bins was unproductive, and Araminta therefore—and with some reluctance—tore some strips from the bottom of her shift to bathe, and later bind, his foot.

Her attentions were not welcomed. The dog growled and then, when that failed to deter her, he snarled. His heavy-jowled face, lugubrious in repose, became both ugly and menacing when he snarled, but the Earl had instilled into his children the first principle of animal management which was, he maintained, that if you showed no fear, the worst you could expect was threats.

Araminta knew that this was not an infallible rule and, as she dealt with this unprepossessing animal, she did wonder whether anyone had had the forethought to drum it into his head, as well. Despite her occasional doubts, it appeared to hold true and she was able to wipe most of the extraneous blood and dirt away, leaving the mangled foot with one good toe and one that should probably be completely severed. Araminta's nerve stopped at that, and she doubted that the landlord would be willing to oblige, so she contented herself with brushing the foot with tar and then, with far stronger objections from the dog, binding it with strips from her shift.

When she had finished, she sat back on her heels to admire her handiwork and realised that the landlord had been standing in the doorway watching her, two bowls in his hands. When he realised she had finished, he brought them in.

'I takes me hat off to you, and that's a fact,' he said. 'I thought that brute was going to have you any minute. I don't know if you was scared or not, but if you was, you had me fooled. I dare say he'll be a bit sweeter-natured when he's put himself outside this little lot.' He handed her a large wooden bowl generously full of kitchen scraps. Bread, Araminta was glad to see, formed the greater part. Bread would fill the dog up and, now that she looked at him in daylight, he looked even more in need of it than he had felt last night. The second bowl contained water.

Araminta took them from the landlord and placed them by the dog's head. 'There you are, you ugly brute,' she said affectionately. 'Eat that and go to sleep—and don't hobble off.'

'Ah, well, now,' the landlord said. 'The last thing I want is that thing wandering around and bringing the wrath of every landowner for miles around on my head.

If it's all the same to you, we'll tie him up,' and he produced from his pocket an aged iron collar and a piece of rope.

Araminta looked at the collar, which had long ago lost its soft protective lining. 'I shan't need that,' she said. She made a loop at one end of the rope and threaded the other end through and then slipped the noose over the dog's head. The rope was a long one, and she tied the other end to one of the wooden bars that divided one stall from another. 'I hope the timbers are sound,' she remarked.

'So do I,' the landlord replied with feeling.

Araminta picked up her bundle and her cloak and followed him into the tavern. As soon as she stepped over the threshold she realised that efficiency stopped at the stable door. To someone whose previous experience was limited to those hostelries that accommodated the gentry on their journeys to and from the capital, this one was a revelation although, had Araminta but known it, she could without much difficulty have found many that were worse. The floor was covered in sawdust, the roughly hewn tables looked as if they had never been wiped, and the ceiling and walls were so blackened by smoke from the huge hearth that it was difficult to distinguish where one began and another ended.

'Sit down there,' the landlord said, pointing to a table near the fireplace, from which the previous night's tankards had been removed. Since there were drinking vessels on the other table and on the counter, Araminta assumed that he had made some effort to prepare this table for her meal. He slapped down in front of her a large wooden trencher on which was half a loaf of bread, a large wedge of cheese, four thick slices of ham and some butter. Then he added a knife and a tankard, the latter full of a dark liquid.

'Wine'll be more to your fancy, I reckon,' he said grudgingly. 'The fire's out, so you'll have to drink it cold, but it'll be none the worse for that.'

To Araminta, the meal was one of the best she had ever tasted, and the wine, which at first she sipped with caution, proved to be quite remarkably good—at least as good as anything she had drunk at home, and possibly, she thought after the fourth or fifth mouthful, even better. She wished the tavern were as good as its food and drink, and, looking around the taproom now that the edge of her hunger had been blunted, she could not feel optimistic about the state of any bed she might be offered. Damp sheets were likely to be the least of the ills she might encounter. The stable would be preferable, and when the landlord returned she told him so.

'Have you any objection if I sleep in the stable?' she asked. 'I'd like to keep an eye on the dog.'

He seemed surprised but not offended. 'You can sleep where you like so long as you pays me first. I don't want to find you sneaked away without settling up.'

Araminta paid him the shilling he demanded, knowing that it was too much, but too grateful for the food—which was more than adequate—and the shelter—which at least would be dry and comfortable—to cavil.

He bit the coin before pocketing it, and when she left the taproom with her bundle she was unaware of the speculative gaze that followed her.

Halcyon was in the stall nearest the loft-ladder, at the end of the run of eight, and the dog was curled up at the foot of the ladder in the straw that covered the access passage. Araminta had originally intended to sleep there, too, but closer investigation proved that the straw was not deep enough to guarantee comfort and, since it would be easier to sleep in the loft than to climb up just to knock some more down, she changed her plan accordingly. This had the added advantage of enabling her to snuggle down into hay rather than straw, and thus secure a bed that was both warmer and softer. She removed her boots and, with her blanket as well as her cloak to cover her, she was very cosy indeed.

Two things about the stable bothered her slightly. It was most unusual to leave stalls in the state of preparedness she had found, though she supposed a posting-inn might well do so. This establishment seemed to have no horses of its own, and it was not on the sort of road which was likely to see many travellers. Water, in particular, was not usually drawn and waiting, simply because it would soon have a film of particles from the fodder and bedding and horses disliked dusty water. Even more strange was the layer of straw covering the passageway between the stable door and the stalls. In every stable Araminta had ever seen, the head groom took a personal pride in keeping this area scrupulously clear of anything, someone being directed to remove any wisp of straw that had the temerity to settle beyond the shallow, tiled drainage-gulley separating stalls from passageway. These were oddities, but they could be explained, and when she had slept she'd ask the landlord— taking care to phrase her questions tactfully, of course. She had no wish to imply that things were being badly done. She was beginning to devise appropriately tactful ways of putting it when her mind first blurred and then faded, and she was asleep.

She was awoken some hours later by a low growling from the foot of the ladder and opened her eyes to find the sun streaming through the open door. It took her a few moments to collect her thoughts and remember where she was and in what circumstances.

'You're a vicious brute,' she heard. The voice was unfamiliar, its tone coarse. She resisted the impulse to move across so that she could peer down from the loft. Whoever it was probably had no idea she was up here, and he didn't sound like the sort of person whose ignorance she wished to dilute. 'Now, I wonder if you belongs with that nice piece of bloodstock there,' the voice went on. 'Lady's saddle, too, I see. Hmm. Caleb Fetcham's got a few questions coming.' Araminta heard the slight rustle of straw as he made his way to the door, followed by footsteps across the yard outside, and then a silence broken only by the sound of Halcyon's munching jaws.

She snuggled back under her blanket and tried to recapture her interrupted sleep, but it had fled. The worst of her exhaustion had been slaked and the man's visit had sharpened her attention to a point that could not be immediately blunted. All the same, she lay there for a long time. She was warm and comfortable, and not until she began to feel hungry again did she give serious consideration to getting up. Besides, she would like to give her visitor time to get his questions answered and go on his way before presenting herself at the taproom again.

Eventually the pangs of a good, healthy hunger could no longer be ignored so she brushed and combed her hair and then tied it back with the ribbon the dog no longer needed and hoped, in the absence of a glass, that she looked reasonably respectable. She wrapped everything up again in her blanket and put the bundle behind the dog. People seemed very wary of him, so she decided it would be quite safe there. Halcyon was content and there seemed to be nothing wrong with him that a good grooming wouldn't put right. She would have to ask the landlord if he could lend her some tools. The dog, too, seemed quite happy. She renewed his water and wiped her own face over in one of the still-unused buckets. Then she buttoned up her jacket, crammed her hat back on her head and went over to the tavern.

She lifted the latch and went in. There were two men in the taproom, one of them the landlord. Both stopped talking as the door opened and they watched her cross the room in silence.

'Well, well, well,' said the one she didn't know. 'What have we here?' Araminta had no difficulty in recognising the voice of the man in the stable.

She smiled brightly. 'Good afternoon,' she said, managing to include them both in her greeting. 'Landlord, do you think you could find me something to eat?'

'I dare say,' he said. He opened a door behind the counter and put his head round it. 'Peg!' he shouted.

A buxom countrywoman of more than middle years and older, Araminta guessed, than the landlord, appeared. She looked the sort of woman who might have been in service until she had married, and Araminta thought her out of place in such a hostelry, though no doubt she was responsible for the excellent victuals.

'She wants some food,' the landlord told her, nodding his head towards Araminta.

'There's stew in the pot,' Peg informed their visitor defensively. Araminta might look unkempt, but Peg Fetcham knew a lady when she saw one and doubtless this one expected an array of dishes. Well, she'd be disappointed. 'It's a good thick one, and there's suet dumplings in it, but I can't offer you pies and kickshawses—we don't have much call for that sort of thing out here.'

'Stew will suit me admirably,' Araminta told her, 'and if you've any of that delicious bread I had last—I mean, this morning, that, too, will be very welcome.'

Mrs Fetcham was no more impervious to compliments on her cooking than any other woman, and mellowed noticeably. A lady, undoubtedly, and a real one, at that, with manners to match.

'And who might you be?' the man from the stable enquired.

Araminta looked at him as if she had scarcely noticed him before, and raised one eyebrow. She had the satisfaction of seeing him wriggle uncomfortably, although he took care not to look too abashed.

'A traveller,' she said briefly.

'Aye, and that's your horse out there, I take it?'

Since there was only one horse, and little point in denying it, Araminta conceded it was.

'Your dog, too, I don't doubt?'

Araminta hesitated. The dog had been preceded by his reputation. It might not be a good idea to admit ownership. On the other hand, he was less likely to be shot if he were thought to be hers, and she had become quite attached to him. 'That's right,' she said.

'Caleb here reckons you had holsters on your saddle. Reckons they wasn't empty, neither.'

Araminta looked him straight in the eye. 'Would you expect me to travel alone at night without some sort of protection?' she demanded.

'If you asks me, I wouldn't expect the likes of you to travel nowhere alone, at night or any other time.' He looked her up and down. 'In fact, if you was in breeches, I'd reckon you was on the bridle-lay, only whoever heard of a female Jack Ranton?' This sally struck him as hilariously funny and he roared with laughter, thumping his fist on the counter as he did so.

Araminta's heart skipped a beat and then turned a somersault at the reference to Jack Ranton. She reminded herself that she must now be in his territory, and her spirits lightened imperceptibly. All the same, her instinct was to reveal nothing to this man, so she stared at him, apparently unmoved by his sally, and any need for a retort was obviated by the appearance of Mrs

Fetcham with a bowl of steaming stew, a trencher of bread and a tankard of wine.

'Take no notice of Ned Nacton,' she advised. 'The good Lord must have had His mind on other things when Ned was made, for He gave him too much mouth and not enough brain.'

Far from being offended at this blunt and accurate appraisal, Ned Nacton burst out laughing once more and assured the landlord that his Peg was quite a one.

The landlord did not seem inclined to share his customer's jocularity, and instead suggested that maybe it was time Ned was on his way. 'You've got a long way to go, Ned, and I needs you there ahead of time, just in case.'

'Aye, well, maybe you're right.' He glanced across at Araminta. 'She'll be going, I take it?'

'You mind your business and I'll mind mine,' the landlord told him.

For all his coarseness, Ned Nacton did not seem to be a man who easily took offence. 'Fair enough,' he said. 'Can't grumble at that.' As he passed Araminta's table, he made an exaggerated gesture of pulling his forelock. 'Happy travelling,' he told her. 'If I was you, I'd keep that dog out of sight.'

The landlord followed him to the door and watched him go. He didn't doubt that Ned would do exactly as he was told, but it paid to make sure. It would never do to have him take the easy way of reaching his destination—on the back of the only horse in the stable. When he came back in, he sat down opposite Araminta.

'Your wife makes a very good stew,' she told him, 'and this wine is truly excellent.'

He smiled briefly. 'I prides myself on the cellar,' he said.

'With good cause, if this is typical,' Araminta said. 'I'm only surprised there's much call for it in this little hamlet.'

'There's not,' he said cautiously. 'Come market day, though, we've quite a passing trade.'

'Indeed?' Araminta recalled the narrow track leading to this place and wondered. 'Is market day the reason for keeping the stable ready?'

'You wondered about that, did you? We don't get travellers very often, but when we do, they usually want to rest—like yourself, in fact. Saves a lot of bother if everything's ready.'

'Yes, I suppose it must do,' Araminta agreed. The explanation was plausible, but she didn't entirely believe it.

'You'll be thinking of moving on,' he went on hopefully.

'Yes, but I'd like to wait until the dog's better able to travel.'

Fetcham frowned, but made no comment. Instead, he asked, 'Where was you heading?'

Araminta hadn't the slightest idea, but she had no intention of saying so. 'London,' she said.

'London? Pity.'

'What makes you say that?'

'Ned Nacton's not the cleverest man in England, but in a way he's right: it'd be better if you wore breeches. Now, I don't know who you are, nor I'm not asking,' he added hastily. 'What I don't know, I can't tell, and that's how I likes it. The fact is, in breeches and a cross-saddle, no one's going to look twice at you—not even close up, if you're lucky. But ladies don't travel alone—and, whoever you are, you're a lady, of that I'm sure—and if they're foolhardy enough to try, they gets seen, and sooner or later they gets waylaid.'

'I've been travelling at night,' Araminta told him.

'Then you've been lucky, but the further south you goes, the less lucky you're likely to remain. There's a lot of folks about after dark in these parts—and I tell you this: your luck held when you stumbled on this place, for I don't hold with slitting of throats, and it's good for you there wasn't anyone here when you came because not everyone shares my views.'

'I'm not sure I follow your drift,' Araminta told him, puzzled.

'Maybe that's just as well. All I'm saying is, if you wasn't going to London, you'd get further safer in breeches. Only I don't reckon you'd be safe on London streets for long dressed in men's clothes. That's all.'

Araminta, who had said 'London' because it was the one place she had never had the slightest intention of going to, pondered this. All this talk of slitting throats was hardly encouraging and the landlord's suggestion made sense. She passed her mind over the rest of Ned Nacton's remarks. 'Who is Jack Ranton?' she asked.

The question took the landlord aback. 'Not someone the likes of you would want to meet,' he said.

Mrs Fetcham was more specific. 'He's a legend round these parts. Some say he's a highwayman, some say he's a smuggler. It's my belief he's nothing more than a name to give the Revenue men when they starts asking questions.'

A highwayman. One of Georgie's bizarre suggestions, and one less likely to lead to immediate discovery than the Navy or the Army. 'Could you get me breeches and a cross-saddle to fit Hal...my horse?' Araminta asked.

'I could. I'd have to take your lady's saddle by way of exchange, and I'll not have what you needs tonight, neither, but you'd best be gone, and I don't know as it's a good to stay here any longer than you must.'

'Will one more night hurt?'

'Depends which night,' Fetcham said cryptically.

'Are you determined on London?' Mrs Fetcham asked.

'Not *absolutely* determined,' Araminta told her cautiously. 'Why? Have you an alternative suggestion?'

Mrs Fetcham looked at her husband. 'Jem?' she suggested.

Her husband screwed up his face in contemplation, and then nodded uncertainly. 'Could do worse, I suppose. Better than here, at all events.'

'Who's Jem?' Araminta asked, looking from one to the other.

'My sister's husband,' Mrs Fetcham told her. 'Jem Hoby, landlord of the Red Lion at Rake. Respectable hostelry, busy road. Might suit you better than here—give you more choice.'

'Of what?'

Mrs Fetcham shifted uneasily. 'Of what you do next. We're not daft, you know. It's as plain as the nose on your face you're running away from something, and it's none of our business what, but whatever it is there's a limit to what you can profitably do next—and respectability's not going to play much part. Now, if you decide to turn things around and go back to whatever you left, the Red Lion's as respectable-seeming a place as you'll find to do it from. And if you decides to carry on, well, there's opportunities there, not to mention Portsmouth on the one hand and London on the other. But we neither need you on the premises tonight nor wandering in the woods around—not you or your horse or that cur.'

'We can account for the horse,' Fetcham corrected. He reached across the table and handed Araminta's tankard to his wife. 'Fill it up again, Peg,' he said. 'She'll want to wash the stew down.'

All sorts of loose ends inside Araminta's head spliced themselves together as he spoke, though it was the tankard rather than the words that made them do so.

She took a sip from the replenished vessel. The wine really was exceptionally good.

'Could it be that your cellars are not so full at the moment as you would like them to be, Mr Fetcham?' she asked.

He frowned. 'They're only empty enough to let me and Peg sleep easy in our beds,' he told her.

'And tomorrow they won't be?' There was no answer to Araminta's question, but she hadn't really expected one. 'Mr Fetcham, your sister-in-law's at Rake sounds just the place for me, but I shall need men's clothes and a man's saddle, and I think it would be extremely inadvisable for me to be loose in the woods, don't you? You say you can explain my horse. Good. That leaves only me and the dog. If everything is ready in stalls beneath, no one needs to come up into the loft. Why can't I spend the night there? All we have to do is to get the dog up there as well.'

Fetcham hesitated but his wife nodded. 'Better than a bedroom,' she said. 'Not much talk in the stable.'

'Jack Ranton won't even know I'm there,' Araminta said lightly, and was surprised that the sally evoked no smile from her hosts.

'Can you keep that brute quiet?' Fetcham asked.

'I think so. I fancy the greater difficulty will be in getting him up there.'

'Aye, well, we'll haul him up in a sling. The saddle had better go up there, too. You make sure you settle yourself down right at the back.'

'Where I can't be seen and won't fall out,' Araminta agreed. 'If there's nothing else to be decided, I'll go and see to the animals.'

When the door closed behind her, the landlord shook his head. 'I'm not happy,' he said. 'She's a sight too sharp, that one. I'm not at all sure we shouldn't have found out who she is and handed her back to whoever she belongs to.'

'And have the gentry all over the place when the gentlemen come?' his wife said scornfully. 'You've addled your brains, Caleb Fetcham.'

'Then we'd better make sure the gentlemen don't get wind of her, for if she's found with her throat cut it's us as'll swing for it.'

'She'll sleep sound enough. Leave that to me.'

CHAPTER SIX

ARAMINTA did not sleep as soundly as Mrs Fetcham planned because she was perfectly familiar with the taste of laudanum, not quite disguised by a wine she had sampled twice before. She attributed nothing sinister to its presence and made no comment, but quenched her thirst in water afterwards, meanwhile tipping the wine unobtrusively into the sawdust under the table, where the shadows disguised the darker patch.

Grendel, as she named the monstrous dog, whacked the floor of the loft with his tail in pleasure at having her with him, and she admitted to herself that she felt a great deal more secure for his presence. Her only anxiety was that he would growl and thereby alert any visitor to the fact that he was there.

She had no doubt at all that Caleb Fetcham's wine— and no doubt his brandy, too—had paid duty at no port, and that within a very short time of arriving it would have found its way into those cellars whose owners could afford the best but saw no reason for paying the ungrateful government for the privilege. No wonder so out-of-the-way a tavern had such excellent liquor. To most people, including impressionable girls, smugglers were daring, romantic figures whom they saw in much the same light as Robin Hood. Smugglers might not exactly rob the rich and give to the poor, but at least they deprived the government of its iniquitous taxes and let people buy what they considered themselves entitled to by custom. Those whose job was to collect the duty or catch the smugglers viewed them in a somewhat different light, and Araminta, recalling Mr Fetcham's ominous talk of slitting throats, was sufficiently fair-minded to acknowledge that he might know rather more about the customs of smugglers than she did. Nevertheless, she couldn't help feeling a degree of excitement as she snuggled down in the hay, one arm across Grendel's chest and with every intention of staying awake.

It was a stiffening of the dog's body that woke her up, rather than any sound he made, and she woke completely, her eyes wide open and all her senses alert. She placed a warning hand over Grendel's head, but he had no inclination to growl so long as his mistress was this close. If someone came up the ladder, things might change, but for the present it was enough that she was awake.

The sound of hoofs shuffling through straw ascended clearly enough. She heard the clink of a bit being mouthed and then the unmistakable sound of a bridle being removed and hung up. Munching followed, and then another horse came in.

'See this, guv'nor?' a voice whispered. 'I ain't never seen this one afore.'

There was a pause and the next voice to speak took the unseen listener by surprise. It was the voice of a gentleman. A trifle light, perhaps, but pleasant and well modulated—not at all the sort of voice one associated with running contraband. Furthermore, it was familiar. 'A cut above anything this stable's seen before,' it said. 'Doubtless Fetcham can explain it.'

It was the voice of the highwayman.

It seemed the landlord expected some unease over the presence of a strange horse, for he left supervising the safe stowing of his goods in the cellar and came over. Araminta guessed him to be standing in the door. 'Leave the end stall,' he said softly, as if assuming no one had noticed Halcyon. 'There's a beast at livery.'

'Since when have you taken in liveries?' the gentleman asked, suspiciously.

'Since he sprained a tendon cub-hunting,' Fetcham retorted. 'I said he could rest up here and they're paying me handsomely for the favour and that's good enough for me. Took him out too soft after the summer, that's my guess.'

'Bit lightweight for a hunter,' the pleasant voice commented, not to Araminta's surprise.

'Lady's 'oss. Leastways, a girl's. Groom took her back pillion. Took the saddle, too. Didn't trust me, I reckon.'

'Who was she?'

'No idea. Didn't ask. The groom belongs to Mr Hodnet, the magistrate.'

'Risky,' the gentleman said, but he sounded satisfied.

The slow-moving file of horses into the stable seemed never-ending, but Araminta knew it could number no more than eight, unless they were doubling them up— a dangerous practice, but quite feasible if the horses were staying only a short time. Then the stable door was closed and she heard a bar being put across it on the outside. It was just as well she had no thought of going anywhere. Grendel relaxed and Araminta wriggled a little deeper into the warm hay and wondered how long it would be before men and horses left.

She never found out. When she woke up, it was broad daylight again and the stable was empty except for Halcyon. Had it not been for obvious signs of recent occupation, Araminta would have concluded she had dreamed the night's brief episode. She attended to Halcyon's needs before thinking about breakfast, and then unbound Grendel's foot and had a close look at that. It seemed to be coming along quite nicely with no signs of heat or pus, so she left it unbound. He would have to stay up here until the landlord could help her get him down.

There was no sign of anyone other than Mrs Fetcham when she entered the taproom, and that lady put a generous trencher of bread, cheese and ham in front of her.

'Sleep well?' she asked, when she brought over the customary tankard of wine.

'Yes, thank you.' Araminta wanted to ask about the night visitors, but she remembered the laudanum and thought better of it. 'Is Mr Fetcham about?'

'No, he's been gone some hours. Won't be back for another hour or two yet. He's hoping to get you some breeches and a cross-saddle.'

'But he was going to give them my saddle in exchange, and it's still in the loft,' Araminta told her.

'Too heavy to carry if you don't have to,' Mrs Fetcham explained. 'The people he's doing business with will trust him. He won't be approaching strangers.'

'I don't suppose you have anyone who comes in to clean out the stables when it's been used?' Araminta asked.

'And let everyone know we've had visitors? You suppose right.'

'That's what I thought. Then I'll do it. It will keep me occupied until he returns and be a small way of thanking you both for your help.'

'If you think you can manage,' Mrs Fetcham said doubtfully. 'It would be appreciated. Don't refill the buckets, though. We don't have them standing around until we've been warned to be ready.'

Cleaning out one stall was no great task, but cleaning out eight was another matter, and long before she had finished Araminta was beginning to realise just how much hard work went into being a groom. Nevertheless, she was a determined woman and had undertaken to do the job, so she persevered, and had just heaved a sigh of satisfaction at its completion when Caleb Fetcham returned.

He nodded approval when he saw what she had done. 'Don't reckon you've ever worked half as hard as that in your life before, have you?' he remarked with the hint of a smile.

'I don't reckon I have,' Araminta agreed.

'Ah, well, hard work never hurt anyone. Now, then, I've got you a saddle. It's old and it's well worn, but it ought to fit and it's got a good, deep seat which you'll find more comfortable than the straight one you're used to. I just hopes that animal's carried a cross-saddle before.'

'I suppose he may have been broken to one,' Araminta said doubtfully. 'And the breeches?'

'I've got you some, but I'll not guarantee the fit.' He looked her up and down. 'They'll be too big, but too small would be worse. Caused some comment, they did, but in the end I found someone only too glad to sell her husband's clothes, pour soul. Killed by a bull, he was, and the family left destitute. Still, except for a bit of blood, his breeches were undamaged.' He hesitated. 'I gave her a shilling for them. It's more than they're worth—quite a lot more—but her need was considerable and she threw in some spatterdashes as well.'

Araminta held the breeches up. They were made of brown homespun in an old-fashioned style with lacing at the back and buttons down the front instead of the 'fall' which had been *de rigueur* for decades in more fashionable circles.

She disappeared into the loft with them, and when she emerged she had created a passable shirt out of her shift. Her own stockings and riding-boots were long enough to cover the buckles that fastened the leg-bottoms below the knee and her tricorne completed the picture.

The landlord seemed to think she had done quite well, but his wife shook her head. 'It won't do,' she said.

'You'll have to have a proper shirt. Caleb's got a spare one.'

She paid no attention to her husband's protestation that if he had a spare one, it was because he needed it, but sought it out and gave it to Araminta together with a side strip of linen. 'Don't try to make a cravat of it,' she told the younger woman. 'Just tie it as a stock. I'll get you a glass.'

When Araminta had taken her advice and had had the opportunity of seeing what she looked like—which proved to be better than she had expected—Mrs Fetcham declared herself satisfied. She was anxious to be on her way, and the Fetchams were no less anxious to see her gone, but first there was the matter of seeing how well she could ride astride.

Halcyon took to the experience better than his owner. It felt odd to Araminta to be sitting much lower in a saddle. Gone was the feeling she had always taken for granted—that of being perched up high. It was odd, too, to have her hands as low as the pommel of the saddle and not resting at the height of a knee several inches higher. It took her time to become accustomed to using her right leg as an aide to controlling the horse instead of the long whip which replaced it when one rode aside.

Grendel was another cause of delay. Fetcham reluctantly agreed that he was in no state to follow a horse, but expressed the opinion that, if Araminta carried him in front of her, she could leave on the morrow, and that in a couple of days the dog would be able to hobble along, so long as she didn't expect him to show any speed.

'Tomorrow must see you on your way,' he told her. 'I don't want my cellar full any longer than it must be, and there's some I does business with that I don't want asking any questions. We'll risk it tonight, but tomorrow you go.'

Araminta could only be grateful. She was nothing to the Fetchams and there was no reason why they should be as kind to her as they had been. She made a tentative suggestion that she should travel at night, but they would have none of it.

'We can tell you how to reach Rake,' Mrs Fetcham told her, 'but it's not an easy route and you don't know the locality. If you try to find it at night, you'll fail. No, you go by daylight. We'll take a chance on tonight.'

There were visitors again that night, but they didn't come into the stable and Araminta guessed they hadn't been expected to, because the bar had been put in place some time after she retired. As far as she could tell, the visitors didn't stay long and, although she didn't hear the bar being removed, it was gone in the morning when she woke up and let herself out.

The Fetchams seated themselves either side of her as she ate her breakfast. They described the route she should take and made her repeat it over and over until she was word-perfect. Araminta privately hoped that there would prove not to be too many dead oaks or forded streams, because she suspected that a route that relied as heavily as this one did on such landmarks could easily be lost.

The Fetchams told her she should reach Rake before nightfall if she maintained a steady speed and didn't get lost. The journey was through heavily wooded country which disguised the steep contours of the hills and valleys clothed by the trees. Araminta was glad she had been made to learn her directions by heart, and found it by no means easy to adhere to her first instruction; a steady speed was not something easy to achieve in this landscape.

Nevertheless, dusk was still some way off when she rode down the steeply sloping path into Rake, a village of some dozen cottages, so far as she could tell. That so small a place should be served by two hostelries was less surprising when one realised that the road through it, which Araminta was approaching at a right-angle, was the main London-to-Portsmouth road and therefore one of the busier ones in the south of England. Araminta drew rein where the path met the road and looked about her. To her right stood the Flying Bull. To her left and across the road, she could make out the roof of what must be the Red Lion. She put her heels to Halcyon's sides and rode over.

The mellow brick walls and terracotta tiles of the hostelry nestled beneath the steep slope of the wooded hill behind. It was not as obtrusive as coaching inns generally were, but Araminta supposed that, if Mr Hoby was in the same line of business as his brother-in-law, then some discretion was to be expected. All the same, an ostler ran out to take Halcyon.

'Just show me where the stables are,' she told him. 'Then fetch Mrs Hoby. I've a message from her sister.'

Margery Hoby was a younger, plumper version of her sister but her eyes were harder. She took one good look at her visitor and sent the ostler packing. 'You can thank God he's simple-minded and doesn't see nothing beyond the end of his nose,' she told Araminta. 'It'll take him ten minutes to fetch in the wood I've sent him for. Settle your horse in that time and rap on that window over there. You won't want to go in, the place is full.'

Correctly deducing that Mrs Hoby thought it inadvisable for word to get around that she was not what she appeared, Araminta did as she was bid, though as soon as she had seen to Halcyon she took her habit skirt from her bundle and put it on over her breeches. It was therefore conventionally dressed that she rapped on the indicated window, and Mrs Hoby visibly relaxed when she saw her changed appearance.

'That's better,' she said. 'Go round to the door and I'll let you in.'

She led Araminta to a small sitting-room and frowned at Grendel, hobbling behind his new mistress. 'Does that cur have to come too?' she asked.

'Grendel goes where I go,' Araminta said firmly.

'Hmph. Well, you'd better keep that foot of his out of sight. Any landowner worth his salt will shoot him on sight if they see it. Only poachers' dogs get caught in traps. Is that your lay?'

'I'm not a poacher, if that's what you mean,' Araminta told her. 'I'm here at Mrs Fetcham's suggestion.'

'Oh, yes?'

It wasn't a promising omen and, since Araminta still had only a very hazy idea of what she was going to do, she did her best to explain to Mrs Hoby without either revealing too much about herself or telling her hostess any of the irregularities in the way the Fetchams ran their business. If the Hobys had the same sort of friends they would prefer evidence of her discretion; if not, it could be dangerous for the Fetchams.

'Can you pay for your keep?'

'For a while, yes.'

'No reason why you can't stay here while your money lasts, but this is an inn, remember. Not an almshouse. Don't go thinking we can offer you work, either; we've all the help we need and they're people we know we can trust.'

This was not quite what Araminta had hoped for, but at least she had been offered a respite, though not a very long one when she considered how much money she had left with which to support the three of them.

Jem Hoby took much the same view as his wife, though he was a little more forthcoming. 'If Peg and Caleb sent you, they must have thought this was the place for you,' he said thoughtfully. 'I wonder just what they had in mind? Margie said you rode over in breeches.'

Araminta laughed. 'That came about because one of their customers remarked that if I'd worn breeches I could be taken for a female Jack Ranton. They had to explain what he meant.'

'Which of their customers would that have been?'

Araminta cast her mind back over what she had already told him. She could think of no reason for not naming the man, though she doubted whether his name could convey much to Jem Hoby. 'Ned Nacton,' she said.

'Ned, eh? Too much mouth, that man, but as shrewd as he can hold together. What are we going to call you?'

The question was a natural one, its phraseology interesting. Araminta knew she should have foreseen it and been prepared. She thought very quickly. 'Jane Shore,' she said, settling for something quite inappropriate that had come unbidden—and inexplicably—into her head.

'Jane Shore. That should be easy enough to remember. It's plain enough.' He clearly had no idea of its connotations which, since it was too late to think again, was probably just as well.

The Hobys let it be known that she was Caleb Fetcham's niece, and no one thought it at all surprising that she should be staying at the Red Lion. Araminta slipped quietly into the part, giving a hand here and there, as much to occupy her time as for any other reason, but was no nearer deciding what to do and her steadily diminishing stock of coin caused her a steadily increasing concern.

Then, quite out of the blue, she heard that same, familiar voice. She had just finished grooming Halcyon and had barely noticed the sound of hoofs in the yard but there was no mistaking the light, pleasant tone she had heard elsewhere.

'Good morning, Billy,' the voice said. 'Rub him down for me, there's a good lad. Since when has Jem had a dog? Ugly brute, too. Looks as if it's been roaming where it's no business.'

'Oh, that's not the master's,' the lad assured him. 'Belongs to his niece.'

Araminta came out of the stable. This man had seen Halcyon and the explanation he had been given had made no mention of nieces. Perhaps suddenly seeing her would distract him from the inconsistency.

The sun was better placed for assessing his appearance than it had been at their previous meeting. Now she could make out more than just his height. He had broad shoulders upon which a coat of brown broadcloth sat easily. It was well cut and it fitted, but he would have been able to shrug himself into it without the help of a valet. His brown hair was of only moderate length and was tied with black ribbon. He was long limbed and well shod, and he had grey eyes in the pleasant, rather lean face that matched his voice, though perhaps with rather more character. Araminta judged him to be about thirty. 'The dog is mine,' she said.

For a fleeting second she thought she saw sheer astonishment on his face, but if she did, it was soon gone, to be replaced by the impassive expression of someone who had never seen her before and was not unduly interested to do so now. She was conscious of a flicker of disappointment. Obviously their previous encounter had meant little to the highwaymen. Of course, she no longer looked like the undoubted lady of that occasion, but even so...

'So you are Hoby's niece?'

'No, sir. I'm his brother-in-law's niece.'

'Which one? He has several, I believe. A widely scattered family, the Hobys.'

Araminta hesitated. If by some misfortune he later spotted Halcyon, at least the fact that she was supposed to be Fetcham's niece would explain his lie about the horse's origins. 'Caleb Fetcham.'

His eyes narrowed. 'Indeed? The ramifications of these families never cease to amaze me. And what do they call you?'

'Jane Shore,' she told him.

He made no attempt to disguise his smile. 'Dear me— a name which could be regarded as auspicious or unfortunate, depending upon one's point of view. I won't ask you how you see it,' he went on.

Araminta flushed. The connotations of her new name were not lost on this man, she thought, annoyed, and wished she could demand his, but the niece of a country landlord did not ask impertinent questions. If the Hobys knew, as seemed probable, she would ask them afterwards. She forced herself to pretend not to understand him. She smiled.

'Shall I take you to...Uncle Jem?' she asked.

'Thank you, I know my way. "Uncle Jem" is a fortunate man.'

Araminta saw him go with mixed feelings. There was relief that he had not seen Halcyon and had stopped asking questions that might be difficult to answer. It seemed as if he really hadn't recognised her—a depressing thought, though she supposed she should be glad of it. All the same, she would have been much happier had his eyes lighted up with recognition and had he swept her once more into his arms.

She reminded herself that he was a smuggler and a highwayman and she was a married woman. It was the first time since she had run away that this latter inconvenience had struck her, and she began to see that her flight might have other consequences than simply throwing herself on her own resources. She therefore took herself off to the little room under the eaves that she had been allocated as suitable for a relative by marriage of the landlord.

Here there would be no chance of her bumping into him again. She would have to hope Billy brought his horse round for him, thereby ensuring he did not catch sight of Halcyon.

Araminta reckoned without the softly spoken man's long acquaintance with Billy. The lad could be entrusted to unsaddle a horse, but saddling up again was quite another matter and something the visitor preferred to do for himself. He saw Halcyon and recognised him. He also remembered Caleb's story. There was no reason on earth why Caleb Fetcham shouldn't have his niece's horse in his stable or his niece in his house, and no reason to lie about it either. There was some kind of double game being played here.

Caleb had always been trustworthy. Why should he have lied? And why should Jem Hoby be conspiring in that lie? The pleasant-voiced man decided that it might be a good idea to watch his back. He wasn't sure whether the 'niece' had recognised him, and he doubted if she were anything more than an unwitting pawn in whatever game was being played. It was the nature of that game that worried him.

Neither Jem Hoby nor his wife was naturally vague, but both became so when Araminta asked them the identity of their visitor. If it suited people not to volunteer their real names, it wasn't for the likes of the Hobys to ask and, no, they didn't know where he was from, but it couldn't be from these parts or they'd have known him, wouldn't they? Araminta was tempted to ask other members of their household, but to do so would be to reveal the sort of interest that would arouse unwelcome comment, so she forbore.

Ideas as to how she should support herself were not coming in with the same speed that her sparse funds were going out and so, when she counted the pence one evening, and then counted them again and could still make them come to no more than would support the three of them for two more days, she sought out Mrs Hoby and asked whether there was still no work for her at the Red Lion. The landlady was adamant.

'Now you knows no one's left since you came, so how should there be work for another pair of hands? Nor is it likely to change—all the people we have have been here for years. They're not going to flit away. And the Flying Bull's in much the same position,' she added, seeing Araminta glance across the road.

'Do you think I might find employment in Portsmouth?' Araminta asked.

'Bound to. Whether you'd like it is quite another matter.' She returned to her work with that comment, thereby declaring the subject closed, but when Araminta dejectedly left the room, she watched her go, her expression speculative.

When Araminta had had the opportunity of passing an unproductive night pondering her dilemma, Jem Hoby took her aside.

'I hears your funds is running out,' he said.

Araminta confirmed the rumour.

'Maybe I can put a little something your way,' he suggested.

Araminta brightened. 'You've work for me after all?'

'In a manner of speaking, though not what you'd call *regular* work. Still, it'd keep the wolf from the door.'

'Tell me more,' Araminta said warmly.

'Remember telling me what Ned Nacton said? About a female Jack Ranton?'

'Yes.' Araminta's reply was guarded.

'Well, why not? You've got the horse, the saddle, the breeches and the pistols. What more do you want?' He looked at her horrified expression. 'Think about it,' he said.

Araminta did—for most of the day and well into the night. From what the landlord had said, she deduced that it was Jack Ranton's exploits on the bridle-lay that he was suggesting she emulate, and not his smuggling activities. Georgiana would no doubt have jumped at the suggestion. Indeed, now that Araminta thought about it, it had been one of her silly ideas—and now it was being put forward in all seriousness. It was unthinkable, yet Araminta found herself thinking about it and her thoughts became increasingly positive. There could be few better roads for such an activity than that linking the great naval dockyard city of Portsmouth with the capital, and, although Araminta was unfamiliar with any of that road other than that which ran through Rake, she could appreciate that there could be few more suitable stretches than the three miles between Rake and Sheet. The road climbed steeply up out of Rake and then fell away equally steeply towards Sheet so that vehicles in either direction were obliged to slow down. Indeed, someone had mentioned that in winter passengers often had to get out of coaches travelling north and help push them up the incline. The road was heavily wooded on either side and nothing could be easier than to disappear into the trees. The trees continued north of Rake, too, but the road here did not have the advantage of such steep inclines.

It might be inadvisable to work so close to the Red Lion but, on the other hand, if she adopted this ludicrous scheme she would only have to get back very quickly, change into her skirt, hide her jacket, and she could pass as any tavern wench. If she were careful to avoid Petersfield, she could range as far south as the wooded slopes of Butser, another great hill that effectively slowed down all traffic.

There were risks, of course. Araminta, who had no intention of carrying out this hare-brained scheme, made herself think about them. It wasn't only public vehicles that carried armed guards. Some private ones took the same precautions; she had only to remember Lord Cosenham's armed outriders to realise how careful some travellers were. It was true that very few travellers had Cosenham's enormous wealth, but even so there was a strong probability they would have a pistol somewhere about their person. How did Araminta view the prospect of being shot? Not with any great enthusiasm, she unhesitatingly admitted. She had even less enthusiasm for being hanged, and hanging was the inevitable punishment for highway robbery. It would be a powerful incentive for not getting caught—if one went into such a foolish undertaking which, of course, Araminta had no intention of doing.

The rewards might be worthwhile, of course. If one avoided taking identifiable objects, such as watches, and limited oneself to coin, it was reasonable to assume one might live very comfortably for some weeks on the proceeds of just one sortie.

There was the shame to one's family to consider but if one were using a different name—as Araminta already was—there was no reason why anyone should make the connection. In any case, she had brought enough shame on the name of Wareham by leaving her husband on their wedding-night; a career as a highwayman could hardly make it worse. It was unfortunate that highwaymen tended to have exceedingly brief careers, and it would make sense to ensure that the proceeds of such a venture should be husbanded carefully in order to enable one to go somewhere a long way away—France, or Italy, for example—and set up in some sort of respectable occupation there. If the Hobys were willing to teach her their trade in the intervals of highway robbery, she would be able to open a hostelry in whatever place she chose to settle. With a goal in mind beyond the simple act of robbery, the risks seemed to diminish because exposure to them had acquired a limited, if unspecified, time-span.

The clinching argument was that Araminta hadn't the slightest idea what other course she could pursue.

Next morning she sought out Jem Hoby. 'I'll do it,' she told him. 'How do I go about it?'

'Can you use those pistols?'

'No.'

'Then that's the first thing. We'll take a gig out to a quiet spot and I'll teach you.'

Araminta hesitated. 'I don't think I want to be able to use them,' she said. 'Surely it will be enough just to point them? No one will know they're empty.'

'Don't be daft,' he said scathingly. 'If you're going to do this, you're going to do it properly, and if you hold up a carriage whose owner suddenly produces a pistol you need to be able to use yours. You don't have to aim to kill,' he added by way of reassurance. 'You just need to be able to incapacitate him. Once you've mastered that skill, we'll consider other aspects.'

'You're overlooking the fact that I've no more money left,' Araminta pointed out. 'It sounds as if it's going to be some time before I'm ready.'

'Don't worry—I'll frank you. From now on you pays me a percentage of what you takes. How does that strike you?'

Araminta didn't like it at all. It would be much easier to calculate whether she was earning her keep if she paid a fixed amount by the week but, since she would be living at the Hobys' expense for the time being—and not only she, but Halcyon and Grendel, too—it seemed churlish to cavil.

Jem Hoby sensed her reservation. 'It's the usual way,' he said.

'Then so be it,' Araminta agreed.

She was an apt pupil and quick to learn. The pure mechanics were soon mastered. Aiming took rather longer, and Araminta discovered that flintlock pistols were extremely temperamental in their willingness to perform with complete predictability.

When the landlord decided she was sufficiently adept with pistols, he turned his attention to the horse. 'That's a real pretty animal, is that. Just the sort to stick in anyone's mind who's seen him. Now, either you gets rid of him for something more ordinary, or you lets me doctor him up a bit so's no one takes much notice of him.'

Araminta could see his point, but she had no intention of being parted from Halcyon. 'You doctor him,' she said promptly.

'It won't be too drastic,' he told her. 'We'll get rid of those nice white stockings and we'll get rid of the blaze. That may be enough to do the trick. I hope so, because then we can change him from bay to brown and later from brown to black when word gets around about what colour horse you're riding.'

Araminta had heard of horse-copers before, but this was the first time she had seen one in action, and it began to dawn on her that Jem Hoby's knowledge of pistols, horses and the tricks that made banditry successful was rather more extensive than might be expected of any law-abiding citizen. She was uncertain whether this realisation should be a comfort to her or a cause for concern.

She was soon to learn that Jem Hoby gave a wider interpretation to his task than merely instruction. When he decided she was proficient enough to put into practice what she had been taught, he took her aside.

'I've a job for you,' he said. 'There's an elderly gentleman travelling north tomorrow—broad daylight, I'm afraid, but that can't be helped. He has an elderly coachman and slow horses. The coachman always carries a gun, but they say he's frightened silly by it and it's never loaded. He'll be carrying mostly cash, but don't take more than you can comfortably stow in your pockets and in a saddle-bag I'll give you. The best place to catch him is north of Sheet, where Adhurst Wood comes down to the road. It's a bit close to home, maybe, but you'll be able to be back here—and in skirts—before he's recovered his wits and gets here himself. Couldn't be better.'

'It would be better at night,' Araminta corrected him.

'If ever you hears of someone travelling unarmed at night and carrying coin, you mistrust it,' he said and, upon reflection, Araminta was obliged to admit he had a point.

She slipped out early, before the household was about. With some reluctance, because she liked his company, she left Grendel behind. Jem Hoby said his missing toes made him too easily identifiable and she knew he was right. Halcyon was now a bright bay with black points and not a trace of white on him, and together they slipped into the trees behind the Red Lion. Araminta planned to waylay the gentleman towards the end of a long, slow, gruelling incline. She might have as long as an hour to wait, and she kept well back. It would hardly serve her interest if some other traveller caught a glimpse of her.

Her heart was beating furiously and the pit of her stomach felt clenched and knotted. As the time passed, she began to shiver uncontrollably and an unexpected rustle behind her made her spin round and reach for one of the pistols. Her fear turned to relief when she saw it was Grendel. Someone must have let him out and he had presumably followed Halcyon's scent. It might be a risk having him here, but Araminta wasn't sorry to see him.

She began to feel fidgety as well as nervous. Then, at last, she heard the sound she had been listening for:

something heavier than a gig and with more than a single horse. She edged Halcyon closer to the road and peered southwards through the trees. This must be it. An old-fashioned carriage, a coachman and two horses which had been selected for their stamina rather than their speed. There was nothing behind the carriage, and a glance in the other direction showed that to be empty, too.

Araminta pulled a muffler up over her mouth and nose, removed one pistol from its holster and cocked it, gathered up her reins and emerged from the trees exactly abreast of the coachman, her gun pointing at his head.

Like his passenger, he was an old man. There was no need for Araminta to say anything. He took one look at the gun and drew rein so hard that the horses were thrown back on their breechings.

'Get down,' she ordered.

The coachman did as he was told.

'Open the door.'

He did that, too.

Now she had both men covered and she could see what she took to be the money-box lying on the seat opposite the passenger. That gentleman was hastily unfastening his pocket-watch, a handsome gold piece which was of no use to Araminta.

'Not that,' she said, and gestured with the gun-barrel towards the box. 'Unlock the box.'

The old man hesitated. 'There's nothing in it,' he said. 'Nothing of value, that is: it's my travelling bureau.'

Araminta hesitated. It could very easily be the sort of box that opened into a sloping desk with compartments for ink, quills, sand and paper. Then she reminded herself that Jem Hoby's information had been accurate so far. 'Then you won't mind opening it,' she said.

The old man fished about in his pocket and finally, reluctantly, produced the key. The coin was mostly silver, though some gold gleamed here and there, and there was a great deal of it. Araminta handed the old man the saddle-bag. 'Fill that,' she told him.

When he had done so, she transferred some of it to her pockets and then returned the bag to him to be topped up. Not until it was full did she pronounce herself satisfied. There was still some coin in the box so she took the container from him and emptied it on the ground, correctly guessing that he would stop to pick it all up before carrying on with his journey, and thereby giving her a little more time to get away.

She rode off into the trees at some speed, Grendel on her heels, and made no attempt to slow down until she was well away from the road and in a patch of particularly heavy cover. Then she stopped.

She had been shaking before the old man's carriage had arrived, but it was nothing compared with the way she was shaking now. It was as if she had been struck with an ague and her stomach, its knots miraculously untied, was now heaving like a swollen sea. She realised with dismay that she had ridden off at high speed with a cocked pistol in her shaking hand, and she hastily—but very, very carefully—uncocked it and put it safely back in its holster. Now that they were no longer obliged to function, her legs were shaking, too. It took a very determined effort of will to pull herself together and get back to the Red Lion, and, even when she was in the woods behind the inn, she knew she had to restrain her impulse to rush down, stable Halcyon and change back into her female clothes. The fewer people who saw her dressed like this, the better. She therefore waited until the yard was empty and then, Halcyon settled, she wrapped the enveloping folds of her cloak around her to disguise her apparel and went straight to her little room.

Neither the landlord nor his wife commented on her appearance in the small dining-room, nor did they show any curiosity about the success of her outing.

A farmer came in to quench his thirst after a long day at Petersfield market. A tankard of ale to wash the dust away was his first requirement, and then he imparted the gossip and news, the exchange of which was a vital part of any market's existence.

'What's more,' he announced, after telling them about the body found in Nursted Copse last Sunday, and Jude Whiteland's new bull, 'what's more, it looks like Jack Ranton's got some competition.'

'How so?' someone asked.

'It seems some old man from Emsworth way was robbed this morning just north of Sheet. A young whipper-snapper on a bay horse took most of his money—left him some, though it beats me why—and then disappeared, surrounded by a pack of ravening hounds.'

Jem Hoby's outward uninterest vanished. 'Surrounded by *what*?' he asked, pausing on his way back to the bar-counter.

'A pack of ravening hounds. That's what he said. I heard him. Slavering away, they was, frightened the life out of him, he said, though it's my belief it wouldn't take much to do that.'

'How much did this youngster get away with?' one of the customers asked.

'You've got me there. That was a matter he was very cagey about,' the witness said regretfully. 'Mind you, money was all he took. Didn't take a gold watch and wasn't interested in silk kerchieves. Just the money.'

'Risky place to pick,' one listener commented. 'I don't know as how I'd want to hold up a carriage in broad daylight on that stretch of road on market day.'

'I don't know,' another commented thoughtfully. 'Keep a careful lookout and you'll be all right. Good day for rich pickings—and no one ain't going to follow you into the woods, now are they? Not if you've got a gun.'

'To say nothing of a pack of slavering hounds,' someone added, and everyone roared at this sally. It was one aspect of the story they all disbelieved.

'At all events, he was too scared to continue, so he had his coachman turn round and they went back to Petersfield,' the bearer of news continued. ''Course, without his money, I reckon his journey wasn't necess-ary any more.'

They all laughed again. There seemed to be re-markably little sympathy for the victim, and then one of the listeners remarked, 'I don't reckon Jack Ranton'll be too happy about it. Not seeing as how it's right on his patch.'

There was general agreement with this opinion, but one man was heard to say that Ranton's patch was big enough to let one or two others work there so long as they weren't greedy. There were some uneasy exchanges of glances at this, and the subject was changed by common, if tacit, agreement.

It was Margery Hoby, not her husband, who knocked on Araminta's door later that night and slipped quietly into the room. 'Jem and I have been discussing our share,' she said. 'Now we've a living to make, as well as you, and there's palms to be greased if it's not to be a hit-or-miss business, and Jem's spent a lot of time teaching you a few tricks. Normally we'd take a quarter, but this time we thinks it fair enough to take half. That'll pay for Jem's time and your keep since your money run out—to say nothing of the horse and that dratted dog. What do you say?'

'Half of it is a lot,' Araminta said.

'Yes, it is, but it'll only be for this time. From now on we goes to a quarter. More if we has to fence things for you, of course.'

Araminta knew what 'fence' meant. The arrangement was fair, but it was a very good reason for limiting her takings to coin. 'Very well,' she said.

The two women knelt down on the floor and divided the spoils between them. When they had finished, Mrs Hoby straightened up.

'It's a good haul,' she said. 'Mind if I gives you some advice?'

'Not at all.'

'Go easy with it. A haul like that don't come often. As likely as not, you'll never make another to compare. Generally speaking, it's a handful of guineas and a pocket-watch. Don't fritter it away.'

Reflecting that there wasn't much opportunity in Rake for frittering anything, Araminta promised that she wouldn't. She didn't add that this was the start of her provision for the future. 'And now may I ask a question?' she went on.

'You can ask,' Mrs Hoby said unpromisingly.

'This Jack Ranton people keep talking about. I heard his name at the Fetchams' and that's a long way from here. Who is he?'

Mrs Hoby looked uneasy. 'You'll hear his name all over the south of England,' she said. 'It wouldn't surprise me if you heard it in the north, as well. As to who he is, well, that I can't say. I only knows *what* he is.'

'A highwayman, I presume,' Araminta said.

'So they do say. I'm not so sure. He's no friend of the Revenue men, that I do know, and there's not an innkeeper in the country that doesn't agree with him, to say nothing of half the magistrates and most of the landowners.'

'And he lives round here?'

'I've no idea where he lives. Probably somewhere else altogether—that would be safer. He's not around sometimes for weeks, even months, on end. He's a pleasant-spoken fellow. There's some as says he's got another, entirely respectable life. I don't believe it myself. More likely he *had* a respectable life and then fell on hard times and had to do something about it—not unlike yourself, in fact.'

Araminta flushed. 'At all events, he's not a legend. That's what I had been told.'

'You would have been, wouldn't you? After all, you weren't one of us then.'

She left Araminta with much to think about. Oddly enough, her morning exploit figured less prominently in her thoughts than might have been expected.

She was far more interested to learn that Jack Ranton was one man and not, as her father believed, a composite of several. It increased the likelihood that that was the identity of the highwayman who had waylaid her. She had already encountered him here, and might well do so again. True, he seemed not to have recognised her, but she refused to let such considerations daunt her.

Nor would she allow thoughts of Justinian Fencott, Marquess of Cosenham—and her husband—intrude upon a far more pleasant dream, and she finally fell asleep, not in the least perturbed by the fact that Lady Araminta Wareham, well born, well bred, well connected and nothing if not respectable, was now considered by the owners of what her father would have castigated a thieves' kitchen as being one of themselves. Furthermore, she slept very soundly.

CHAPTER SEVEN

JEM HOBY advised Araminta to lie low for several weeks after her successful first sortie. 'Word'll have got round and they'll be expecting you if you goes too soon—and at the same place. Give 'em time to think you've gone somewhere else, or been so successful you've given up. I'll tell you when to go.'

Araminta's second robbery took place at Petersfield, where she relieved an elderly dowager of several guineas. The robbery went off without a hitch save for the fact that, despite her precautions, Grendel once more escaped to join her.

She heard nothing at all about her exploit for several days, when Jem Hoby took her aside.

'I've found out your other name,' he said teasingly.

Araminta's heart leapt into her mouth and she coloured self-consciously. This was one of the things she had been dreading.

He laughed. 'Rest easy—not your real one. I thought you might like to know as how you're generally reckoned to be a young stripling called Bay Peterkin.'

'Bay Peterkin? What an extraordinary name! How did anyone come to that conclusion?'

'Bay is for the horse, you see. We'll have to darken him a bit, otherwise we'll have lost part of the element of surprise. Peterkin—well, I suppose Peter's as good a boy's name as any, and the nursery ''Peterkin'' just underlines your youth. So Bay Peterkin you've become, and it seems you left most of your pack of hounds at home because the dowager can't remember more than three. You'll have to shoot that dog.'

'I shall most assuredly do no such thing,' Araminta said indignantly. 'It can't be beyond the power of human intelligence to keep him contained for just a few hours.'

'Then I suggest you puts your human intelligence to the task of working out just how to do that very thing. That dog is fast becoming a liability.'

Araminta knew he was right, but she had no intention of allowing Jem Hoby or anyone else to shoot Grendel. Next time she would fasten the window *and* tie him to the leg of the bed. That ought to be sufficient.

She thought of her family often, and with affection, but never with regret. Araminta was a practical woman. She had made her choice. She had considered that her straightforward, unexplained disappearance would give her family less public shame than any course of action other than remaining with her husband. The marriage could be quietly dissolved without anyone outside the family being any the wiser and, if anyone enquired after her, they could be told she was abroad. Her family would be anxious about what might have befallen her, and for that she was sorry, but at least it would be a private grief. She was far less concerned about Lord Cosenham. She judged him to be a man of shallow feelings other, perhaps, than pride and vanity, and she saw no reason to pander to those, and she very much doubted whether any more laudable feelings would have been outraged.

Having decided that the one thing she could not bear to do was that which was conditional to the marriage, she had chosen to abandon that marriage completely, and not only the marriage but the life that went with it. It was a choice she had made and no useful purpose would be served either by regretting it or by wondering whether a better alternative might have been found— and in fact she genuinely did not regret it. Her new life had an excitement totally lacking in her old one, and she enjoyed that. There was an element of risk but, to a woman in whose life risk had been an unknown component, its sudden appearance was exhilarating. Furthermore, she had met Jack Ranton. It was true this gentleman had exhibited no particular interest in Jane Shore, and quite probably she would never see him again though, given his occupation and her place of residence, there must be a reasonable chance that she would. The fact remained that she very much wanted to meet him again. He was, she told herself, the sort of person with whom one would wish to become much better acquainted. It crossed her mind that these must be improper thoughts for a married woman, but she found it difficult to think of herself as such and told herself that she was unlikely to remain one for very long.

Several weeks of caution on Jem Hoby's part passed before he felt it advisable for Bay Peterkin to ride again. The year was slipping quickly into autumn, with mists early and late increasing cover and making positive identification more difficult. He took Araminta aside.

'A little bird's been talking to me. There's a big one coming up. Interested?'

'If it's that big, won't there be guards?'

'It seems not. There's this very fashionable gentleman who'll be driving himself in one of these new-fangled curricles—and that means he'll just have a groom up behind. Now it's likely the groom'll be armed, but the driver won't be—his attention will have to be on his horses. This one usually protects himself pretty well and is left alone by the gentlemen of the road on that account. But it seems he wants to see how this vehicle goes so he's driving himself down to Portsmouth and his baggage will have preceded him by some hours.'

'You know a lot about this man,' Araminta commented doubtfully.

'So I'd expect to. I pays enough for my information and I expects it to be accurate—accurate and detailed. Have I let you down yet?'

Araminta agreed that he hadn't, and between them they settled upon a stretch of road where the trees were thickest and the hill steep enough to slow the keenest of prime horse-flesh, let alone a pair that was coming to the end of a long, hard run.

It was a dull day, heavy and overcast. The morning mists scarcely lifted and showed signs of descending again early. From Araminta's point of view, it could hardly be better, a sentiment she felt obliged to qualify because she found the muffling effect of the mists unnerving, prompting her to want to look over her shoulder for fear someone might come up behind her without her having heard them. As protection against that, she insisted that on this occasion Grendel should accompany her, despite Jem Hoby's strongly expressed objections.

She had taken up her position in the trees just below the crest of the hill before she realised that she had ridden out without her gauntlets. She must hope her fingers did not become too numb to handle a pistol. It was eerie waiting here in the mist, and she was very glad she had insisted upon bringing Grendel. She even caught herself talking to him from time to time.

By the time the traveller was within earshot, the mists were eddying, now thick, now thin. She strained her ears to gauge the speed of the curricle's advance, and when she was ready she rode out of the mist-laden trees. The traveller was driving his team in tandem, and such was the shock to the leader of this sudden apparition that he half reared and then jibbed and sidled until he was standing across the wheeler's forehand, a position from which it was impossible for even the most experienced whip to extricate his team with ease.

No sooner had the groom realised the carriage was immobile and the highwayman armed than he pulled out his own pistol and let fly without a second thought. It was fortunate for Araminta that he was so anxious to shoot that he omitted to take the careful aim necessary to hit a rider on a far from stationary horse. Consequently, he missed and dared not reload because his adversary would be able to shoot him, with plenty of time to take accurate aim while he did so.

Now, for the first time, Araminta was able to divert her attention to its true object, the driver. She held him in her sights—and gasped.

She was staring straight into the glittering eyes and white-painted face of the Marquess of Cosenham. The man she had waylaid was her husband.

Her instinct was to flee, but that would provoke more questions than a straightforward highway robbery. She tightened her hold on the reins and, as she did so, the waning light caught her memorial ring. Lord Cosenham saw it and frowned and Araminta, catching his glance, immediately changed the angle at which she was holding the reins so as partially to hide the ring. If Lord Cosenham recognised it, he might guess her true identity. More probably, he would assume that the highwayman before him had taken the ring from Araminta's corpse. There were advantages in his reaching that conclusion, not least the fact that it would make him a widower and thus do away with the need for legal annulments.

She paused before she spoke, and not only lowered the tone but also forced it so that the effect was both lower and more harsh than normal. She also decided to keep words to the minimum.

'Your money,' she demanded.

Lord Cosenham, who had recognised the ring immediately, appeared to be giving this demand due consideration. If he was at all frightened by being faced with an armed robber, he disguised it very well. Araminta found this disconcerting.

'*All* of it?' he asked. The fashionable drawl was undiminished. Indeed, if anything, it seemed more pronounced than Araminta remembered. If he could retain it even at a time like this, she thought scornfully, perhaps long usage had made it second nature.

'All you have,' she said.

'I take it you mean all I have *with me*?' he persisted.

Araminta's ambition to say as little as possible seemed destined to be thwarted. 'Of course.'

'One should always phrase these things precisely,' he told her, the quiet sibilance of his voice imparting menace to an otherwise unobjectionable statement. 'It prevents misunderstanding. One should always endeavour to prevent misunderstanding, don't you think?'

Araminta assumed the question was rhetorical, and responded only by moving the muzzle of her pistol in a gesture indicating that he should obey his instructions.

Lord Cosenham surveyed the barrel and raised one eyebrow. 'Ah, yes, of course. My money.' He kept his eye on the gun but spoke over his shoulder. 'Tell me, William, do I have any money with me?'

'No, me lord,' the groom replied promptly.

'My apologies, dear sir, but, as you heard, I have no money with me on the present occasion.'

Again, Araminta was being obliged to speak. 'You've money,' she said. 'You've lodging and livery in Petersfield to pay for.'

'Dear me, you seem remarkably well informed, young man. Don't you agree, William?'

'Remarkable, me lord,' the groom said grimly.

'You are, of course, correct,' Lord Cosenham went on in the tone of one who wished to establish the facts of the matter in a way that precluded misunderstanding. 'Money is being carried for that purpose. Gold, to be precise. But look at me, dear boy. Do I look like a man who would willingly spoil the line of a coat by filling the pockets with gold?' And he threw both hands out as if to demonstrate the absurdity of the suggestion.

'Then your groom must have it,' Araminta said, wondering for how much longer she would be able to sustain this peculiar and unnatural voice.

'Note, William: a young man of deductive logic. He wastes no time considering whether I might be foolish enough to put it in the box along with the nosebag and water-bucket.'

'Very bright, me lord,' the groom agreed. He seemed no more put out than his master. Araminta, on the other hand, was becoming increasingly disconcerted.

'Hand it over,' she said, and such was their combined effect on her that she almost added 'please'.

'You heard the young man, William. Hand it over.'

'All of it, me lord?'

'Perhaps not quite all. We shall need a little for expenses, but I'm sure we can manage on far less than we allow ourselves.' He turned to Araminta and said with exaggerated courtesy, 'Will that arrangement suit you?'

Araminta was completely taken aback. Nothing in her past—and admittedly limited—experience or in Jem Hoby's sound advice had prepared her for a victim who behaved with such complete sang-froid. Travellers were expected to hand over their valuables without question, grateful to have lost nothing more vital. They were not expected to haggle.

'All of it,' she said shortly.

The Marquess sighed, much as a parent sighed when dealing with a recalcitrant child. 'Dare I venture to suggest that your otherwise astute intelligence is letting you down? If you rob me of everything, I shall naturally seek out the constable as soon as we reach Petersfield. I shall be obliged to because otherwise innkeepers will be loath to grant me lodging and livery on a note-of-hand. If, on the other hand, you leave me enough money to take care of that, you may take the rest and be welcome to it.' He watched what he could see of her face. 'I appreciate that you only have my word I shan't go to the constable anyway, but you do have my word as a gentleman. I should have thought it was a chance worth taking.'

Araminta was inclined to agree. She knew very little about her husband and disliked most of it, but she had never heard it suggested that he was anything other than a man of his word.

'Very well,' she said grudgingly.

'William, you will extract ten guineas from the purse and toss the remainder to our young friend here,' Lord Cosenham instructed, and his groom did precisely as he was told. 'And now,' he went on when she had stowed the leather bag away in her own pocket, 'perhaps you will leave us to continue our journey.' He raised his quizzing-glass and stared at Grendel through it. 'And take that unsightly hound with you,' he concluded.

Araminta had forgotten Grendel's presence, and she knew from the way in which the Marquess had studied him that he would have not the slightest difficulty in recognising him again. No one could disguise the loss of a dog's toes. She reined Halcyon backwards until they were in the trees. It would not have surprised her had Lord Cosenham or his groom—-or, indeed, both of them—produced another loaded pistol, so she kept her own trained on them until it was safe to turn away and ride off, uncocking it as soon as the mist had enveloped them.

The meeting with her husband had unnerved her more than she would have imagined, and her only reassurance lay in her certainty that he had no inkling that the highwayman was anyone other than he seemed. The meeting also served to confirm her belief that in running away she had done the right thing. The man was every bit the same affected, superficial person she had married, and nothing in his behaviour inclined her to think that perhaps marriage to him might have been tolerable. Only two things surprised her. The first was that he had driven his own team—and tandem, too, which suggested he was no mean whip. It didn't quite accord with the carefully cultivated picture of himself that he put forth. But then, she remembered, neither had his black saddle-horse. The other cause of surprise was, quite simply, his courage. It might be that he so lacked imagination that he had not foreseen the possible consequences of finding oneself facing the barrel of a pistol at almost point-blank range. No, that had shown courage, and for that she accorded him a grudging admiration. She wondered idly how Jack Ranton would have reacted in a similar situation.

She told Jem Hoby nothing of what had transpired. She gave him his share and when he asked his usual, 'Any problems?' she shrugged.

'Not really. The groom loosed off his pistol, but he didn't take his time so he shot wide. Very wide.'

'Did you fire back?'

'No.'

Araminta was grateful for Jem Hoby's network of informers whose whispered words provided such infallible guidance. She was less happy about the long interval the Red Lion's landlord considered necessary between each sortie. Her sole purpose in this undertaking was to accumulate funds to set herself up in some entirely respectable business. She had already done better than she would have thought possible, but it was taking a long time.

Although she was anxious to acquire the necessary funds that would enable her to give up this life, Araminta was also quite pleased to have a respite after discovering that she had robbed her own husband, a situation whose piquancy was overshadowed by the sheer shock of the occurrence, but as time passed her impatience grew. She was therefore in a very receptive frame of mind when two riders, well armed and of comfortable means, stopped for refreshment with a tale of an elderly man they had observed at Guildford. This gentleman had insisted that the landlord stow his money-box—there was dispute between them as to whether 'money-box' was an adequate word, one of the pair preferring 'treasure-chest'—in the cellar for safe keeping, where the gentleman's manservant would sit up with it as if it had been a sick horse. The old man was on his way to Southampton and would put up the following night at Winchester where, doubtless, he would cause as much of an upset as he had at Guildford.

Araminta had pricked up her ears at mention of the money-box. She did some quick calculations and decided that it began to look quite promising.

She knew the area and mentally reviewed the road between Guildford and Winchester to select the most appropriate spot. She decided against telling Jem Hoby what she planned. She wanted to prove to herself that she could plan and execute a foray on her own, and it crossed her mind that it would be no bad thing if Jem Hoby learned she could do so.

The plan was made carefully and nothing could have been smoother than its implementation. No one saw her leave the Red Lion, she made better time than she had allowed for and passed no one on her journey. Grendel was with her; she would have preferred to leave him behind, but those occasions when she had succeeded in leaving him while she exercised Halcyon had been marred by the fact that he had howled all the time she was absent, and she had no desire to alert the Red Lion to the fact that she had gone.

It was a clearer day than she would have liked and the parish with responsibility for this stretch of road did rather too good a job of keeping the underbrush at bay. All the same, there was plenty of cover, and she positioned herself to take best advantage of it. The only problem was that, although she would have no problem hearing the approaching carriage, she would be unable to see it until it was nearly upon her, and more than one carriage could be expected along so important a road.

The wait seemed interminable and the emergence of self-doubt did nothing to shorten it. At last Araminta heard the sound she had been listening for. It was the heavy sound of one of the old-fashioned, cumbersome coaches still in use by those of an age to consider that improvements were rarely for the best. It was accompanied by the sound of more horses' hoofs than she had anticipated. She cast her mind quickly back over the conversation she had heard. Had they mentioned whether it was drawn by two horses, or four? She couldn't remember. Perhaps she had simply assumed it had been two. If so, it had been a false assumption, for there were certainly more than that.

Calculating when the leaders would round the bend, Araminta cocked her pistol, covered her face, and rode out.

No sooner had she materialised in front of the foremost horse than she realised her mistake. An armed manservant to spend the night in the cellar was not the only assistance this traveller had brought with him. There was a coachman in front, a footman behind and, more immediately significant, four armed outriders, two before and two behind.

Araminta's mind raced and in seconds she had begun to rein Halcyon back, at the same time lowering her pistol, but it was too late. The outriders wasted no time in questions. A masked rider with a gun appearing suddenly before them from the trees could mean only one thing and they knew what they were being paid for. The two at the front fired. Fortunately, Halcyon was already moving rapidly back and one ball went wide while the other skimmed the horse's head, missing his skull and his rider by inches.

Araminta made no attempt to return their fire. She pulled Halcyon's head round towards the trees and dug her heels into his sides. As he leapt in obedience, another ball whistled past her left shoulder and then she felt a tremendous impact on her right, as if a fist had thumped her, hard. At the same time her pistol slipped from her loosened grasp. She heard horses behind her and knew they must be giving chase. More shots rang out but, oddly, none came in her direction, or so it seemed. She was confused and so was Halcyon, who found the hand on the reins was no longer directing him, though the panic he sensed in his rider made him weave his way through the trees at as great a speed as they allowed.

Araminta was dimly conscious that the pursuit continued though the firing had ceased. For some reason, presumably connected with that blow, she was only able to use one arm. She felt dizzy too, and, though she wanted to look back over her shoulder to establish how far behind her pursuers might be, she was quite unable to do so.

She was aware of a huge liver-chestnut drawing level and of Halcyon being brought steadily to a halt, though not by any effort of hers. The next she knew was that an arm was round her and a light, familiar voice said,

'We've shaken them off and bought some time. I'll take you up in front of me and we'll make for a place of safety.'

Araminta was too dazed to do much more than attempt to follow his instructions, and transferring from one horse to another was far from easy. It took precious minutes to accomplish the move, and the comforting sense of physical support from the body behind her and the arms that encircled her brought a feeling of overwhelming relief to Araminta's muddled senses.

'Don't leave Halcyon,' she murmured.

'I won't,' the familiar voice reassured her, and then they were moving.

CHAPTER EIGHT

WHEN Araminta opened her eyes, she saw nothing familiar, so she closed them again. When she opened them for the second time, nothing had changed but she decided to keep them open anyway. Wherever she was, it was dark, though there was a lamp in one corner. She was lying down in a bed of some sort. A narrow bed that sagged, and she hurt. A dull, nagging ache centred somewhere in the region of her collarbone and radiated outwards from there, diminishing slightly as it went. She shifted her position and the ache changed to a sharp pain that made her cry out.

Immediately, the lamp moved from the corner to a spot just above her. She supposed someone must be holding it but she couldn't make anyone out in the dark behind it.

'So you're awake,' said a pleasant voice that was familiar but which she couldn't quite place. 'How are you feeling?'

Araminta considered the question. 'Not good,' she decided. She turned her head away from the lamp and the speaker and winced at the effort. There were shapes dimly illuminated by the odorous oil-fed flame. They were familiar, but not what she would expect to see in a bed-chamber. Barrels. Several barrels in a neat row. 'Why am I in the cellar?' she asked.

'Cellars are secluded places,' the voice told her.

That was true enough, she supposed, but she was unsure of its relevance. 'What happened?' she asked.

'You don't remember? You were shot. The ball caught you in the shoulder. You were lucky.'

Araminta managed a faint, disbelieving smile. 'I was? It doesn't feel like it.'

'You were lucky because it was your right shoulder so there was no question of its hitting the heart; furthermore, it missed the actual shoulder-joint and passed right through. The doctor is satisfied it isn't lodged inside.'

Araminta frowned. 'I've seen a doctor? I don't remember it.'

'He's a trusted friend of mine, well able to keep his own counsel. He gave you some laudanum. You've lost a lot of blood and it will be several days before we can even think of letting you out of here. You need to regain your strength.'

'But Jem Hoby doesn't like strangers in his cellar,' she told him.

'You're not in Jem Hoby's cellar. This isn't the Red Lion.'

'Then where am I?'

'Safe. It doesn't matter where.'

Araminta tried to gather her wits together. 'And Halcyon?' she asked.

'In the stable. Last time I looked in on him, he had reverted to his original colour. It seemed the best way of disguising him. Now go back to sleep.'

'You won't go?'

'I'll be here when you wake up.'

Araminta closed her eyes obediently and was asleep again almost at once.

The only thing that had changed when she woke up was that she felt much less hazy, and the area of nagging pain was smaller but the sharp pain was more pronounced. Her attendant had been true to his word, but when he saw she was awake he left her briefly and returned with a bowl of broth laced with what Araminta took to be brandy.

He put his arm behind her neck and shoulders. 'This will hurt,' he told her. 'I can't help that, but you need to be sitting up to drink this. You must be half starved by now.' He propped her up with cushions and pillows against the cellar wall behind the bed and fed her spoonfuls of the broth. Araminta realised for the first time that her arm was in a sling.

'Being fed like this makes me feel as if I'm three years old again,' she said, feeling foolish that it should be necessary.

'Make the most of it,' he told her. 'How often do adults get so thoroughly coddled?'

'Where's Grendel?'

The abrupt change of subject did not seem to take him by surprise. 'The dog? He ran off when the shooting started and I've not seen him since.'

'Perhaps he'll go back to the Red Lion,' Araminta suggested unhappily.

'Perhaps he will. There's nothing you or I can do about it for the time being,' he said. There was no point in telling her how far the Red Lion was and the improbability of a badly frightened dog finding his way back there. That would have to come later, but the later, the better.

Later that day—or it might have been night; it was impossible to tell in the windowless cellar—Araminta asked her companion exactly what had happened.

He shrugged. 'There's not a lot to tell. You attacked—very inadvisedly, I may say—an extremely well-guarded consignment. I admire your courage in tackling it but not your judgement. To be sure, if you had succeeded, you would have been able to retire from the road, but the odds were so heavily stacked against success that I can't think of anyone else who would have tried. By sheer good luck, I had business in Four Marks, heard the fracas, guessed what was happening and came to assist. It wasn't till I saw the dog that I realised I had come to the aid of Bay Peterkin.'

Araminta digested this. 'How long have you known about Bay Peterkin?' she asked.

'I knew you must be he as soon as I heard about the dog.'

'And are you indeed Jack Ranton?'

'So they tell me.'

It was a cryptically worded answer and Araminta guessed it might well not be his real name any more than Jane Shore was hers. She changed the subject. 'Jem Hoby will be worried about me,' she said.

'You flatter yourself. He may wonder what has become of you, but he won't worry. If you galloped into the yard at noon on market day dripping blood, then he would worry, but his concern would be less for your health than for his own freedom.'

'You're very cynical!'

'Not at all. I merely face facts. However, Jem Hoby should by now not even be wondering. He will have had a message and, since he will be expecting your eventual return, I think we may assume your little hoard of silver and gold will remain untouched. Without such a message, Mr Hoby would undoubtedly have appropriated it for his own use.'

Araminta opened her mouth to protest and then closed it again. Mr Ranton was almost certainly correct. 'How long must I stay here?' she asked.

'You can go nowhere while you need a sling. They know they hit you and there's a hue and cry out for you, but that will eventually die down.' He paused as if uncertain whether to continue and then asked, 'Did Jem put you in the way of this job?'

'No. I heard about it myself. Two men came into the Red Lion talking about it.'

'And you still decided to tackle a convoy that included four outriders?'

Araminta flushed. 'I didn't know about them,' she said. 'They only mentioned an old man and an armed manservant.'

'Then it's a great pity you didn't check with Jem. That consignment is well known, my dear. Every quarter that old man takes a similar amount of money down to Portsmouth. A Navy is an expensive toy, you know, and he's the paymaster who sees to it that ships can be provisioned and fitted out and that sailors can sometimes get paid—if Parliament doesn't have a more pressing use for the money.'

'But he wasn't going to Portsmouth. He was going to Southampton. The travellers I overheard said so—and, besides, he was on the Southampton road.'

Jack Ranton sighed. 'That, my dear simpleton, is his very rudimentary ruse. One quarter he makes no bones about it and heads straight down the Portsmouth road, the next he opts for subtlety and gives out that he's going to Southampton but leaves Winchester on the Portsmouth road instead. It must be nearly twenty years since anyone tried to waylay him and the last one hanged. They won't abandon the search easily, if only to set an example to others.'

'I'd better become accustomed to life in a cellar,' Araminta said miserably. 'It will serve me right for being such a fool.'

'Two statements with which I am in whole-hearted agreement,' her companion said. 'The rest will do you no harm at all and, since they'll be looking for me as well, I shall be obliged to spend much of my own time down here, too, so you will at least have some company.'

'I'm sorry,' Araminta said sincerely. 'It was never my intention to embroil somebody else.'

Jack Ranton stood up and made an exaggerated bow. 'Think nothing of it. I frequently lie low for long periods for one reason or another and I can think of no more agreeable companion.'

Araminta laughed and she felt herself blush. His compliment was mere *badinage* and it would never do to let him think she took it seriously. She was glad the dim light covered her confusion.

She slept frequently during the next day or two, and the time was punctuated by the arrival at regular intervals of food. The fact that this was of a simple nature—stews, bread, cheese and ham and only very rarely roast meat—suggested that the cellar belonged to an ale-house rather than an inn, and the landlord's appearance confirmed this. His visits to the cellar were infrequent, and when he made them he took no notice of Araminta whatsoever, not even glancing in her direction. It was as if she weren't there. Food was either brought down by Jack Ranton or, if he were already in the cellar, handed to him through the door at the top of the stairs by the landlord, whose apparent desire not to see Araminta stopped him from bringing it in.

Time began to drag heavily once Araminta had slept off the immediate effects of her ill-conceived escapade. Jack Ranton obtained some books for her, but the lamplight was too poor to allow her to read for very long and quite inadequate for her even to contemplate needlework. He taught her chess and piquet which they played for ten-pound points, winning and losing such astronomical sums that they had to stop in case their laughter penetrated to the rooms above.

Such shared merriment in so confined a space induced a warm camaraderie that Araminta had never experienced before. The strong feeling for Jack that their first encounter had engendered did not diminish in their present proximity, but she felt obliged to suppress it because she had no idea to what extent—if at all—it was reciprocated. She found it was gradually becoming overlaid with a sense of friendship and a genuine liking that had very little to do with the passionate yearning beneath, and she suspected that these might even prove to be more valuable commodities. She was in no doubt that Jack Ranton enjoyed her company, and her only nagging unhappiness lay in her uncertainty as to whether his feelings went any deeper than that, or even whether he had recognised in Jem Hoby's niece the woman whose carriage he had held up and whom he had treated on that occasion so disgracefully.

She was eventually up and moving around the confines of the cellar from time to time. The lack of light, air and proper exercise became irksome, and her situation was not made easier by the fact that her companion left her alone for increasingly frequent periods for which he offered no explanation on his return. The time passed unbearably slowly when he was away, and there was no denying the fact that her heart beat that little bit faster when she heard his step on the cellar stairs. She longed to join him in the daylight above—and not only for the pleasure of being with him—but the highwayman was adamant.

'No one knows you're here except the landlord and if people see you they'll ask questions. They may even put two and two together, and we don't want that.'

'They must see you,' Araminta objected.

'They've seen me before, several times. There's nothing unusual about me.'

But perhaps her greatest embarrassment was caused by her wound. The doctor had removed the ball, but the wound itself had to be dressed. Because of its position, this was not something she could do herself and, since a doctor's arrival and disappearance into the cellar would occasion remark at the very least, there could be no question of a physician's being sent for. Jack Ranton must dress it.

A rough but clean shirt had been found to replace the one torn and bloodied by the ball's impact. The right sleeve of this hung empty, that arm being bandaged across her chest so that the hand rested on the opposite shoulder. Her embarrassment the first time her companion changed the dressing was acute. Never in her life had she been undressed by a man, and there was an intimacy in the very fact of his removing the shirt that brought the colour flooding to her cheeks. When the sling was removed and her naked breast inevitably revealed, her confusion was complete and she turned her head away, ostrich-like, as if by doing so she might pretend nothing was happening.

Jack Ranton was as fully aware as she of the delicacy of their situation, and executed his essential task in as impersonal a manner as any physician, for which Araminta could only be grateful. It did not cross her mind that it might be as difficult for him as it was for her, nor did she realise that her gratitude for his tact enhanced the deeper feelings she had for him.

At their first meeting he had aroused in her a purely physical passion which, because of its strength and the fact that she had never experienced such feelings before, she had assumed to be love. This was the passion which had caused her to fly from her husband. That passion was still there, and grew stronger as her strength returned, but now, added to it, was a different, deeper and more satisfying emotion in which a strange mixture of affection and friendship played their part. Araminta enjoyed the company of her highwayman-rescuer. When he was absent, the cellar seemed empty, lifeless, and cold; when he returned, life became worthwhile once more.

As the early days stretched to a week, and the first week merged into the second, their companionship became such that they spoke very little, not because there was nothing to say but because there was very little that needed to be said, and the long silences were entirely natural, leading to no desperate feeling that they should be broken. They were the companionable silences of old friends.

During their early conversations, Araminta had explained what she hoped to do with the proceeds of her exploits, but she took great care to reveal nothing about her origins or her reasons for having adopted her present mode of life. In return, she learned nothing about her companion beyond what she already knew or had guessed. She wanted to know and longed to ask, but she knew that any confidence he gave would have to be reciprocated and that was not something she was prepared to do. Whatever illegal activities he was currently engaged in, he was a gentleman, and she could imagine all too clearly his reaction to learning that she was a married woman. She found too much pleasure in his company to want to risk losing it.

It was bad enough when he left the cellar. He slept elsewhere and whenever he left, whether for that purpose or on his increasing diurnal absences, she saw him go with an ache that was almost physical and that certainly hurt more deeply than the pain in her shoulder. When he returned, her spirits lifted and her eyes shone.

She knew now what Isabella felt for Thomas Kineton, though she still found it difficult to conceive what there was about that young man to inspire such feelings. Doubtless Izzy would have the same reservations about Jack Ranton. At all events, Araminta was going to do nothing that might give him a disgust for her—and revealing that she was a married woman who had left her husband immediately after the ceremony would undoubtedly have that effect.

She had been in the cellar some three weeks when he returned from a prolonged absence and, instead of coming straight in, put his head round the door.

'There's a visitor for you,' he said. 'Can I let him in?'

Araminta glanced up, surprised. A visitor, and a man? The only person it could conceivably be was Jem Hoby. She checked the buttons on her shirt and smoothed her breeches with her one sound arm as if they were skirts. 'Yes, of course,' she said.

He opened the door fully and, to Araminta's delight, a large, lolloping, long-tailed brute of a dog burst past him down the steps and into the cellar.

'Grendel!' she exclaimed delightedly. 'Where have you been?'

'It appears he's been turning up every day for two or three days now. The landlord chased him off every time—with renewed energy when he realised his missing toes would connect him with the robbery—but he refused to stay chased. It seems he spent last night with Halcyon, a circumstance that didn't make the landlord any happier, so he told me about it and suggested I shoot the brute.'

'You didn't,' Araminta said, trying with her sound arm to fend off the worst excesses of Grendel's effusions of delight.

'So it would appear,' he said drily.

Araminta looked up at him with shining eyes. 'You can't imagine how grateful I am. Wondering what happened to him has been—oh, the cloud on the horizon, I suppose.'

'Yet you haven't mentioned it.'

'How could I? Your intervention probably saved my life and it certainly found me a safe hiding-place. I could hardly expect you—or anyone else—to search for my dog.'

'Then it's as well he searched for you.' He hesitated. 'Are you really so attached to him? You surely realise he's a liability?'

'I don't care about that,' she said firmly. 'I found him caught in a trap when I was ru-riding some months ago,' she amended hastily. 'I nursed him back to health then and I'm not abandoning him now.'

'Admirable loyalty. I hope it doesn't misfire on you.' The words were cynical, even harsh, but the tone in which they were uttered was neither. 'I've just come from the Red Lion,' he went on. 'Hoby will take you back as soon as you can ride without your sling. He's not too happy about it, though, and we are agreed that you won't go on the bridle-lay again.'

'*You've* agreed?' Araminta stared at him. 'What right have you to make such a decision on my behalf? You know what I'm doing it for, why I need the money.'

'I know what you intend to do with the money,' he corrected her. 'That's not quite the same thing as knowing why you want it and, since your activities on the Southampton road put at risk anyone who had helped you, the Hobys in particular, I don't think it's unreasonable for the risk to be removed while he continues to help you. Do you?'

Araminta reluctantly conceded that it was different, put like that. She looked so crestfallen that Jack took her chin and raised it so that he was looking down into her eyes. 'Don't look so dejected,' he said softly. 'You're nothing if not resourceful. You'll think of something else.'

Araminta opened her mouth to demand what and found it stopped by a far from gentle kiss. Her startled eyes flew to his face and her one arm, its fist clenched, rose to strike his shoulder, but instead changed its mind and rested there while she was gently drawn closer to him.

He raised his head briefly. 'I'm not hurting you?'

Araminta smiled and shook her head. She lied, but the increased ache in her shoulder was a small price to pay for the realisation that her feelings were reciprocated. That was what she had dreamed of and hoped for, but with no real expectation of its being so and there was as much relief as passion in the vehemence with which she returned his kisses.

He released her at last with a final brief kiss. 'I've brought more suitable clothes back with me,' he said. 'The skirt of your habit and a side-saddle so that when you return to the Red Lion it will be with an aura of respectability. There's also a workaday dress and a clean shift, I gather, as well as some softer shoes.'

Araminta laughed ruefully. 'There's no longer anything very respectable about my habit,' she commented. 'It has been worn day in and day out for so long now it would be better described as thoroughly disreputable.'

She was glad to get out of her breeches. There had been an element of adventure in dressing as a man, as if it had been a gesture of rebellion, an indication that she would lead the life she chose and not that imposed upon her by family, no matter how well-intentioned, or husband—and his intentions had been unfathomable. The adventure had fled with the musket-ball and the rebellion was complete. There could be no going back now, even had she wanted to. It was more important now that Jack Ranton should see her as a woman. True, he didn't appear to be encountering too much difficulty with the concept, but it would do no harm to drive the point home. She evaded facing up to the fact that there could be little purpose in driving it home while she remained married and he was in ignorance of that fact. If she gave it any thought at all—and she tried very hard not to—

her conclusion was always to the effect that something would turn up, a naïve opinion with no basis in past experience.

It was not very long before Araminta learned that one of the consequences of being in love was an unquenchable desire not just to be with the object of one's affections but to touch and be touched. The feel of his arms, the passing brush of his lips in her hair, these were things that made her heart glow and the warmth shine through her eyes for anyone to see. Her dreams changed, too. She no longer had need to imagine his embrace or the tenderness in his voice. She welcomed his touch with as much avidity as she had shunned her husband's and she knew that, were Jack Ranton her husband, there would be no thought of duty when it came to ensuring an heir.

There was just one small mote in the beam of light that seemed to illuminate her days. Jack Ranton behaved as Araminta assumed a man in love would behave, but no word of love passed his lips and there were times when she felt his emotions were kept so firmly under control that she doubted their spontaneity. Surely, if he loved her, he would tell her so? And surely the natural progression from that would be to suggest marriage?

She told herself it was just as well he didn't, since she was already married and would have to decline, with only the choice of giving the real reason, a false one, or none at all. She knew that honour would demand they saw no more of each other once a declaration had been received and rejected, and the thought of never seeing him again was unbearable. Yet perversely she wished he would declare himself. She felt a desperate need to know he felt as she did and, increasingly, a desperate need to prove to him in the only way left to her the strength of her own love for him. Yet this, too, was denied her. Jack Ranton might be a smuggler, and quite possibly a highwayman too, but sadly there seemed to be a limit beyond which he was not prepared to go when it came to compromising a lady.

Araminta greeted with mixed feelings his opinion that she was fit to travel. It would be a joy to escape the confines of this dark, chilly cellar after nearly five weeks of confinement. She had latterly come back into the outside world at dusk before any customers appeared, and had been able to get some fresh air and a little exercise. It would be good to ride again, and even better to see the sun and feel the breeze. On the other hand, this was the place where she had encountered the nearest thing to true happiness that she had so far experienced, and she was loath to leave those associations behind. She also had an unhappy feeling that their return to the Red Lion would spell the beginning of the end.

She put on her habit and Jack tied her other clothes in a neat bundle and strapped them on his horse. She looked around the cellar before ascending the stairs.

'I shall never forget this place,' she said.

Jack slipped his arm round her waist and guided her to the steps.

'No one would,' he said grimly, glancing round at the brick walls with their barely discernible sweat-beads of damp. 'We must just hope this is the closest either of us comes to gaol.'

Araminta glanced up at him over her shoulder, surprised. 'That isn't what I meant. I meant——'

'I know what you meant,' he interrupted with finality. He leant over and kissed her cheek. 'Don't let sentiment cloud your judgement,' he said.

Araminta frowned, unsure what he meant, but suspecting she wouldn't like it if she knew. The need to mount up and be gone before anyone saw where they came from took precedence over explanations, however, so she said nothing and hurried through the ale-house taproom to where Halcyon was waiting. Jack threw her into the saddle and then mounted his own horse. He glanced down at Grendel.

'Will that confounded hound be able to keep up or shall we have to adjust our speed to suit his mutilated foot?' he asked.

'He manages very well,' Araminta told him. 'Besides, I'm in no condition to ride hell for leather. He'll cope.' They rode out of the yard and pointed the horses' heads towards the east. 'Why do you dislike him so much?'

'I don't. I've become almost attached to him, as a matter of fact. The only thing I don't like about him is something we can do nothing about. He's identifiable.'

The Hobys expressed no surprise at their lodger's return, nor could Araminta detect any sign of either pleasure or displeasure although, in the circumstances, the latter would have been understandable. Jem nodded approval at Halcyon's restored white blaze and stockings but frowned when Grendel frisked around his boots.

'Keep that dratted dog out of sight,' he said.

It was a joy to return to the civilised world of feather mattresses and sheets, and one small anxiety was annihilated when she found her small hoard of plunder was exactly where she had left it. Her greatest dread had been the need to say goodbye to Jack, an eventuality she had assumed would follow hard upon their return. Happily, there was no sign of his going, a fact which did not escape the notice of the rest of the household, some of whose members teased Araminta unmercifully about it, though she noticed they said nothing to Jack or in his presence.

'You two was away long enough,' was one typical comment. 'Helping him run a cargo, was you? Or did you take the opportunity to wed over there?'

Araminta had no difficulty laughing off such comments, but she wondered whether Jack knew about them and what he thought. She wondered, too, how much longer he would stay in Rake.

In a way, things were easier here—there were too many people about for Araminta and Jack to spend much time in each other's pockets, and that meant that the distance between them which Araminta knew her own position demanded was easier to maintain. She supposed she should welcome it, but she didn't. She longed for the small gestures of affection that the presence of others prevented, and hated the need for snatched kisses in odd moments.

She was grooming Halcyon one morning, immersed in hard work and her own thoughts and oblivious to what was going on around her. A rustle of straw caught her attention and she glanced round and gasped. A tall figure stood there, black against the sunlight streaming at its low, late-autumn angle through the doorway. It was not the suddenness of its appearance that made her gasp so much as something unexpected about its unfamiliarity—an impression that fled as soon as it had been received and which was impossible to define.

'What's the matter?' Jack's voice asked.

Araminta laughed nervously. 'You surprised me, that's all. I was miles away.'

'I noticed. Leave that, Jane, and come with me—but shut the dog up first, for goodness' sake.'

'Why? Where are we going?'

'Away from here. Oh, nothing dramatic, just a walk. Somewhere where we don't have to be perpetually looking over our shoulders.'

She returned the grooming tools to their shelf and took Grendel up to her room. She closed the window, tied him to the bed-leg and locked the door behind her. He would howl the place down, but never mind. Jem Hoby was perfectly capable of explaining it away if anyone asked. She ran down the stairs and joined Jack outside, entirely oblivious to the nudges and winks their departure provoked.

He led the way along the road and then, taking her hand and tucking it into his arm, led her off into a narrow ride through the woods.

'You've not been here in spring, have you?' he said. 'Imagine what this is like then—bluebells as far as you can see and the pale green of the first shooting leaf-buds of the trees.'

'I love them,' Araminta told him. 'We have them at home and I always...' Her voice tapered off as she realised the careful guard she kept on her tongue had slipped. She glanced up at her companion, but he appeared not to have noticed. 'I love the woods,' she finished lamely.

'How's your shoulder?' he asked when they had gone a little further.

'Much better. Almost completely healed,' she said.

'Don't overdo the grooming. You'll open it up again.'

'I'll be careful.'

He stopped suddenly and turned her towards him. His face was suddenly harsh and a little frightening, and Araminta realised why no one at the Red Lion teased him. She had never seen this face before. They probably had.

'How much longer do we go on playing games—Jane?' There was a slight hesitation before he said her name, as if to emphasise it.

'I've not been playing games,' she said.

'No? I thought—I let myself believe—that you'd come to love me.'

Araminta's heart swerved uncomfortably. 'Do you believe it no longer, then?' she asked.

'I don't know what to believe. I thought when we returned to the Red Lion that our...our friendship would deepen. Instead I've suspected you were holding me at arm's length, teasing me with the odd kiss, unwilling to be alone with me.'

'I've come with you now,' she pointed out, deliberately keeping her voice calm, afraid of where this was leading. 'Besides, I thought it was you who were cool—no, not cool, exactly, but perhaps unwilling to compromise me.'

He stared at her. 'Unwilling to compromise you? I don't give a damn about compromising you! It's your feelings I'm unsure of.'

Araminta laughed unsteadily. Her head was whirling. There were so many conflicting paths she needed to tread at the same time. She stretched out her hand to his sleeve in a gesture of appeal that spoke louder than words. 'My feelings are perfectly simple,' she said. 'I love you, Jack.'

He swept her to him then with all the force and vigour he had until this moment kept in check. Araminta's breath was crushed out of her body in his embrace and she welcomed it, responding with a fire and passion that she had barely suspected she possessed. Hers was no submissive body to be coaxed to an appreciation of the heights of desire and then taken gently, lest fear should overcome delight. This was a body that would fight for what it needed with lips and tongue and teeth, matching his demands with her own, seeking his exploring hands, his searching lips, striving for a closeness she did not yet know but knew she longed for.

It was Jack who broke across her newly aroused and still unfettered instincts. His whispered, 'Are you sure?' shattered the mood. It was not so much the words as the voice. It was the wrong voice, the voice of the man she loved but not the voice of the man to whom she was married. She withdrew infinitesimally from him, not physically but in spirit, and he sensed it.

'I'm sure I love you,' she said, but there was melancholy in her voice where there should have been triumph.

Jack looked down at her, his body tense as if at last something he had waited for would happen, but only if his luck held. 'What's the matter?' he asked.

Araminta turned her head away, unable to look him in the eye, and then rested her dark curls against his willing shoulder, desperate not to lose the physical closeness that meant so much to her.

'Nothing,' she said and then, since that was patently untrue, she added, 'Nothing we can do anything about.'

He kissed the curls nestling against his shoulder. 'Tell me,' he suggested.

There was nothing Araminta wanted to do more, yet she dared not. Jack Ranton appeared to be a gentleman, and he had certainly thrown convention to the winds by running contraband and, if rumour was correct, by taking to the highway. That did not mean that he would condone her own unconventional behaviour. True, her chosen career on the same lines did not seem to bother him unduly, but fleeing from a husband on one's wedding-night for no better reason than that one had no wish to be touched by him came into a category of unconventional behaviour that few, if any, men would view with equanimity.

She shook her head. 'No. It's something I have to unravel on my own.'

Now it was her turn to sense that he had drawn away from her in some indefinable way, and her heart cried out that it should not be so, but she knew she could only put things right by telling him what lay between them.

There was silence for a long time and then Jack dropped another gentle kiss in her hair. 'I've been here too long. I must move on in the next few days.'

Araminta's universe whirled, and when it stopped she knew it was upside-down. Was this the reward of silence? Was she to lose him either way? The unjustness of it made her bitter and anger was the quickly ripening fruit of bitterness.

'You knew that, yet you could suggest . . . so much?' The question was an accusation.

'Nothing happened,' he replied, a hard edge to his voice.

'No, it didn't—and if it had, when would you have told me you were leaving? Immediately? Or should I have been left in happy ignorance another day or two?'

His voice was a little softer. 'Perhaps it is still too soon. I had hoped . . . I had thought . . . It seems I was mistaken, that's all.'

'What had you hoped?' It was a question she was almost afraid to ask.

'I said I must move on. I said nothing about never returning. I had a foolish, sentimental picture—but it seems I was mistaken. Your own instinctive reaction tells me that.' It was a statement, but he left it in the air so that it became almost a question.

Araminta clung to him. She had not thought it possible to feel more miserable than she already did. Perhaps she had been wrong. Perhaps there had been in his mind the very thing she longed to hear him express, the one thing she could not grant him.

'Believing that, will you now not return?' she asked, dreading the answer.

'Would there be any point?'

'I don't know.' Never had telling the truth hurt so much. 'I just don't know.' She hesitated. 'How long will you be gone?'

'I can't be sure. Several weeks. Perhaps as much as two months.'

'But definitely more than two or three days?' Araminta persisted.

'Unquestionably. Does it make a difference?'

She deduced that he must have business in France. A combination of tides and Revenue men would be likely to increase rather than lessen delay. Who knew what might not be achieved in two months, given the incentive to expend some concentrated effort?

She moved slightly away from the protection of his arm and looked up at him shyly, uncertain how wise she was to read into either his words or his deeds those things she wanted to read there. He had not, after all, so far mentioned the word 'love', not even when she had done so herself.

'Can the realisation of this picture not wait?' she asked.

His eyes narrowed and he looked at her speculatively. 'Is there any reason why it should?'

'I suppose that depends upon its nature—and its intensity,' Araminta said, hoping his response would go some way towards enlightening her of his true intentions.

It did not. 'I suppose it does,' he said. 'Perhaps it also depends on you. Why does the possible length of my absence matter? What do you propose to do?'

'Untangle a ravelled skein, I suppose—or try to.'

'Very cryptic. Can't I help? I could always—um—hold one end?'

Araminta laughed. 'I think I shall succeed better alone.'

'As you wish,' he said, but he looked doubtful. 'And if you don't succeed? What then?'

Araminta looked stricken. 'Don't even think such a thing,' she implored him. 'If that happens, I suppose— at least I shall be obliged to tell you.'

He put a finger under her chin and raised it. 'Bear in mind that secrecy between a man and a woman is a corrosive force,' he murmured as he bent down to kiss her again, and Araminta wondered whether it was entirely her imagination that detected a hint of menace in his tone.

He was gone before nightfall and he went without a touch, a kiss, or even a backward glance. Araminta was desolated and took refuge with Grendel in her room. She was torn with the suspicion that, had she but told him everything, she might now be dancing on air. That was to assume her revelation would not have shocked him. True, he had suggested she tell him what was bothering her and had indicated his willingness to help resolve it, but that had been said in ignorance of what was involved. Araminta knew she would not be able to bear seeing the first unguarded expression of shock and the subsequent disgust before he schooled his features once again into polite impassivity and perhaps did not return from his next enforced absence. The risk was too great.

Nor would her own sense of honour permit her to say nothing, but go with him as his mistress. It was to his credit that he had not suggested she should, and probably that was just as well—he would have interpreted her refusal as an indication that she considered herself insulted. The truth was that, while she would infinitely prefer to be his wife, there was no denying that being his mistress would be the next best thing. At least it meant they would be together. Unfortunately, her married state and her own sense of what was honourable precluded that course of action, even had it been offered.

No, there was only one avenue open to her: somehow, in the next two months, she must extricate herself from this misguided marriage. Not only would she then be free to marry Jack Ranton, but there would be no necessity to tell him anything about it. Goodness knew, it had been brief enough—so brief, she doubted whether she would even recognise her husband again if she saw him. She pulled herself up. Now she was letting her imagination run away with her. The Marquess of Cosenham, once seen, could never be forgotten. All the same, there had never been anything between them except a legal contract and, she supposed, a religious vow, and she was a little ashamed of herself to realise that it would cause her no qualms at all to override both considerations. She would very definitely not be a suitable wife for a clergyman, she thought, recalling her mother's thoughts on the subject.

She knew there was no question but that the marriage could be dissolved. How easily and—more importantly—how quickly that could be achieved, she had no idea at all. Her father would know and she toyed briefly with the idea of going back to Cassington Hall to consult him. Appealing as the idea was, she rejected it out of hand. She had brought enough shame upon her family by her flight and the eventual dissolution of the marriage would rekindle their humiliation. To ask their help on the grounds that she had fallen in love with a smuggler who was said to waylay coaches for variety would be to stretch their bonds of affection beyond reason. By the same token, she dared not approach her father's lawyer in London: he must have been apprised of her disappearance and would be duty-bound the tell Lord Cassington if she contacted him.

There was only one person who would know how to get out of this mess and be in a position to arrange it, and that was Lord Cosenham himself.

He must have been as greatly humiliated as her family, though in the Marquess's case it would be his pride rather than his feelings which had been hurt. He was all the more likely, then, to want to be free of this legal encumbrance so that he could find another woman through whom to secure the succession, and would undoubtedly prefer to do so with as little noise as possible. Even so ridiculous a figure as Lord Cosenham would not wish to become a public laughing-stock.

Araminta begged paper and ink from Mrs Hoby and spent several hours drafting letters to her husband. They were all totally inadequate, ranging from the purely selfish to the pathetic and encompassing the accusatory on the way. She could send none of them. There was only one thing left she could do.

She must tackle him in person.

This prospect would have been marginally more attractive had she believed him to be the complete fool he seemed, but their brief converse in the knot-garden had led her to quite another opinion. Despite his lazy, affected drawl and the general nonchalance of his demeanour she had not judged him to be easygoing, and suspected he might well have a vindictive streak. In the circumstances, it would be churlish to deny him the right to that, she supposed. In any case, she had behaved appallingly and had no right to expect to be released for the asking. A bigger problem was to discover his whereabouts. Had she not run away, he would have been in Italy. Might he have gone there anyway, perhaps to demonstrate how little he cared? Araminta didn't know him well enough to guess, but thought not—had she suddenly reappeared he would have wanted to be in a position to demand an explanation with the minimum of delay. He had a country house, but by all accounts spent little time there. He was a man of fashion and at this time of year men of fashion were in London. What better way could there be to still gossiping tongues than to demonstrate one's disregard for them by plunging oneself into the Season as if the cause of their whispers was of little moment? There was a good chance he would be at Cosenham House, so to Cosenham House she would go.

CHAPTER NINE

Araminta's only qualm when she left the Red Lion was that the Hobys would be unable to keep Grendel in. Jem had recommended to her a tavern in Guildford with whose landlord he did business and where she would be entirely safe, and another in London itself where the landlord would also be happy to oblige an old friend by accommodating that friend's niece by marriage and her horse. If the Hobys wondered what was behind this visit, they gave no sign of it, merely commending her intention of leaving the dog behind together with anything that might identify her with Bay Peterkin, such as breeches and a cross-saddle. For safety's sake, Jem gave her a flintlock, retaining at the Red Lion the pair to the one she had dropped in that last, fateful incident.

The pistol proved unnecessary, both days' journeys being without incident. Neither tavern was the sort that either Lady Araminta Wareham or the Marchioness of Cosenham might have been expected to lodge at, but Araminta had long ago learned the value of a roof, four walls, hot food and a bed, though she did take the precaution of locking her door at the second establishment.

She located Cosenham House without difficulty. Enveloping herself in her cloak, and with her tricorne pulled down well over her eyes, she further protected herself from identification by positioning herself within a clump of trees. She surveyed the house with dismay. She had known the Fencotts were enormously rich, and her father had told her she would be mistress of a very fine Town house. Neither information prepared her for the veritable palace before her. She supposed she must have seen it during her previous visits to London, situated, as it was, in the heart of the most fashionable area, but, having had at that time no acquaintance with its owner and no particular reason for taking note of it, it had barely registered with her.

It was not only large, but ornate, calling to mind the work of Vanbrugh rather than Wren and, although Araminta had no doubt it suited the taste of Lord Cosenham very well, she guessed it had been built by a previous holder of that title. The house was set back behind ornate iron gates in a way that suggested that it might well have been surrounded by fields when it was first built. Now there was just a narrow lane on either side and then terraces of houses that were mean only by comparison with the splendour in their midst. It was not the sort of house to which a woman looking as Araminta knew she looked would be likely to gain admittance— and she most assuredly could not present herself at the door, claim to be the Marchioness, and expect to be believed!

She crossed the road and made her way down the narrow alley beside the house. A high wall surmounted by a formidable array of iron spikes surrounded a large garden and burgeoned into a stable block at the end furthest from the house. At no point in the garden wall was there anything useful to her, such as a small door, and the wall itself was far too high for her to consider climbing over, even had it not been so effectively protected. She returned to her vantage-point having discovered nothing to alleviate her dismay, and found herself being watched by a small urchin with sharp eyes and a large besom.

'New to Lunnon, are you?' he asked observantly, and Araminta admitted that she was.

'It's a very splendid house, isn't it?' she observed.

He screwed up his nose. 'I bet it ain't cosy,' he said. 'I likes to be snug. Somethin' a bit smaller'd suit me better.'

Araminta looked at Cosenham House again and conceded the point. 'Still,' she went on, 'I dare say it suits the Marquess.'

'I dare say it does,' he agreed. 'So you're not quite as green as you looks at first sight, are you?'

Araminta was startled. 'Is that how I strike you—green?'

'What's more,' the urchin went on relentlessly, 'you're a cut above what you looks. You talks more like His Lordship than me, f'r instance.'

Araminta, recalling Lord Cosenham's languid drawl, was not sure she welcomed the comparison, but let it pass. 'You've spoken to him?' she asked.

''E's been known to toss me a sixpence,' he said with some pride, 'and I always says thank you. And once he told me to go round to the stables and tell the coachman's wife to give me a square meal. Which I done, and very square it proved to be,' he added, his eyes glowing with the memory of what was probably one of the few square meals he had ever had.

Araminta frowned. It was difficult to equate that episode with what she knew of her husband, yet the boy had no reason to lie.

''Course,' the urchin went on, 'you're wasting your time, you know.'

'Am I? In what way?'

He looked her up and down. 'No one ain't goin' to let you in the front door, you'll never climb over—and the stables is too well supervised for you to slip in that way.'

Araminta flushed. 'What makes you think I want to get in?'

The urchin tapped the side of his nose and winked knowingly. 'You're flash, for one thing—the sort His Lordship probably knows—but you looks as if you've fallen on bad times. Then again, that cloak covers up a multitude of sins, I'd say. Know what I thinks? It's my belief His Lordship's got you in the family way and you wants him to do somethin' about it, that's what I thinks.'

Araminta opened her mouth to deny this gross calumny, but thought better of it and closed her mouth again. The boy's opinion of her might be unflattering and his words unpleasantly direct, but his tone was not unsympathetic. She lowered her eyes as if she felt suddenly self-conscious. 'I wouldn't have put it quite like that,' she said.

'Don't suppose you would. That don't make it wrong, though, does it? Still, you ain't the first and I don't suppose you'll be the last. What was you aiming to do— get some money out of him?'

'Something like that. I thought if I could see him face to face—in private, you understand—we could discuss things and perhaps reach a mutually acceptable solution to our difficulties.'

'If you gives him a mouthful like that, he'll 'ave indigestion,' the boy remarked dispassionately. 'Ain't you got *any* money?'

'I've a few shillings,' Araminta admitted cautiously.

The boy grinned. 'What's it worth to tell you how to get in?' he asked.

Araminta glanced across at her goal. 'If you can really do that, then I'll give you a shilling for the information and a further shilling when I've been successful.'

'Throw in another sixpence at each end,' he suggested.

'Agreed.' Araminta fished in her pocket and gave him one and six. 'Now—how do I get in?'

'Well, you won't get in now. You'll have to wait until His Lordship goes out for the evening. If he's goin' to be very late, he tells his people not to wait up for him. There's a little postern door in the front door. You can't see it from here; it's made to fit the panels. When 'e gets back, the carriage drops 'im off and in 'e goes. Now, if you was to wait till they've all gone to bed, you could be in there waiting for him. See what I mean?'

Araminta did indeed. It was brilliant by virtue of its simplicity. There was just one small snag. 'How will I know when he's going to be out late?' she asked. 'If I'm seen to be observing the place day after day, I rather fancy the constable will be called.'

'That's easy—but it'll cost you another shillin'. You got somewhere to stay?'

Araminta named the tavern.

He whistled through his teeth and looked at her with something close to respect. 'You know some funny coves, and no mistake,' he said. 'I'll tell you what—you go back there and I'll come and fetch you when I hears anything. A crossin'-sweeper gets to hear most things what's goin' on, and this time of year it's likely you'll not have long to wait.'

A shilling did not seem to be an excessive sum for being able to wait in the relative comfort and undoubted inconspicuousness of the tavern, and Araminta began to search for the coin.

The boy held his hand out in a gesture of prohibition. 'Not yet. Don't you give me nothin' more until I've delivered. That'll be soon enough. That way, if the wait's longer than I expect, you won't be thinking I've run off with it and go and do something stupid yourself.'

Araminta thanked him for his honesty and returned to wait for three interminable days before the landlord told her that a scruffy individual was demanding to see her in order to collect a shilling he claimed he was owed.

She paid her debt and was glad to have the boy's escort to Cosenham House. A persistent mizzle mingled with the smoke from the sea-coal fires that kept Londoners warm and cooked their victuals. It made Araminta cough in a way the wood-smoke she was used to never did, and the corner of her cloak that she kept across her face was not only to disguise her features. There had been rain earlier in the day and the road outside Cosenham House had had no need of the sweeper, horses and carriages having churned it into the sea of mud it became each autumn. It would stay like this until early summer, its only respite coming with the winter's freeze. She carried the loaded pistol under her cloak, but acknowledged to herself that it was the presence of the city-bred urchin that made her feel safe as cloaked figures loomed out of the miasma, bustled by with muffled footsteps and disappeared again.

When they reached their destination, only the flambeaus either side of the door indicated that the house was occupied, and their tar-stoked smoke added its mite to the fog that thickened as the mizzle imperceptibly eased.

The urchin led her to the clump of trees where they had first done business. 'The gates is to but they ain't locked. You'll be able to slip through, but just make sure you pushes them to again behind you. You never know when someone might look out of a window, and they're always left like that. The door you want is over there to the left. Like I said, you can't see it from here, not even on a clear day. I knows where it is 'cause I've seen His Lordship go in, but I don't know what sort of catch it's got—there ain't no 'andle in the usual sort of way. Still, no one won't be able to see you from the 'ouse, and in that cloak I don't reckon you'll be spotted in the shadows of the porch from the street. I'll stay 'ere until I sees you go inside. Then I'm goin' 'ome and you're on your own.'

Araminta thanked him and, pausing only to pay him the two and sixpence she owed him, ran swiftly across the muddy road, slipped through the iron gates which, she was relieved to discover, her husband kept well oiled, and up the short flight of steps to the door. The flambeaus cast an adequate light on the steps, but their guttering flames deepened the shadows cast by the beading of the doors' panels and, had she not been assured of the postern's existence, she would have given up, for the double doors themselves could clearly only be opened from the inside. Finally her fingers detected the crack, slightly wider on the hinge side of the postern, and then she was able quite easily to trace it round until it yielded under pressure. It seemed a simple enough mechanism once one knew it was there.

The door swung open and Araminta poked her head cautiously round it, more than half expecting to see a barrage of servants waiting for her. The hall seemed empty. A lighted oil-lamp stood on a side table and beside it a branched candlestick so that the Marquess need not carry the unpleasant smell of oil upstairs with him.

Having ascertained that the hall was clear, Araminta glanced back outside to see if her guide was still there. The glance told her nothing; she could barely make out the small group of trees where he would be standing. She stepped in and closed the door. The catch went home with well-oiled precision and very little sound, but that little seemed a lot and Araminta stood stock-still for several seconds, in partial expectation that someone would come to investigate.

An ornate ormolu clock told her it was a quarter past ten—late enough for the household to be asleep, but not nearly late enough for there to be any expectation of the Marquess's imminent return, and she looked about her with the interest natural in a woman surveying what might, had the circumstances been different, have been her own home. It was undoubtedly impressive but, as the urchin had said, by no stretch of the imagination could it have been called cosy. She was tempted to explore the saloons which opened off the hall, but resisted. No doubt all the doors opened with the ease of the postern, but she was wearing boots, not little satin slippers, and had no desire to find that the sound of leather on highly polished wood brought servants to find out what was going on. Instead, she curled up in the huge, hooded leather chair by the door. Its original purpose had been to provide a draught-free seat for the footman whose sole duty it was to answer the door, and in most households when the master was out it would have been occupied by that individual, dozing until he heard the carriage.

It was the perfect place from which to await Lord Cosenham's return, since it would be impossible to miss him when he came in, and Araminta amused herself by planning changes she would make to the furnishing of this vast, draughty room were she in a position to do so. There would be carpets on the marble-flagged floor and a fire—a wood fire—would burn permanently in the huge grate. She toyed with the idea of replacing the marble with a wooden floor, such as the other rooms almost certainly had, but reluctantly conceded that a hall needed something harder wearing, and then found herself wondering whether anyone as rich as the Fencotts bothered about such considerations. She kept the footman's chair—it really was most comfortable—but mentally re-covered the few chairs that stood around the walls and rather thought the hall would be improved by the addition of a large, round table in the middle.

Such thoughts as these occupied her mind with ever-diminishing importance, and two or three times she caught herself dozing off. She told herself this would never do, and on each occasion returned to her domestic plans with renewed vigour, devising different schemes and finding herself unable to choose between them.

When the Marquess of Cosenham returned home in the early hours, she was sound asleep in the footman's chair.

The shadow cast by the chair's hood and the dark cloak in which Araminta had enveloped herself served initially to hide her presence, and it was not until Lord Cosenham had lit the branch of candles and turned to check that all was well before he put out the lamp and retired that he realised the chair was occupied. He stepped cautiously over, the candelabrum held aloft and his other hand on the hilt of his small dress-sword, useless though that weapon might be in serious combat. He had little difficulty in recognising his wife, for her hat had slipped over to one side and the candle-light was more than adequate for the purpose. He moved the candles to one side so that the light no longer fell full on her face and let go the sword-hilt. Two questions bothered him. The first was why she was there at all. The second was how she had got in. A clever wife, one who wanted to coax or wheedle her husband into acquiescence with one course of action or forgiveness for another, would have made sure she was discovered in the bed-chamber, seductively attired in satins and lace, not curled up in a footman's chair, wearing mud-caked boots and a mud-bespattered cloak. He raised the candles so that the light fell directly on her sleeping eyes and they were so close that the flames warmed her skin. When she stirred, he placed them on the small table beside the chair.

Araminta opened her eyes and was momentarily bewildered. Her surroundings were unfamiliar and it took her a few seconds to place them. That done, the identity of the tall exquisite before her, languidly observing her through a quizzing-glass, presented no problems. Her stupidity in falling asleep was another matter. She had lost the advantage she had sought—the advantage of surprise. In fact, not only had she lost it, but she had handed it to the Marquess, on a plate and garnished.

She straightened herself up. 'You must be wondering why I'm here,' she began defensively.

'Not at all,' he answered politely. 'You are, after all, my wife. In what more natural place might I expect to find you?'

Araminta flushed. 'Yes, well, that's what I'm here to discuss.'

'Indeed? In the hall?' He stood aside and one graceful hand indicated the staircase. 'The bed-chamber might, perhaps, be more appropriate, don't you think?'

At the mention of the bed-chamber, Araminta involuntarily shrank back into the chair, a fact that did not go unnoticed. 'I don't think so,' she said, quickly regaining her self-possession. 'Perhaps you have a...a...study, or something?'

He inclined his head courteously. 'I do indeed have a study. I have even been known on occasion to use it for that purpose. Follow me.'

Even though this was a perfectly reasonable instruction, Araminta caught herself glancing round suspiciously as if she needed to get her bearings in anticipation of a hurried escape. She need not have worried: the study proved to be one of the rooms immediately off the hall, and, when Lord Cosenham had lit the candles in the wall sconces, she exclaimed, 'Oh, what a cosy room!'

'So glad something meets with your approval,' he drawled. 'The fire seems to have gone out. Would you like me to relight it for you?'

Araminta was oblivious to the hint of sarcasm in his voice. 'Not at all. I shan't be staying.'

'Indeed? You find me desolated.'

The word was so far removed from any that might have sprung to Araminta's lips to describe the Marquess that she chuckled. 'No, you're not. I've been a great inconvenience to you. I should think you'll heave a sigh of relief when I leave.'

'"Inconvenience" is a nicely understated word to use in the circumstances, though not inaccurate. I am relieved to find you are alive and, apparently, safe and well—and so will your family be, or have you forgotten them? I imagine I am more likely to feel angry if you leave without fully explaining yourself.'

Araminta coloured. 'I've not forgotten my family and I shall be very much obliged if you would assure them that all is well with me. However, you're my husband and my first duty is to you.'

'A somewhat belated realisation,' he suggested drily. 'May I suggest you sit down? I have the uncomfortable feeling this interview is likely to be prolonged and quite possibly unpleasant.' He poured brandy from a decanter and handed her a glass. 'That will warm you. When the servants are up, they can get you something to eat.'

Araminta accepted it gratefully and settled herself in one of wing-chairs by the still-warm embers of the dead fire. 'I shan't be here that long,' she said firmly. 'My lord, there's no point in beating about the bush. Our marriage was a mistake, but fortunately it was never consummated so it can be set aside. I've no idea how one goes about arranging that, but I'm sure you do and I'd be grateful if it could all be settled as soon as possible.'

Lord Cosenham was standing by the hearth, and at these words he raised his quizzing-glass and studied his visitor in a lengthy silence, an experience Araminta found distinctly disconcerting.

'Would it surprise you to learn that my experience of "setting aside" a lawful marriage is as limited as your

own? It isn't something of which I've ever made a habit,'
he said at last.

'I didn't think you had,' Araminta replied sharply.
'But I'd be very surprised if you hadn't taken steps to
find out what you could about it when you discovered
I'd disappeared.'

'You credit me with more perspicacity than most,' he
murmured.

'I've never taken you for a fool,' she replied.

'Dear me, was I so transparent? Very well. You are,
of course, correct. Just how soon had you in mind?'

Araminta softened. He was being less difficult than
she had anticipated. 'Can we say a month? Six weeks at
the most?'

He laughed softly. 'My dear, it takes months—years,
even—and such annulments attract an unacceptable
amount of scandal and gossip, to say nothing of the en-
suing stigma. I don't think you would enjoy it at all.'

'Enjoyment was not a consideration,' Araminta told
him. 'Are you sure about the length of time?'

'Quite sure. There is another small problem as well...'

'Yes?' Araminta felt her suspicions returning. He was
too bland, too objective.

'When you left, your family and I agreed to put it
about that we had gone to Italy as we planned, but instead I went to Copenore and lived in tedious seclusion
in the hope that word would eventually come to me of
your whereabouts. I couldn't remain in purdah indefi-
nitely, of course—sooner or later even the best-trained
servant lets something slip—so I returned to Town. The
reason my wife does not accompany me is that she is
seriously indisposed. I understand the general belief is
that you are increasing and are having a particularly difficult time. We can hardly claim the marriage was
unconsummated.'

'But it was!' Araminta exclaimed.

'As you and I both know. Convincing others might be more difficult.'

'Not when nine months had passed with no birth,' Araminta pointed out.

'Your ambition was six weeks at the most. And then, of course, there would be the question of blame. I am not an energetic man: you may have noticed that I rarely exert myself. Put yourself in my shoes, my dear. Just imagine the sheer effort I should be obliged to expend in demonstrating to Society that the blame wasn't mine.'

'I'm perfectly happy to accept all the blame,' Araminta assured him.

He shook his head. 'No one would believe you. They would look at you and then they'd look at me and snigger.' He sighed. 'Oh, the shame of it!'

'If that were their reaction,' Araminta told him, suspecting that it all too probably would be, 'then you've only yourself to blame.'

He became very still, and when he spoke that strange, strained, rather high-pitched voice with its pronounced sibilants had become very soft and very menacing. 'Perhaps I may be permitted to know why an annulment is so important to you—and why there is such urgency?'

Araminta swallowed hard. She should not have allowed herself the luxury of saying what she thought. She had no wish to tell him about Jack, and when she had set out on this expedition she had determined not to mention him. Nevertheless, the Marquess's questions were perfectly reasonable. She owed him some sort of explanation, though the less detail he was given, the better.

She hesitated, unwilling to lie but knowing the truth was unlikely to be palatable. 'I've no wish to...to hurt your feelings, my lord. Or your pride,' she added, suspecting that that might be closer to the mark. 'It's simply that…well, I should like to be free to…to marry someone else.'

'May I enquire whether you have a candidate in mind, or is this just a general convenience you would like to have to hand should the need arise?' His voice was the epitome of polite but uninvolved interest.

'I am in love with someone else.'

'I don't recall its being mentioned when our respective fathers were discussing our marriage.'

'I hadn't met him then.'

'From which I deduce that this is an acquaintance made since our marriage?'

Araminta nodded, shamefaced. Put like that, it somehow seemed far more reprehensible than she had thought, and she began to have some inkling of just how seriously the rest of the world would view it.

'Forgive my bluntness, my dear, but in view of the urgency and the circumstances I don't think it is unreasonable of me to ask whether by chance you're increasing by this man?'

'No!' It had never crossed Araminta's mind that he might come to that conclusion.

'You relieve my mind, but I'm no wiser as to the need for speed. Won't he wait? Has he given you some sort of ultimatum?'

'He doesn't know I'm married,' she said, her voice a mixture of misery and defiance.

'So you are not sure enough of his love for you that you dare tell him the truth?' Lord Cosenham persisted.

She shook her head. 'It's not like that at all. I shall tell him, of course, but I think it would be better if I were no longer married when I did so.'

'That might depend very much on the nature of the man. Happily, it is purely academic. There will be no annulment. I have little faith in the power of love. I suspect its potency soon wears thin. I have a better suggestion. You return to me and give me, as soon as may be, an heir—and preferably a second son by way of insurance—and then you may do exactly as you wish, short of divorce, which I will not contemplate. You may even set up house with your lover with my blessing— and my financial support, which is probably more to the point—provided you do so well away from Society's eyes and ears. Cornwall, perhaps, or Cumberland. I demand only that any children you bear before you leave my roof are mine.'

Araminta stared at him. 'But that could be years!' she objected. 'I could have several daughters before I bore a son. I might take after my mother and have only daughters. I could be quite old before I had my freedom.'

'Very true. Are you afraid your lover won't wait?'

'I don't think it would be reasonable to expect him to,' she retorted.

'I agree, but I thought we were talking about love, not reason.'

Araminta was confused. Somehow he had succeeded in twisting her own words around and using them to trip her up, and she had the feeling that, if only she could see how he had done it, she might somehow retrieve her position.

The Marquess watched her for several minutes, shrewdly guessing what was going through her mind. When he judged her to have had long enough to realise there were no obvious loopholes in his argument, he decided it was time to press the matter home.

'You arrive at a most opportune moment,' he went on, substituting affability for menace. He rifled through the papers on his desk and held up a card of invitation. He handed it to her. 'As you see, the Earl of Pembroke invites us to Wilton. I understand some of the Royal Dukes will be fellow guests. Your presence would indicate that the worst of your indisposition is over, and

I really do think that, if you are so very determined to attain a degree of freedom, the sooner we set to work, the better, don't you?'

Araminta studied the invitation which was, she knew, a most flattering one, despite Lord Cosenham's more exalted title. 'If I decline, will you still go?'

He raised one faintly surprised eyebrow. 'My dear, I've already accepted on behalf of both of us. Had you not reappeared, I should have made your apologies based on your continued indisposition. If you decline, nothing will have changed.'

Araminta looked up at him, appeal in her eyes. 'No, my lord, I shall not come with you. Nor shall I return to your roof. To do as you suggest would be to live a lie. I've met someone I love and I am truly sorry I didn't meet him until after we were married, but if I am to bear children I want them to be his. Can you not set me free so that they can at least be legitimate?'

'I can't keep you with me against your will, but if you go to this man you go as my wife, and my wife you will remain. You will be an adultress. I wonder if you will tell your lover the truth?'

'I suppose I must, and give him the choice.'

'That will take courage. I hope for your sake it doesn't prove misplaced.'

'So do I.' Araminta got to her feet and put the empty glass on the mantelshelf. 'Goodbye, my lord. I doubt if we shall meet again.'

'One never can tell, I find. Tell me, Araminta—why did you run away in the first place?'

Her startled eyes flew to his face but saw nothing there save glittering eyes in a white maquillage, a beauty spot on one cheek and artificially red lips. The height of fashion, but it contrasted oddly with the image she carried of Jack Ranton's face—a face which fitted roughly into the same shape but was lean and unfashionably tanned—and the way he contented himself with tying his unpowdered hair back in a simple bow, a far cry from the ornate, powdered tower above Lord Cosenham's features. She knew then that she had made the right decision.

'The truth, my lord?'

'What else?'

'I couldn't face the marriage-bed.'

'With me?' He seemed to demand the clarification.

'Precisely.'

He made no further comment and his face betrayed no emotion. He opened the study door and escorted her across the hall to the postern. Outside, dawn was fighting its way through the fog.

'Will you be safe?' he asked. 'I can send a man with you.'

'No need. I know my way.'

Araminta ran down the steps and slipped through the gates and across the road, knowing that the fog would soon conceal her completely, rendering it useless for him to dispatch someone after her even if he had a mind to.

Justinian Fencott watched her go. Dawn was less dangerous than dusk and she seemed to have a genius for survival. Now he must calculate what she was likely to do next. He closed the door and cursed. He still had no idea how she had got in.

Even the best sense of direction could be disorientated by fog, but Araminta had learnt the route here rote-fashion and found her way back to the tavern by the simple expedient of applying it in reverse. She was soon back at the tavern, where she devoured a breakfast which would have defeated a huntsman. Then she went to bed. Somewhat to her surprise, she slept soundly. She had expected to toss and turn, going over and over the night's converse, but the truth was that, quite apart from her sheer exhaustion, she had made a decision from which there was no going back. The rest of her life had been settled for good or ill this night, and her body's response was the unconsciousness of pure relief.

She had decided to return to Rake in the morning since she was unable to delude herself that a further interview with her husband would be any more productive than the first. To that end she had the landlord's wife wake her up in the course of the afternoon. She had no desire to sleep herself out during the day and then find herself tossing and turning all night with a long day's ride before her.

There were two unpalatable facts to be faced. Justinian Fencott was not prepared to release her from this mockery of a marriage, and she had no idea how Jack Ranton would react when she told him the truth. Had their situations been reversed, she would have been unhappy, but it would have made no difference to her feelings or to her willingness to continue the association, but there was no guarantee Jack would feel the same way. Men all too often had a disconcerting way of seeing things very differently from women. Jack's scruples did not appear to affect his willingness to disregard the law by running contraband, and her own unlawful activities certainly didn't bother him unduly. All the same, there was sometimes a reserve in his manner which suggested that laissez-faire was not necessarily the essence of his philosophy. She tried to imagine what her life would be if he recoiled in disgust when she told him her story, and the most frightening thing about that particular speculation was that she could all too clearly imagine him doing so.

The more she thought about it, the more sure she became that her only chance of happiness lay in at least being able to assure him that she was no longer married, assurance that Lord Cosenham had removed from her grasp.

Or had he?

She wiped her trencher clean with a hunk of bread and sought out the landlord.

'Which road would you take from here to Salisbury?' she asked.

'On horseback or by carriage?'

'By carriage—and with outriders and a baggage-wagon.'

He pursed up his mouth. 'I'd head for Winchester, lay over there and make Salisbury in one day after an early start. It's a shade longer than the direct route, but a bit safer if you haven't got speed on your side. Mind you, with outriders safety might not matter.'

Araminta thanked him. His suggestion made sense. The road from Winchester would avoid the dangerous wilderness that was Salisbury Plain. Most travellers would need to be in a very great hurry indeed to tackle that.

Two days later she was back at the Red Lion, being greeted by an enthusiastic and half-starved Grendel.

'We did try feeding him,' Mrs Hoby assured her, 'but he refused to touch a morsel. Still, at least we succeeded in keeping him in, though we haven't been so good at keeping him quiet. It'll be real peaceful with you back again.'

The voracity with which the lugubrious-faced hound broke his fast testified to the fact that there was nothing wrong with him that his mistress's return wouldn't put right, and any anxiety Araminta had felt when she first saw him was soon allayed.

'Has there been any sign of Jack Ranton while I've been away?' she asked.

The Hobys were surprised. 'Why should there be?' Jem asked. 'He's only just gone and we sometimes don't see him for weeks, even months, on end. He wasn't reckoning to be back soon this time, anyway.'

'No, he wasn't. I just wondered if perhaps he'd changed his mind.'

'He might have changed his mind but he can't change the tides or the weather, and they say it's been rough between here and France. You'd do better to give your mind to other things.'

Which was, Araminta thought, exactly what she proposed doing.

The idea had come to her in the tavern in London. She was determined to be free to marry Jack Ranton, but her husband was equally determined not to release her from their contract. Very well. There were, as the proverb said, more ways than one of skinning a cat. If he wouldn't release her by legal means, she'd obtain her freedom illegally. Bay Peterkin would waylay His Lordship and, in the process of an apparently normal highway robbery, her pistol would accidentally discharge itself and she would flee, a widow.

There were certain snags attached to this course of action, not the least the fact that Araminta had never killed anyone in her life and had no particular desire to start; even smaller was her desire to hang which, if she were caught, would be the inevitable consequence. The chances of her being caught were quite high; she recalled the entourage with which he had felt it necessary to surround himself when he had visited Cassington Hall for a few days although, to be sure, he had been on his way to a longer stay with friends in Oxford. Still, it was unlikely he would travel in any less style to a place such as Wilton. She might very well be killed herself, or caught, and it would be wise to plan for that possibility rather than to assume her husband would be travelling as light as he had been when she had waylaid him without realising who he was. Either way, it would be Bay

Peterkin's last sortie and she must do everything in her power to ensure that that decision was carried through voluntarily and not forced upon her by events.

She knew nothing of the road from Winchester to Salisbury, but she had a more than passing familiarity with that stretch north of the ancient capital that had been the scene of her last, and far from successful, enterprise.

The Hobys had to be told that Bay Peterkin would be riding once more and they were far from happy at the news.

Jem shook his head. 'Jack won't like it,' he said. 'He wants an eye kept on you so's you comes to no harm, and anyway, why bother? You've enough to live on for the time being, and if you hadn't I don't doubt he'd settle your tab when he comes back.'

'I've no desire to be beholden to Jack Ranton,' Araminta informed him with a fine show of indignance. 'I know this one. I know how he travels—and I also know that if I'm successful I'll be set up for life.' All of which, she reflected, was absolutely true, though not perhaps in quite the way Jem Hoby would assume.

But Jem could not view her forthcoming escapade in anything other than a pessimistic light, and, when he saw her slip quietly out on Halcyon with Grendel at her side, he had the unhappy feeling that she would not be back.

CHAPTER TEN

ARAMINTA knew when she reached her hiding-place that she might well have as much as a full twenty-four hours to wait. She had calculated how long it would take the Marquess to reach Wilton and guessed that, if the Royal Dukes were to be among the other guests, he would be unlikely to time his arrival to be more than a day outside the date specified.

The wait would not be pleasant. The air was damp and bitterly cold and both elements seemed to seep through her cloak and her coat and on into the very marrow of her bones. Her feet in their cold leather boots became heavy and numb, making it difficult to gauge the strength of any leg-aids she gave Halcyon, one consequence of which being that on a couple of occasions he leapt forward suddenly instead of simply moving off. Her fingers, too, became colder and colder despite the gauntlets she wore, and this was more worrying: manipulating the reins, to say nothing of cocking and firing a pistol, needed accuracy, and benumbed fingers were no tools for precision. She tucked her gloved hands as far into her coat-sleeves as the reins permitted and felt them gradually return to a sort of half-life with which she supposed she would have to make do. At least the muffler was useful: its purpose was to disguise her features, but it effectively kept her nose, ears and chin snug and warm.

As dusk descended, she began to wonder whether there was much point in keeping a nocturnal vigil. She longed to be free to curl up inside her damp cloak and try to sleep but this scheme was too important. She saw it as her only opportunity to get rid of her husband and thereby be free legitimately to love Jack Ranton. Lord Cosenham was unpredictable. Dared she risk his driving past while she slept? True, few people travelled by night if it could be avoided, but the Marquess could afford armed guards on and around his carriage. Perhaps in those circumstances the dark was less of a deterrent.

She was still undecided when she heard the thud of approaching hooves, the rattle of wheels and the faint metallic jingle of harness. She sat up straight and strained her ears through the trees. Yes, whoever it was was travelling southwards. Araminta gathered up her reins, took the flintlock from its holster and cocked it. Then, her numbed feet urging Halcyon on, she edged forward until she was in a position from which she should be able to identify her quarry. There were outriders which, if this should be Lord Cosenham's carriage, was a nuisance but not unexpected. Two horses under the control of a postilion followed and behind them the un- mistakable shape of a post-chaise. A very large crest decorated the door. This was precisely the sort of equipage in which the Marquess had been travelling when he had visited Cassington Hall. She had very little time in which to identify it before riding forth, especially since she must come from the side to be sure of her mark, and Araminta was not one to waver over important de- cisions. She clapped her heels to Halcyon's sides, raised the pistol and galloped forward through the trees.

Her aim was unerring. The ball smashed through the window above the crest and, as it did so, Araminta saw to her horror that the crest was not Cosenham's and the passenger whose terrified face appeared at the window was an elderly lady. The woman's vigorous scream was evidence that Araminta might have hit the carriage, but she had mercifully missed its occupant. She tugged at

Halcyon's rein to pull him out of his headlong charge, and by so doing felt the whistle of air as the ball from one of the outriders' pistols skimmed past her head.

Halcyon heard it too, and shied. This unexpected action coming, as it did, when the horse was still in mid-swerve, unseated his rider and, finding himself unburdened, Halcyon fled into the trees, followed by a startled Grendel, for whom the noise and confusion was too much. The postilion had brought his pair to a halt by this time and one of the outriders remained on his mount, his pistol trained on their assailant, while the other one dismounted to inspect their catch. Having satisfied himself that there were no arms concealed about the robber, he called out to his colleague, 'I reckon we've done Hampshire a service, Ned. Unless I very much mistake, this here's Bay Peterkin.'

'Aye, likely he is,' the other replied. 'The horse and the hound disappeared in the trees. Any good going after them, d'you reckon?'

The first one shook his head. 'Not in this light. We'd best get him to Winchester and hand him over to the magistrate. How's Her Ladyship standing up to it?'

Her Ladyship, her recovery from the fright she had received considerably speeded by the observation that its source had been captured, declared herself to be standing up to it very well, but demanded to know how they proposed to get their prisoner to Winchester when his horse had vanished.

The dismounted guard had the solution to that. 'If you don't mind me riding with you in the chaise, my lady, we can truss him up and put him on my horse and Ned can lead him in. It's not what you're used to, of course, nor me neither, but I dare say you'll not object to having a guard a bit closer for once.'

His employer expressed herself emphatically in agreement, and so this plan was put into operation and

Araminta, her hands tied behind her, was manhandled into the saddle and her feet tied into the stirrups. Ned took both reins, and the sensation of riding a horse over which one could exert no control whatsoever was not one Araminta had any desire to repeat. The post-chaise took the lead, the two riders followed on, and in this manner they finally clattered into Winchester where Ned handed her over to the gaoler and went in search of a magistrate.

Three quarters of an hour later, another post-chaise, but this time an unescorted one, slowed down to tackle the slight but steady incline. An observer would have noticed that the passenger kept a particularly close watch on the deepening gloom beyond the carriage and, as it approached the bend at the top of the road, he put his head out of the window and called to the postilion to stop.

'What, here, my lord? Is it wise?'

'What's that over there, in those trees?' Lord Cosenham's voice had suddenly lost the high-pitched, sibilant drawl he affected and the postilion grinned to himself. He'd always suspected it was put on. Now he knew.

'I don't know, my lord, and if it's all the same to you I'd as lief not find out. It's my belief we didn't ought to have set out without guards, and movements in the trees is just the sort of thing I had in mind.'

'Don't be impertinent, man—and don't be a fool. Whatever it is, it's not human. Mind the horses.'

With these words, Lord Cosenham opened the door and jumped down. The postilion took some comfort in the fact that he kept one hand on the hilt of a very businesslike sword, but decided he would have been happier had His Lordship had a pistol instead. He also considered it the height of folly on His Lordship's part to leave the chaise at all, and plain stupidity to go walking in the woods, sword or no sword.

Whatever it was that His Lordship had seen, it didn't seem at all alarmed and, even though it was very large, the manner in which it leapt around could not be interpreted even by such a Jeremiah as the postilion as being anything but friendly. He was therefore not particularly surprised when Lord Cosenham returned to the chaise accompanied by a large, lumbering hound.

'That's an ugly brute,' he remarked, and then, realising it carried one hind leg oddly, 'What's wrong with its near hind?'

'It's lost two toes but the wound's an old one. It's fully healed. Strain your eyes. See if you can make out a horse. Not a large one. Bay, probably with four white legs and a blaze, though not necessarily.'

But the postilion was still thinking about the dog. 'I know that brute,' he said. 'I've seen him before—and so have you, my lord. It's the one the highwayman had that time we was stopped on the road to Portsmouth. Bay Peterkin, they call him.' His voice became anxious. 'Get in, my lord, and I'll whip them up. This is no place to be stopped.'

'Nonsense. The dog's here on his own and it's my guess the horse isn't far. What can you see from up there?'

Resigning himself to his inevitable fate, the postilion sighed meaningfully and did as he was told. The sooner His Lordship couldn't find the horse, the sooner they could get on to Winchester. The postilion's fear was that they might indeed find the horse—with Bay Peterkin astride him.

'There is something,' the Marquess said. 'Over there— to the right. Can you make it out?'

Grudgingly, the postilion was obliged to admit that just possibly there was something. 'A deer, I reckon,' he volunteered.

'A deer? After all the noise we've been making? I hardly think so. I take it you'd prefer me to investigate?'

The postilion was delighted to accept Lord Cosenham's offer, but he was beginning to revise his opinion of his master. He had been in the Marquess's employ for some three years and had formed the opinion that there was little to like and nothing much to respect in his master except for some of his odd quirks, like not expecting the indoor servants to wait up for him, and going off for weeks on end and leaving everyone to their own devices. It was beginning to look as if His Lordship might have more courage than you'd expect, though that courage might well turn out to be nothing but foolhardiness.

The Marquess made his way into the trees and the postilion had no difficulty following his progress, his master having elected to travel in a coat of dove-grey with silver-thread embroidery, and with a matching cloak for warmth lined with cloth-of-silver. It was unnervingly like watching a ghost among the trees, and the postilion profoundly hoped that was exactly how it would strike Bay Peterkin.

When Lord Cosenham returned with the horse, there was no sign of a rider and one of the reins had snapped.

Lord Cosenham slid the stirrup-irons up their leathers and secured them so that their flapping did not alarm the horse, then he fastened the remaining rein to the back of the carriage. He turned to the dog. 'In,' he commanded, and the dog, after a brief, uncertain hesitation, jumped into the carriage.

The Marquess turned his attention to the postilion and, when he spoke, the languid drawl was once more in evidence.

'We would appear to have accomplished all we're likely to do here, don't you think? I suggest we make such

speed as we may to Winchester, if the effort won't inconvenience you.'

'And what do I do, my lord, when they sees that dog
and that horse and decides you must be Bay Peterkin
and takes you into custody?'

'In that event you will naturally inform my father, but
I don't imagine anyone will have the temerity of making
that mistake, do you?'

Not if you uses that tone of voice, the postilion
thought, but wisely kept his opinion to himself. In fact,
come to think of it, Lord Cosenham was just about the
last person on God's earth that any right-minded individual would confuse with a bridle-cull.

Dark had fallen long before they clattered into
Winchester and drew up before the Saracen's Head. The
Marquess of Cosenham was a regular and valued guest
at this hostelry, and a porter was quick to open the chaise
and take down the step so that His Lordship might alight
with the unhurried languor that characterised everything he did. Lord Cosenham was not a man one warmed
to, but there was no denying he rewarded good service
very generously. The porter was far more taken aback
by the hound that followed His Lordship out of the
chaise than by the cloth-of-silver lining of his master's
cloak. The Marquess wasn't noted for his restrained
dress, but the porter would have thought one of those
little lap-spaniels or a curly-coated Teneriffe would have
been a more natural accompaniment to his usual flam-
boyance. The chaise rattled into the stable-yard and Lord
Cosenham raised one enquiring eyebrow at the landlord.

'Your usual room is waiting, my lord, and a private
parlour has been set aside. You'll find your man is
waiting. I trust everything will meet with your approval.'

Lord Cosenham permitted the merest hint of a smile
to crack the maquillage. 'Rest assured you will be informed immediately should it not do so,' he said.

The landlord smiled with an affability he did not feel. Lord Cosenham looked a popinjay and sounded—well, never mind—but his voice, for all its affectation, sometimes had a nasty cutting edge to it, and if the landlord heard of His Lordship's sudden demise his only regret would be on account of the loss to the Saracen's Head's coffers.

The Marquess's manservant had accompanied his master on the Grand Tour and had few illusions about him. He disapproved of almost everything Lord Cosenham did and had been known to refuse point-blank to assist in some of his enterprises. He never let his dislike of His Lordship's sometimes acid tongue prevent him speaking his mind, but, because he was a man of total discretion and absolute loyalty, he was permitted to express his opinions with a freedom others would not have dreamed possible. He also had an uncanny ability for picking up pieces of information for which he felt his master might have some use.

He eyed the dog with distaste. 'An ugly brute, my lord, if I may say so.'

'It's young Harry's opinion that he'll get me hanged.'

'A bright boy, that. I've often thought so.'

'You don't think I could talk my way out of the noose?'

The valet considered. 'No, my lord. Probably not. You'd have more success with a mixture of veiled threats and bribery. You do that quite well.'

'Let us hope we never have the opportunity of discovering which of us is right.'

'Quite, my lord. You have presumably observed that the beast has only two toes on one foot?'

'The beast, Cerney, is called Grendel, and, yes, I have noticed.'

'A most appropriate name, my lord. I imagine your credit will survive being seen with a poacher's dog.'

'I imagine it will,' Lord Cosenham said affably.

'Or a highwayman's.'

'Ah. You've heard about that.'

'My lord,' Cerney said reproachfully, 'very little concerning Your Lordship's activities passes me by.'

'How remiss of me; I should have recollected that.'

'Doubtless Your Lordship had other matters on his mind. Has Your Lordship heard the great excitement that has overtaken Winchester?'

'I confess that I noticed very little excitement when we arrived.'

'Your Lordship's mind was probably elsewhere.'

'Undoubtedly, but I should have thought a city overwhelmed by excitement might have been difficult to overlook. I take it you feel the cause of this excitement might be of some interest to me?'

'It seems the notorious highwayman, Bay Peterkin, has been taken.'

No change of expression crossed the Marquess's painted face and there was only a brief pause before he spoke to indicate to the observant that the information might be anything more than casual gossip.

'A careless young man,' he remarked.

'So it would seem, my lord. It appears he made the mistake of holding up a carriage with armed outriders—a post-chaise, to be precise.'

'A mistake of some magnitude.'

'Indeed, my lord. It almost makes one wonder whether he mistook the chaise for another.'

'You may well be right, Cerney, though that would hardly be a mitigating argument in court.'

'You think it will come to that, my lord?'

Lord Cosenham flicked a lace-edged handkerchief before holding it elegantly just in front of his nose and inhaling its scent. 'A night in gaol will do him no harm at all,' he said.

Cerney inclined his head in silent agreement, a subservient gesture from which he managed to expunge any hint of subservience. 'Your Lordship will perhaps be interested to learn that the gentleman in question apparently rode straight at the chaise and fired directly at its only occupant.'

'Did he, by God? To what effect?'

'I gather he missed, my lord.'

Lord Cosenham stood up. 'Life becomes disagreeably complicated, Cerney.'

Cerney opened the door. 'Quite, my lord.'

Araminta was also of the opinion that life was becoming disagreeably complicated. Her plan had failed utterly, and no one had the slightest idea where she was or what she had set out to do and, although Halcyon and possibly Grendel as well would probably find their way back to the Red Lion eventually, the Hobys would have no idea where to start looking for her even had they been of a mind to do so, which was doubtful. Far worse, they would be unable to tell Jack Ranton where to start when he returned and found her missing. Araminta had no doubt that he would want to search for her, but he was known to be absent for weeks, even months, at a time and by the time he returned from running the contraband cargo that presumably accounted for his present absence she might well have been hanged.

It was a dispiriting thought and not improved by the reflection that news of the hanging of Bay Peterkin—or even of Jane Shore—should at least let him know what had happened. She was even more worried at the prospect of being identified as Lady Araminta Wareham, to say nothing of the Marchioness of Cosenham. That would attract a scandal which would devastate her parents and be unnecessarily cruel to a husband who, when all was said and done, had committed no offence against her save that of being eminently unlikeable. In fact, now that she came to consider the matter, he had behaved with quite remarkable forbearance and was in no way deserving of the ignominy that would be his lot if her true identity was discovered. It did not strike her as at all odd that she felt this way about a man she had set out a few hours ago to kill.

Furthermore, if her true identity became known, there was a possibility Jack Ranton would never learn what had happened unless he picked up the connection with Bay Peterkin, and the likelihood of that would depend on how long before he returned she had been dead and another story had taken her place.

She had not the slightest idea how long a process the trial of a highwayman might be, nor of the domestic arrangements in a gaol and the consequent probability of her true sex being discovered. Ideally—if such a word could be applied to such an unideal situation—she would like to remain Bay Peterkin, to be tried and, if necessary, hanged with that identity. If, however, she was discovered, it must be as Jane Shore. That way she could at least protect her family, and it really shouldn't be too difficult, provided only that no one recognised her in court.

These thoughts and many less constructive ones went round and round in her head during the ride to Winchester and she rigorously suppressed the most appealing which was that, by some miracle, Jack Ranton would come riding in at full gallop, seize her—she was undecided whether this should be from the gaol or from the very steps of the scaffold—and ride off with her.

The armed guards saw their employer safely delivered to the Black Swan and then took their other charge to the gaol in the Westgate. Being strangers to the city, this was the only gaol they knew of because, standing as it did astride the road out of the city to the west, it was almost impossible not to be aware of it. The porter, however, refused point-blank to take Bay Peterkin in.

'This ain't no place for a hanging offence,' he said adamantly. 'Debtors is what's here mostly, and few minor offences—we've a baker who gives short weight, for instance, but we don't have no murderers nor no bridle-culls. You needs the Bridewell and, if I was you, I'd get hold of the watch: they'll take this young blade in all the quicker if the watch brings him.'

'And where do we find the watch?' demanded one of the guards. 'We've seen nor hide nor hair of any watch so far.'

'Ah, well, now, that depends,' the porter said, tapping the side of his nose with his forefinger. 'I dare say I could put you on the right track—or you could just ride around until you comes across him.'

Rightly construing this as meaning that the porter's co-operation depended largely upon his bribe, the guard cursed and fished a silver shilling from his pocket, taking some comfort from the fact that his employer would undoubtedly reimburse him.

The porter studied this coin carefully from all angles, then bit it once or twice, and finally directed them over towards the castle where, round a brazier in the lee of the walls, they found three watchmen clustered. None of these gentlemen was particularly anxious to tear himself away from the warmth and do any part of the job for which he was paid, but finally one of them, after a threat to have them reported to the Aldermen, consented to lead the way and to hand Bay Peterkin into the Bridewell. It seemed to Araminta that learning the identity of the miscreant had at least as much influence on the man as the threat of losing his job. She wondered how long it would be before he figured in front of his acquaintance as the man who brought Bay Peterkin in—

and reaped the benefit in free ale from his admiring cronies.

Not only had Araminta never been in gaol before, she had never given the slightest thought to what one might be like. She naturally did not expect it to be a pleasant place, but she was totally unprepared for the filth, the stench and the squalor.

Since she had yet to appear before a magistrate, much less a judge, she was thrown—or, more accurately, pushed—into a stone-walled room none too large for the numbers it contained, both men and women alike. With the Quarter Sessions only a fortnight away, every felon and malefactor who had been taken since the last Session was here. They ranged from a seven-year-old boy who had stolen a handkerchief to a man who had murdered his entire family and showed an unpleasant readiness to extend his activities beyond the confines of his home.

The initial hostility of the inmates to the new addition to their numbers changed to a grudging admiration when Araminta identified herself as Bay Peterkin, the family murderer volunteering to join forces with her if she would only persuade the friends who, he was convinced would be buying her out to buy his release as well.

She soon learnt that, while there was a pail of stagnant water for drinking, there was no food unless the prisoners had either the money to pay for it or friends to bring it in daily. She was aghast.

'But surely the gaolers are paid to provide food, even if it's only bread?'

'Oh, they're paid, all right,' one man said bitterly. 'But it goes straight into the governor's pocket. As for the actual gaolers, they supplement their earnings by cheating those of us that have to buy food and their larders by keeping back some of the food that gets sent in.'

A woman nodded. 'It's not a bad life, being a gaoler.'

'But I have neither money nor friends who know where I am,' Araminta protested. 'How do I eat?'

'You've got clothes, haven't you? And what's that on your finger?' The man pointed to her mourning-ring. 'Sell them one by one, and it should keep you going till you're in court. Of course, they'll cheat you—you won't get a quarter of the value of that ring, so don't get too hopeful.'

Araminta was dismayed. The ring meant a great deal to her and she had no wish at all to part with it, although common sense suggested that she would have no need of it once she was hanged, so it probably made little difference if she parted with it first, in order to eat—an activity which she supposed was logically equally pointless in the circumstances. Selling some of her clothes brought other problems. For one thing, it was very cold. There was a fire in the hearth and the prisoners cooked their food over it, but its warmth went mostly up the wide chimney and Araminta suspected she would be glad of her heavy cloak and the man's thick coat she wore underneath. Furthermore, once she started getting rid of her clothes, she increased the chances of Bay Peterkin's secret being discovered. She could then admit to being Jane Shore, but she did not relish the prospect of the increased and quite possibly salacious interest the discovery would arouse in some of her present companions.

She spent a hungry and uncomfortable night, and had finally convinced herself that the ring would have to be sacrificed when the turnkey opened the door and beckoned her over.

'Seems like Bay Peterkin's a man of some importance,' he said sarcastically. 'At any rate, you're to have a room to yourself. Once your name gets into the broadsheets, the governor'll make a small fortune selling a view of you. Come on.'

He led her a short way to a small room which was luxuriously appointed when compared with the previous one. There was a fireplace and a fire. There was a roughly hewn table and a stool and, in one corner, a bench some two feet wide and nearly two yards long, covered with deep straw and obviously intended to be a bed. Straw covered the floor. There was a jug of ale on the table, and beside it a wooden trencher with a large hunk of bread and a small wedge of cheese. Araminta turned and looked at the turnkey.

'Why?' she asked.

He shrugged. 'Like I said. Governor's orders. See that window up there?' He pointed to a small glazed aperture with a substantial grille across it on the inside.

Araminta nodded.

'He'll sell a view through that. You'd be surprised how many people'll pay a few pence to look at a blackguard like you. Them as can pay in guineas'll get to come in and meet you.'

'And what if I don't want to see these people?'

He shrugged again. 'You starves—and you goes back downstairs first. Up here the governor'll make sure you're fed and kept halfway decently; people won't come if they reckons they'll go away with gaol-fever. No, you take my advice, lad: you go along with it.'

He locked her in then, and Araminta sat down at the table and tore a piece from the bread and ate it thoughtfully. Much as she disliked the notion of becoming some sort of sideshow, she had to concede that the prospect had some merits. For one thing, she would eat without being obliged to part with her ring or risk revealing her sex. She would be warm, dry and relatively comfortable. There was no danger of being murdered in her bed, and she would have plenty of time to think, though she was not at the moment able to imagine just what she might be expected to achieve.

She found herself longing for Jack Ranton, an ache inside her that was a very real physical pain. Common sense told her that a gaol was the very last place he was likely to enter of his own volition, yet she told herself that he would surely take the risk if only he knew she was here. What such a visit could achieve was debatable, but at least she would be able to feel his arms around her once more and, who knew? Maybe he could devise a way of obtaining her freedom.

The turnkey had mentioned the broadsheets printing the story of her capture, and no doubt the tale would be recounted with relish and very little regard for accuracy. The thought of figuring in such a publication made her cringe inside but there was one great advantage: it increased the likelihood of Jack Ranton's learning where she was. She must move heaven and earth to ensure that her true identity did not leak out. Neither her parents nor her husband would think twice about the capture of a highwayman except, perhaps, to be glad that another risk to travellers was removed. Lord Cosenham, of course, might be expected to ponder Bay Peterkin's capture for a little longer, if only because he had once been waylaid by him, but in both cases it would be merely a passing interest. They must be spared the humiliation of knowing the truth.

Araminta found herself wondering whether she might not have been better advised to have fallen in with Lord Cosenham's suggestion of first giving him his heir and then setting up her own establishment where she might continue her liaison with Jack Ranton, should that gentleman have been prepared to wait. She had lost that chance—thrown it away in some ill-conceived scheme which was not in essence much different from the activities of the murderer downstairs, though it had seemed so to Araminta. Now she had lost even the chance Lord Cosenham had offered her. She hadn't even seen Jack

Ranton again and might very well not do so. Everything had been to no avail, and if Jack was in France when the broadsheets were published, or returned after she had been hanged—well, there were a lot of other things she would regret, too, and high on the list would be her failure to compromise her honour as a married woman.

There was an additional advantage in having been moved to a cell on her own, which only struck her after she had eaten the bread and cheese and drunk some of the ale. There was no one to stop her curling up on the narrow bed and making up for the sleep lost the previous night.

Only when he was travelling did Lord Cosenham leave his room before midday and, though the sometimes excessively early start might surprise some of the newer members of his entourage, it never caught Cerney unawares. Usually, of course, he had explicit instructions as to when the Marquess wished to be called, but even when His Lordship woke unexpectedly early he would find his manservant ready.

On this occasion, breakfast was ready in the private parlour in time for His Lordship's unhurried descent from his room even though Cerney's services had been required from the moment his master opened his eyes to the moment he left the bed-chamber. Lord Cosenham never remarked upon his man's powers of organisation, but he recognised them, and the value he placed upon them was reflected in the not inconsiderable salary he paid him. At the back of the sideboard were chafing dishes keeping hot such delicacies as devilled kidneys, creamed eggs and the new favourite, kedgeree, while in front of them were the cold meats waiting on the bone: ham, sirloin and a fat capon, together with a game pie, should something more filling be required. Breakfast was a meal which most men preferred to eat in silence, but

Cerney had no compunction about initiating conversation as he served his master.

'I took the liberty of making a few more enquiries about the capture of Bay Peterkin, my lord,' he said, putting a plate of kidneys, eggs and ham in front of his employer.

'Was it productive?' Lord Cosenham asked.

'Extremely, my lord. It appears the intended victim was old Lady Morenish.'

Lord Cosenham frowned. 'I know the name, and I've almost certainly met her, but I can hardly claim an acquaintance.'

'No, my lord. It seems she is a friend—a very dear friend of the Dowager Lady Pembroke and, like you, was on her way to Wilton.'

'Was she, by God? How very convenient! I don't suppose she broke her journey here, by any happy chance?'

'No, my lord. She always stays at the Black Swan.'

'Would it be too much to ask whether your information extends to knowing what time she intends to resume her journey?'

'Not at all, my lord. I naturally considered it my duty to enquire. Her maid has instructions to call her at ten and the carriage is bespoke for noon.'

'Leaving it late,' Lord Cosenham remarked.

'I understand Her Ladyship will be staying tonight with friends and does not intend to reach Wilton until tomorrow.'

'Good. Cerney, when I have eaten I shall require writing materials to be set out for me. I shall also require a messenger to carry a letter to Wilton; and I think eleven o'clock might be an appropriate hour at which to call upon Lady Morenish.'

'Yes, my lord.'

There was in fact an additional letter which Cerney undertook to deliver himself to the governor of the Bridewell, together with a purse containing five guineas 'on account', an arrangement which seemed to suit the governor very well.

Lady Morenish, on the other hand, was not disposed to be pleased to receive a visitor, and her dislike of fops and popinjays did not induce her to take a kindlier view of this one.

'Droxford's son, aren't you? Hmm. Such a sensible man, too. You must be a a great trial to him.'

The Marquess seemed unmoved, but that might be simply because the fashionable heavy maquillage gave nothing away. 'I think not, Lady Morenish. Our paths seldom cross.'

'So I imagine,' she said drily. 'I shall be very surprised if you and I have much in common, either, so to what do I owe this visit?'

'I understand you're on your way to Wilton.'

'I am.' She paused and stared at him before going on in tones from which she made no attempt to remove the foreboding. 'Do I take it you are to be a fellow guest?'

'That was the case, but I've just dispatched a note to Wilton expressing my regrets and crying off.'

She looked startled. 'Not on my account, I trust. You may not be precisely my cup of tea, but I'm perfectly capable of being civil for a few days.'

'The thought never entered my head,' Lord Cosenham said with perfect truth. 'It is more closely connected with the unfortunate incident that befell you yesterday.'

'"Unfortunate incident"? I'll have you know, young man, that I came within an inch of being shot. Why, I heard the ball whistle past my ear. I call that rather more than an "unfortunate incident"!'

The Marquess decided to trim his sails to the prevailing wind. 'Your distress is not to be wondered at—

or your anger,' he added since he suspected that anger probably predominated now that the miscreant was behind bars. 'This whole matter is most embarrassing, especially between two people who claim mutual friendship with the Herberts.'

She looked at him more sharply. 'Embarrassing? How so? If you weren't standing here before me, I'd wonder if you didn't mean it was you playing some stupid prank.'

'No, Lady Morenish. Pranks of that nature are not my style.'

She snorted. 'It is difficult to imagine, I agree. Where lies the embarrassment?'

Lord Cosenham shifted uneasily on his feet and this, together with a noticeable hesitation before answering, did more than words to convince Lady Morenish that embarrassment was uppermost in his mind. She was conscious of an almost malicious pleasure that so apparently self-contained a creature as this indolent, over-dressed, superficial nincompoop found himself at a disadvantage, but she disguised her considerable curiosity as to its cause and awaited his explanation with an outward show of comparative indifference.

'Were you acquainted with the late Peter Sourton—of Hinton Ampner?' he began.

'No. Would you have expected me to be?'

'Probably not. A very keen huntsman. We were at Oxford together—the only thing we had in common, as a matter of fact, so why he should have made me his son's guardian I have never been quite sure.'

'One hesitates to be crude or to attribute ignoble motives to one's fellows, but the Fencott fortune might have had something to do with it,' Lady Morenish remarked.

'You may well be right, though I feel bound to point out that when he was killed in a hunting accident he left the boy quite well provided for. At all events, I am his guardian and I feel bound to say to you, Lady Morenish, within the privacy of these four walls, that I am not the ideal choice for a boy's guardian.'

Lady Morenish permitted herself a small smile. 'I mean no disrespect, Marquess, when I say that that thought had crossed my own mind.'

'I'm afraid the boy has been left very much to his own devices, supervised only by tutors. Excellent men and highly qualified, but not altogether sympathetic to the urges of youth.'

'They rarely are,' Lady Morenish conceded.

'The boy—named after his father, by the way—has gone sadly astray, and I recently learnt had considered it quite a lark to set himself up as a highwayman under the somewhat improbable pseudonym of Bay Peterkin. In short, Lady Morenish, you were waylaid yesterday by my ward.'

There was sympathy in neither the glint in Lady Morenish's eye nor her voice. 'Then your ward will get his just deserts. You know, of course, that he is in prison here in Winchester?'

'I do, indeed—and I also know he will hang unless you are generous enough to withdraw your complaint against him.'

'Withdraw! Why should I do any such thing? He's a menace to society. Besides, he tried to kill me.'

'I appreciate your feelings and, frankly, if that were all there was to it, he might hang and be welcome: the boy's a confounded liability. I have to confess to entirely selfish motives for this appeal.' He paused.

'You intrigue me, Marquess.'

'His father left things decidedly awkwardly,' Lord Cosenham continued. 'In the event of young Peter's premature death—by which his father meant his death before he comes of age and can make his own will—I inherit everything. If he dies, my own motives will be highly suspect.'

'But you are so rich that, no matter how well provided for the boy was, it can only be a drop in the ocean compared with the Fencott fortune.'

'I shouldn't even notice the difference,' Lord Cosenham agreed. 'The trouble is, Society as a whole will view it differently and I will be held to have had some hand in his death. I have no wish to suffer such opprobrium.'

'It would be most uncomfortable, but how on earth could anyone believe you had a hand in his death?'

'Perhaps I shall be held to have encouraged him in his wild ways, hoping he would be shot. I have the reputation of being a gambler. It's a small step in many people's eyes to having gambled away most of my fortune and therefore needing my ward's.'

Lady Morenish knew that these assumptions were all too probable. 'But if I withdraw my complaint, what guarantee do I have that young Sourton won't resume his activities?'

'An absolute guarantee can't be given, I suppose, but I undertake to ship him off to my maternal relatives in France where I fancy he will find things sufficiently different to remove the urge to add excitement to his life.'

'He is welcome to waylay as many Frenchmen as he chooses,' Lady Morenish remarked. Unlike her visitor, she had no French relatives and would have strongly opposed any plan by a member of her family to acquire some. 'I should, however, feel easier in my mind if I could be sure he would remain abroad for some considerable time.'

Lord Cosenham bowed his concurrence. 'He will stay until he attains his majority. Three years should be enough to drum some sense into him. I shall inform him that if he should return before then your charges will be preferred again. That should be enough; I imagine he is well and truly scared by now.'

'Can that be done?' Lady Morenish asked.

'I haven't the slightest idea,' Lord Cosenham admitted. 'However, if neither you nor I know, young Peter certainly won't.'

Lady Morenish still looked doubtful. 'The circumstances are really extremely odd,' she said.

'Unique, I imagine,' Lord Cosenham said blandly, 'but there are times when one just has to rally round, don't you think? I don't suppose the Herberts would be overjoyed to have their name dragged through the courts when it comes out that it was to their house you were travelling, and my father will be most displeased.'

Both statements were undoubtedly true, and Lady Morenish valued her friendship with those who had power to wield should they choose to do so. She moved to the little writing-table and wrote a short and formal note to the governor of the Bridewell. When she had shaken the sand from it, she folded it and handed it to her visitor.

'This should be sufficient,' she said. 'I hope I have no reason to regret this.'

'I have every confidence that Bay Peterkin will vanish from the face of the earth,' the Marquess assured her, and took his leave.

CHAPTER ELEVEN

THE governor read and then re-read Lady Morenish's note. It was unambiguous. She was withdrawing all complaints against the young man who had waylaid her chaise yesterday. It had been a most reprehensible prank and his family would no doubt deal with him most severely. Gaol had undoubtedly proved a most unpleasant experience, but she had no desire to see the matter taken further and had therefore asked the Marquess of Cosenham to take the boy into his own custody. The Marquess was to be regarded as her representative in this matter.

The governor looked at the Marquess and was not enamoured of what he saw. An idle, dissipated fop with a painted face and affected manners. Not a man into whose custody he would want to see his own son released.

'You're aware of the contents of this note, my lord?' he asked.

Lord Cosenham raised one supercilious eyebrow. 'Naturally.'

The governor found his visitor's drawl irritating. 'Highway robbery's a serious business.'

'So I believe.' The Marquess sounded merely bored.

'This Bay Peterkin's held up other coaches. Others may be less keen to see the charges dropped.'

'I was not aware the young man had been identified as Bay Peterkin,' Lord Cosenham pointed out.

'The men who brought him in said he was. They said he had his dog with him.'

'Did that dog accompany them to the Bridewell?'

'No,' the governor admitted grudgingly. 'They said it ran off into the woods.'

Lord Cosenham sighed. 'How very convenient. They catch some young lad barely out of the schoolroom and then decide—presumably to enhance their own reputations—that it must be the dastardly Bay Peterkin. And you were taken in by it.'

The governor flushed. Lord Cosenham had a point: it had crossed his mind when he assigned the prisoner to the common cell that he was younger than the general run of bridle-culls, and certainly better spoken, but he did not appreciate disparaging remarks when he had only been doing his duty. 'Lady Morenish refers to his family,' he said. 'Would that be you, by any chance?'

'I do have the misfortune to be the boy's guardian,' Lord Cosenham admitted. 'He is something of a handful, but I imagine he will be able to see sense after this unpleasant experience. It was unpleasant, I hope?'

'I've never heard anyone claim to enjoy gaol,' the governor told him. 'Perhaps you'd have done better not to have him moved to a single cell this morning.'

'That may have been a mistake.' Lord Cosenham felt the time had come to concede a point. The governor needed to be left with some self-esteem. 'How is he?'

'Not happy. I gather the turnkey assumed he had been moved so that the gaol might reap the rewards of selling a view of him, and told him so.'

Lord Cosenham allowed himself a very slight smile, but nothing large enough to crack the carefully applied powder. 'He wouldn't like that at all.' He felt in his coat pocket and brought forth a heavy pouch. 'The gaol has been put to some inconvenience in this matter,' he said. 'This should serve to recompense you and your staff for the trouble that has been caused. I can only thank you for your co-operation.'

The governor picked up the pouch. It really was very heavy. 'Most generous of you, my lord,' he said, warmth

in his voice for the first time. 'I'll have the boy brought
up.'

Lord Cosenham raised one hand in a dramatic,
checking gesture. 'No. I should prefer to be taken to
him. The shock will be the greater.'

The turnkey was summoned and told to take His
Lordship to the new prisoner. The governor showed every
sign of wishing to accompany him, but Lord Cosenham
stayed him. 'Most kind,' he said, 'but really no need. I
shall be perfectly safe and the turnkey will be outside
should I have need of him.'

There was something in His Lordship's languid tone,
a hint of steel under the silk, that made the governor
disinclined to argue despite his curiosity to witness the
encounter.

He recognised the inevitable when he saw it, and
bowed. 'Very well, my lord.'

The Marquess followed the turnkey.

When Araminta heard the key turn in the lock, she sat
up on the narrow bed where she had been dozing and
swung her legs over the side. She had no idea how much
time had passed since she had been transferred to this
room, but she had long since finished the bread, cheese
and ale and hoped the sound heralded another meal.
When Lord Cosenham entered, pressing a perfumed
handkerchief to his nostrils, she sprang to her feet. She
very nearly betrayed herself by recognising him, and remembered in the split second before doing so that she
was Bay Peterkin, and the Marquess of Cosenham a
stranger—or, at most, a half-remembered victim.

'Who are you?' she asked.

The Marquess waited pointedly until the door was
closed, aware none the less that they could still be overheard through the spy-hole.

'I think you remember me very well,' he said.

Araminta was aware of a rising feeling of panic. Had he heard that the person who had waylaid him had been taken? Had he come to add his evidence to that of the old lady? It was small consolation to reflect that one could only be hanged once, but there was no denying that the appearance of a second victim who could identify her as Bay Peterkin would eliminate any slight chance of acquittal she might have had. There was probably nothing she could do about that now—the very fact that he was here at all removed that hope. There still remained the matter of her true identity. That must remain hidden at all costs. She turned towards the hearth so that her back was to him and leant against the stone, kicking the embers with her booted foot.

'I don't recall having seen you before—and I don't fancy you would be easily forgotten,' she said.

'Precisely.'

How well she remembered that softly sibilant voice. Araminta could not quite repress a shudder. She had no choice but to brazen it out. 'Enlighten me,' she said.

'Let me see, now. Where shall we begin? Cassington Hall, perhaps? Yes, that will do very nicely. The parterre at Cassington Hall. We conversed there, I recall.'

She spun round and stared at him. 'You knew!' she exclaimed. 'How long have you known?'

He took her hand in his and passed his thumb over her ring before letting it drop again. 'Since early on in your career, it would appear.'

'You didn't mention it when I came to see you recently.' Her tone was defiant, but Lord Cosenham was determined that the ears outside the door should carry back to the governor only what he intended them to. He placed his forefinger significantly over his lips and glanced towards the door before speaking.

'I was intrigued to see how far you would take it. You may count yourself fortunate that Lady Morenish and I are sufficiently of a mind for her to have been willing, once she knew your identity, to withdraw her accusations.'

'You told her?'

'I had very little choice. She had been unaware that I had a ward but agreed that, providing you were packed off to France where you could do no more harm—or at least, only to Frenchmen, which I suspect she regards as less heinous—it would be in everyone's best interest to refuse to press the matter. You will therefore accompany me from here.'

'I'm not at all sure I want to,' Araminta said.

'Come, now, dear boy. You have been remarkably foolish, to say nothing of careless. You cannot surely expect me to believe that you *want* to remain here? Not that it will be possible—Lady Morenish has withdrawn her charge in writing.'

'Do we...I...go to France?' Araminta asked. Her mind was working very quickly. Jack had gone to France. At least, that was where she assumed he had gone. Anyone who ran wine, brandy, lace or silk would hardly go elsewhere. If her husband was determined to send her there, it should surely not be beyond the bounds of possibility to find him. Much would depend upon whether Lord Cosenham insisted on accompanying her. Very likely he would come no further than the ship and, once that had set sail, return to London. If, however, he came with her, it would be much more difficult to get away.

'I have given Lady Morenish an undertaking that Peter Sourton will go to France and remain there until he comes of age. Whether he goes alone or is escorted by his guardian is a matter about which I have an open mind. We can discuss it here, if you wish, but I must confess I should prefer more salubrious surroundings.'

Araminta picked up the cloak she had been using as a blanket and crammed her hat on to her head before following him out of the cell.

The post-chaise waiting outside, luggage strapped to it in anticipation came as no surprise. The sight of Halcyon tied on behind and Grendel's lugubrious, long-eared face peering through the window took her completely aback.'

'How did you——?' she began.

'You left them where you had been taken. I recognised them. It seemed a pity to leave them there for anyone who came along.'

Araminta climbed into the chaise and sank thankfully into the comfort of the squabs. Lord Cosenham climbed in beside her and, as soon as the step was up and the door closed, the postilion urged his horses forward.

'What happened to your baggage-train, your cook and the armed guards?' Araminta asked suspiciously, having ascertained as they drove out of the city that no other vehicles joined them.

'The baggage-coach went ahead of me to Wilton and is by now on its way back. One does not take one's cook to an establishment such as Wilton; I chose to travel without guards and my manservant has gone on ahead this morning. Does that satisfy you?'

Araminta made no answer. It all seemed remarkably pat.

'Why did you decide not to take guards?' she asked after she had digested his first explanation.

'I had a strong suspicion I might be waylaid.'

'Hardly an argument for leaving them behind,' she commented.

He leant back against the squabs and closed his eyes. When he spoke, it was in the patient voice with which one answers a child.

'It all depends upon whether one knows the identity of one's probable assailant.'

Araminta chuckled. 'Your confidence could have misfired rather badly had your guess proved wrong,' she said.

'Happily, it did not.'

They continued in silence for several miles. Lord Cosenham seemed in no hurry to discuss the details of her visit to France and Araminta was disinclined to introduce it. She did not seem to be very successful at directing any conversation with her husband along the lines she wished. Instead she turned over in her mind everything that had passed between them since he entered her cell.

'You can't possibly have recognised Halcyon!' she said suddenly.

'I beg your pardon?' The silence had lasted a long time. Its interruption startled him.

'You can't possibly have recognised Halcyon,' she repeated.

He raised one eyebrow. 'Indeed? Why not? You were riding him when you stopped me on the Portsmouth road, weren't you?'

His peculiarly soft voice was as unpleasant as ever, but Araminta thought she detected the merest smidgeon of doubt behind it.

'Yes, I was, but all his white markings had been disguised,' she told him.

He laughed softly, completely at ease once more. If the doubt had been there, she had somehow erased it. 'Your father maintained that you are a horsewoman of some skill. That being the case, you surely do not rely upon markings to identify an animal? Besides, he and the hound were together, and how else might an animal of that quality have found its way, saddled and bridled, into the woods? Of course it had to be yours. One might not have been so sure had the dog not been there, I suppose.'

The silence was resumed and Araminta had the disconcerting feeling that something that had been within her grasp had evaded her at the last moment. It was not a comfortable feeling.

They were travelling through countryside entirely unfamiliar to Araminta, and, when they stopped to change horses and give instructions for the return of the Marquess's pair, she neither knew nor very much cared where they were, except that she assumed it must be on the road to either Portsmouth or Southampton. She was more concerned that she felt ravenous.

'May we eat, my lord?' she asked.

He looked surprised. 'Didn't you break your fast in the Bridewell? They were told to send you food.'

'Yes, they did—bread and cheese and some ale, but there wasn't a great deal and I was exceedingly hungry, not having eaten at all the day before.'

'Then let that be a lesson to you to pursue a more conventional life with regular meals. You may eat when we stop for the night.'

Araminta opened her mouth to argue with him, but thought better of it and closed it again. Nothing would be achieved by antagonising him.

They were still travelling when dusk fell. By this time they had long since left the turnpike roads and were making their rough, uneven way over the ruts and through the mud of narrow lanes. From time to time they passed through villages, several of them with perfectly respectable-looking inns where she hoped they might stop, but they never did. When they had first turned off the turnpike, she had assumed it was a short cut to their destination, but they had never returned to the better road and she knew that the usual route to either great port could not possibly be along such narrow, inconvenient lanes.

'Are we never going to stop?' she asked at last.

'A singularly foolish question,' he observed. 'The condition of the horses would ultimately make it obligatory, I imagine.'

'I'm surprised they haven't dropped in their traces already,' Araminta snapped.

'An unfamiliar road—and in the dark, too—always seems longer than it is,' he told her, with a patronising kindness in his voice for which Araminta could cheerfully have strangled him. She refused to give him the satisfaction of further evasive answers by not asking the questions in the first place, and instead leant against the corner of the chaise and closed her eyes. The road was far too uneven to allow any form of sleep, however light, but she kept them resolutely shut in order to convey the impression that it was nothing to her if her husband chose to be childish about their destination.

She was instantly aware when the surface of the lane improved and when they turned sharply to the right and she felt the wheels crunching on the smooth gravelled surface of a well-kept drive. She sat up and peered through the window, but could make out nothing except the dark shapes of elms against the sky and a solid lump of thicker black that might have been a house.

The chaise swung out to the left and then round to the right and drew up before an imposing double door. No sooner had the hoofs ceased to clatter than the doors were thrown open and suddenly the blackly inhospitable bulk of the shuttered house was transformed as the candle-light streamed out.

A liveried footman hurried down the short flight of steps to open the carriage door and assist first Araminta and then her husband to alight. A discreetly clothed butler greeted them at the door.

'Welcome to Copenore, my lady,' he said.

Araminta was completely taken aback. She would not have been surprised had they gone straight to the dockside, nor if this had proved to be an inn, but she was totally unprepared for being taken to her husband's country estate. Even more unnerving was the fact that the household was apparently expecting her.

'Thank you,' she said. The reply was automatic, even surprise not being sufficient to destroy the politeness that had been drummed into her since childhood.

As she entered the hall she was appalled to see that the entire household was assembled to greet their new mistress, and all had politely schooled their faces to hide their reactions to a mistress who came home dressed as a man. She detected a nudge and a smothered snigger from two of the most junior members of the household at the very bottom of the line and guessed it was probably justified: a day in the saddle, an ignominious capture and a night in gaol followed by over half a day's drive was not conducive to an immaculate appearance in any garb. She threw a look of appeal over her shoulder at Lord Cosenham, who murmured something to the butler and immediately that personage clapped his hands once and waved the waiting servants back to the kitchen regions.

'Supper is ready as soon as you are, my lady,' he said when the hall was once again empty. 'Do you wish to eat immediately, or...?'

Araminta hesitated. She was famished, but loathed the idea of sitting down to eat in her very considerable dirt. On the other hand, a bath took time and she had no other clothes.

As if sensing what was in her mind, the Marquess said, 'The trunks for your wedding-journey were brought here and have been unpacked these many months.'

'Then a bath would be most welcome,' Araminta told the butler. 'We will eat in an hour.'

'Very well, my lady. If you will follow me.'

The instructions must already have been given to the kitchen before Araminta made her decision because, within minutes of being shown into her room, a succession of maids carrying steaming copper jugs was filling the small bath in front of the fire.

Her maid's delight in seeing her mistress again was due in part to relief that she was unharmed and in part to pleasure in having a well-defined role once more, and only Lady Cosenham's obvious fatigue prevented her plying her mistress with questions which might well be impertinent but were also entirely natural.

Araminta's sheer joy at feeling clean again was only slightly marred by the fact that she did not have time to wash her hair, but a really stiff brushing worked wonders and, when she finally looked at herself in the glass before joining her husband in the dining-saloon, she heaved a sigh of satisfaction. She was simply but elegantly attired in an undress-gown of soft, sea-green satin, fastened beneath the bosom with a single button and worn with matching slippers. Beneath the gown the lace of a far from simple shift emerged at elbow, neck and hem, carefully arranged to fall in profuse folds. The maid had little time to dress her lady's hair but, on the suggestion of her mistress, succeeded in combing it backwards and upwards, twisting the ends into a soft knot which she pinned in place. There was a jewel-box, the contents of which were quite new to Araminta, and she assumed they must be some of the Fencott jewels, to which she felt she had no claim. She shook her head when the maid unlocked this and held it for her inspection and selection.

'I think not,' she said and then, seeing the girl's disappointed face, 'A formal occasion would be another matter. I've no dislike of jewels, but they must suit the mood. This will be enough,' and she held up her hand with the mourning-ring on her third finger.

She was not surprised that the Marquess should be in the dining-saloon before her, but she was a little disconcerted that he appeared not to regard the meal as informal. Indeed, he looked more like a man who was dining with his monarch than supping with his wife after a long and eventful day.

'My apologies, my lord,' she said, indicating her undress-gown and staring at his own silver-embroidered rich blue velvet. 'I had no idea...'

He minced forward on absurdly high heels and bowed with unnecessary flourish. 'You look charmingly, my dear,' he said.

Araminta was aware of a surge of revulsion. There were occasions when he spoke like a sensible man and one almost forgot the affectations with which his remarks were uttered. And then he reverted to being the undiluted fop, an individual Araminta found it difficult to tolerate. In so far as she had given the matter any thought at all, she had assumed that at least in the privacy of his own home he might let the mask—the very literal mask—slip. It began to seem as if his affectations had become so much a part of his personality that the mask had become the man.

She supposed they had come here because Copenore was near the coast, so perhaps she was going to be dispatched to France on the Marquess's own vessel which might well be within easy reach, and certainly they could expect a degree of comfort here that no inn could provide. Nevertheless, Araminta was not at all happy that it was to Copenore she had been brought, particularly when she recalled the conversation they had had in London. She smiled to herself. If Lord Cosenham thought the glories of Copenore would make her change her mind, he was very much mistaken. She had no feelings one way or another about the house. Its master was another matter altogether and, the more she was subjected to her husband's posturing, the more appealing became the memory of Jack Ranton.

When they had been served, Lord Cosenham waved a dismissing hand at his household. 'Leave us. We shall serve ourselves. There's no need to wait up; I dare say we shall sit over our supper for some time. I shall need Cerney when I retire, but no one else.' He turned to

Araminta. 'And you, my dear? Will you need your maid?'

'No, not at all,' Araminta assured him. 'I'm perfectly accustomed to putting myself to bed.'

'Just Cerney, then,' Lord Cosenham repeated. 'Goodnight.'

The butler bowed and spoke for everyone else. 'Goodnight, my lord, my lady.'

Eating occupied Araminta's entire concern for some little while after the servants had withdrawn, and she was watched by Lord Cosenham who, despite the fact that he, too, had eaten nothing since breakfast, merely picked fastidiously at a few select morsels. Only when his wife hesitated between one dish and another did he speak.

'I take it your hunger is somewhat abated,' he said politely.

'The edge is blunted, certainly. I'm sorry if it should be a disappointment to you, my lord, but I've never been one to pick at my food.'

'Not at all. Tell me, did you eat with such gusto during your two Seasons?'

Araminta chuckled and looked shamefaced. 'I had no need to. Mama made sure I had something to eat before we left home. Thus I was able to sustain the illusion of being a delicately nurtured gentlewoman.'

'So you're no stranger to dissemblance.'

Araminta flushed, but refused to rise to the lure. Instead she helped herself to some more beef. 'If this beast was raised on Copenore, your stockman deserves credit,' she commented.

'We endeavour to please. I will convey your commendation.'

They continued to eat in silence for some while and this time it was Araminta who spoke. The uncertainty about her future and, more particularly, her husband's failure to refer to it, was making her uneasy.

'When do I go to France, my lord?'

He appeared to give the question careful consideration. 'It's difficult to decide when would be most fitting. You might prefer to wait until after the birth of your first child. On the other hand, if that should prove to be a son, you may well have other plans.'

Araminta stared at him, her fork halfway to her open mouth. 'But you told Lady Morenish I should be packed off there immediately!'

'Not quite. I promised her Peter Sourton, my ward, would be so disposed of. You are neither Peter Sourton nor my ward, except in the strictly legal sense that every wife is the ward of her husband. Peter Sourton has vanished and all Lady Morenish will ever know is that she never encounters him again. She will be perfectly satisfied with that.'

Araminta could feel her heart beating uncomfortably as she saw yet another chance of being reunited with Jack recede. 'Then what happens to me? You will hardly risk letting Lady Morenish recognise me. Am I to be imprisoned here until I'm safely delivered of your heir?' she concluded bitterly.

'Don't be absurd. Lady Morenish will never recognise the young blackguard who shot at her in the elegant Marchioness of Cosenham.'

'Just so long as the elegant Marchioness doesn't have Grendel at her heels.'

He raised one amused eyebrow. 'You will hardly take Grendel to a Drawing-Room,' he observed drily. 'I can think of no other place where you two ladies are likely to meet. You are perhaps not aware that Her Ladyship has already seen Grendel with me and has accepted that he belongs to my reprobate ward.'

'You must have presented an incongruous picture,' Araminta said acidly. Jack Ranton was getting further and further out of reach.

'Fortunately, my appearance in the eyes of others has never been paramount in my mind.'

'Fortunately, indeed,' Araminta murmured, but her husband gave no sign of having heard, a circumstance which deprived her of a certain amount of satisfaction.

Neither of them spoke again until they had finished eating, and then Lord Cosenham poured them both some cognac.

'I hope you won't say you prefer tea,' he commented. 'This is particularly fine.'

Araminta sipped it politely. It tasted like liquid satin. 'Has it paid duty at any port?' she asked.

He looked faintly surprised. 'I doubt it very much. Why do you ask?'

'I just wondered,' she said. The truth was, she didn't really know what had prompted the question, and she could hardly voice her suspicion that it was probably because her mind had been running so much on Jack Ranton that it had seemed entirely natural.

One of the effects of the cognac, when it combined with the wine that had accompanied the meal, was to encourage Araminta to say what was in her mind more bluntly than was diplomatic.

'Will you release me, my lord?'

'Release you?' He seemed bemused, as if she meant the word physically rather than legally.

'From this marriage.'

'No.'

'If I had not mistaken the carriage, your death might by now have freed me.'

'The possibility I admit. The probability is not great. Your aim doesn't appear to have been particularly accurate.'

'I might try again.'

'I very much doubt it. That would suggest a degree of cold-blooded ruthlessness I don't believe you possess.'

He was right, of course, sickening though it might be to have to admit it. She tried another tack. 'You know I don't love you,' she said.

'I seem to recall your mentioning something of the sort.'

'You know, too, it's more than that,' she went on, a hint of desperation in her voice. 'I love someone else. Will your pride let you live with that knowledge?'

'A certain Jack Ranton, I believe.' He appeared to give it his consideration. 'Yes, I think my pride will survive that blow.'

Araminta tried frantically to recall with some degree of accuracy the conversation they had had in London. Had she mentioned Jack's name? Surely not? Yet how else could he have known it?

'I don't think his precise identity need trouble you,' she said with what she hoped was dignity.

'On the contrary, my dear, it's probably the most important single aspect of this whole sorry business.' He got to his feet. 'May I suggest that your ladyship retires to bed and we resume this marriage where we left off? With the difference that I shall not, on this occasion, keep you waiting for so long that you are able to disappear.'

Araminta stared at him in dismay. 'Do we have to?' she said despairingly.

'It is customary for a wife to create at least the illusion that she welcomes her husband's presence,' he pointed out.

'You know perfectly well that I don't. Would you prefer me to dissemble?'

'Perhaps not. I prefer to think that I shall ultimately be able to change your mind.'

'I doubt it very much,' she retorted, rising from her chair and declining his proffered arm.

She hesitated briefly at the foot of the curving stone staircase and then, impelled by a discreet hand in the small of her back, ascended. Lord Cosenham opened the door of her room and gestured for her to enter. A fire blazed in the grate and the light of candles beside the bed and in wall-sconces combined to make the room appear both cosy and welcoming, an aspect she had been too tired before to appreciate.

Araminta hesitated again on the threshold and threw her husband one last, imploring glance.

'Must I?' she said.

'You must—and, to save you the bother of looking, I feel bound to point out that there is no fig-tree outside the window and both the windows and the shutters are, in any case, securely locked.'

Her glance dropped instinctively to the door-handle. She was hardly aware it had done so, but Lord Cosenham saw it.

'This, too, will be locked, I'm afraid. I do apologise for such lack of trust, but I'm loath to be made a fool of twice in succession. I'm sure you understand.'

Araminta did, all too well. 'Perhaps you should make assurance doubly sure by joining me now and not taking the risk of leaving me on my own.'

He sighed. 'If only I could interpret that as an invitation! I suspect it was more in the nature of a challenge, and one I sadly must let lie. Certain...adjustments must be made,' and here he indicated his apparel with the spiral gesture of a Turkish greeting.

Araminta gave a grudging laugh. 'Not the work of five minutes, I imagine,' she said. She looked at him speculatively. 'You know, it hadn't occurred to me before, but I think it entirely possible that I shan't recognise you without your wig and...' Her voice tapered off. There was a limit to the rudeness to which one could subject even a husband one loathed.

'And my face?' he finished for her. 'I'm sure you're right, my dear. We must hope the truth will not prove too unpalatable a taste for you.'

He ushered her in and closed the door behind her. Any faint hope Araminta might have had that he did not really intend to lock his wife in was dashed when she heard the key turn smoothly in the lock. A very brief scrutiny was sufficient to tell her that the shutters were also locked and, although she could probably force them open with the poker, there was no reason to assume Lord Cosenham had lied about there being a suitable tree outside. He had not, she reflected, lied to her about anything, so far as she could tell.

She went over to the hearth and threw a piece of wood on to the fire, not because it needed it but because it was something to do. Then she sank down in the armchair beside it.

Everything she had done was to no avail. She might as well have stayed with him in London—that, at least, would have brought the time when she could be free to go to Jack a few days nearer. Better still would have been not to have run away in the first place. Had she not done so, she would never have met Jack Ranton and—who knew?—might even have come to terms with life as the Marchioness of Cosenham.

Jack Ranton. Her heart cried out for Jack Ranton. With what very different feelings would she be sitting here if it were he whom she was expecting. How could she go to him after tonight? Would he understand that she had had no choice? Would any man really believe that? Was it even true?

Of course it was true, she told herself. Short of taking the carving-knife to her husband—or the poker, she added, catching sight of it in the grate—how could she evade what was, after all, her legal duty? You were perfectly willing to shoot him, a little voice whispered in her ear. What's so different about the poker? It seemed very different, somehow, and not only because there would be no question as to who would have battered him to death, in the unlikely event of his standing still and letting her do so. Still, perhaps the fact that she was prepared to go to such lengths would convince him of the strength of her feelings? It seemed unlikely: he had been undeterred by her readiness to shoot him.

Her thoughts turned back to Jack. What a fool she had been! Every woman wanted the man she loved to be the first, and she had let this stupid thing called honour—a virtue that men held dear and women merely accepted because it mattered so much to their men— stand in the way of the fulfilment she craved. Perhaps the thought of her husband would have become more tolerable had she given herself to Jack, though she suspected that the very reverse might be true. What she would have had was a weapon against her husband. That was something she had overlooked. She doubted very much whether the Fencott pride could have swallowed her adultery with the consequent doubt it must cast on the legitimacy of any children she bore.

It was too late to alter that now. It would remain a piece of foolishness for which she would probably never forgive herself.

The sound of the key turning in the lock broke into her thoughts. Araminta tensed, her face rigid with apprehension. Then, since the door was not immediately opened, she bent down and picked up the poker. When the door opened, she was standing by the fire, the weapon hidden by the folds of her skirt.

The figure that entered was not the one she had been expecting. She gasped and her expression changed from apprehension, through astonishment to incredulous delight.

'Jack!' she cried, and the poker clattered unheeded on to the hearth-stone.

Then the delight was replaced by a disbelieving bewilderment. 'Jack?' she said uncertainly. There were too many unanswered questions here, too much for her mind to grapple with at once.

He stepped forward, his hands outstretched. 'You do well not to trust your own eyes,' he said softly, a smile in his voice.

Araminta went towards him then, and his outstretched hands clasped hers briefly and then released them, the better to envelop her in an embrace which left her breathless. They kissed with the long, deep thirst of parched travellers at a desert oasis, and only when that initial desire was slaked did Araminta bethink her of their circumstances.

She glanced beyond him at the door. 'We must be gone,' she whispered. 'It's madness to stay here. I don't know how you found me, but thank God you did! Now we must get as far away as we can in the few minutes that are all we can have left.' She stopped, puzzled. Jack had made no move to obey her exhortations.

'I've travelled far enough today,' he told her. 'This room will suit me to admiration.'

'But you don't understand, Jack, and there's no time for lengthy explanations. This is my...my husband's house and he will soon be here.'

'I know perfectly well whose house it is.' He held her a little away from him and looked down into her eyes, laughing. 'Oh, my beloved fool, have you still not realised?' He placed a finger under her chin and tilted her head up, and when he spoke his voice had become higher pitched, soft and sinisterly sibilant. 'I'm no more Jack Ranton than you are Jane Shore,' he said. 'Do you think you could change it to Justinian if I undertake to remember only Araminta?'

Araminta pulled back, uncertain. 'You deceived me,' she said.

'That would appear to have been a mutual offence,' he pointed out.

Her mind was racing now, trying to marshal events and images into chronological order. 'In the Bridewell you told me you had known who I was since the beginning of my career. I assumed you meant from the time I waylaid you. But there was that time in the yard of the Red Lion, the first time I met Jack Ranton. You must have recognised Jane Shore for who she really was then.'

'Yes.'

'Yet you said nothing? You did nothing? Did you tell my parents I was all right?'

'The first your parents will know about anything will be when they receive a letter from me tomorrow. Had I been at the Red Lion as the Marquess of Cosenham, doubtless I should have done or said something. As it was, the last thing I wanted was to have Lord Cosenham identified as a notorious smuggler and sometime highwayman. Besides, I had a more than passing curiosity to see what you were going to do next. It isn't very often that a bride flees on her wedding-night, you know. It did cross my mind to wonder what sort of life you preferred to the one I offered.'

'It wasn't the life I objected to,' Araminta told him with some of her old asperity. 'It was the posturing popinjay I had to share it with.'

He kissed her and there was silence in the room for several minutes. 'I should have given you some inkling that I went a little deeper than that,' he admitted. 'I knew it when we talked in the knot-garden, but I couldn't see how it was to be done. We were not then even betrothed, you recall. I vowed that my wedding-night would see an end to the idiot I've been playing—and an end to Jack Ranton's activities, too, though you'd not have been told about them. But I left it too late. By the time I'd plucked up my courage to be myself, you'd flown the coop. When I came across you by chance I decided to make you fall in love with me.'

'And am I supposed to believe that you had fallen in love with me when we met at Cassington Hall? Or perhaps you've been nursing a penchant for me since my first London Season?' Araminta asked sarcastically.

'Alas, I have to confess that I couldn't even remember having seen you in London. As to Cassington Hall, I formed the opinion that you were far too intelligent to be hoodwinked for long, and far more straightforward and honest than I deserved. I thought we might deal together very well. When you ran away, my self-esteem was damaged and I was, to put it mildly, piqued. Having found where you were, it was curiosity which made me keep track of your activities, but it was pique that determined me to make you fall in love with me.'

Araminta turned away, desperately anxious that he shouldn't see the tears welling in her eyes. 'Well,' she said stoutly, 'you were more successful than you planned. Not only did you make me fall in love with you, but you even made me believe the feeling was reciprocated.'

He put his hands gently on her shoulders and turned her round to kiss her wet eyelids. 'You only believed what was true,' he said softly. 'I realised when I was nursing you in the cellar that I had come to love you at least as much as I intended you to love me. But there was always your husband between us. I didn't know whether to rejoice or weep that you wouldn't betray a man you disliked and with whom there had never been any sort of physical bond.'

'There was a legal one, to say nothing of the vows I'd taken,' Araminta pointed out gently.

'Few women would have felt them binding in the circumstances.' He paused. 'Are you happier in your mind?' he asked.

'If by that you mean do I now believe you're Lord Cosenham—I mean Justinian—then, yes. I'm still bewildered beyond belief.'

'We have as long as needs be to come to terms with all the implications,' he told her. 'I think we should put the remaining night hours to better use, don't you?'

He undid the button that secured her gown and
Araminta shrugged herself out of it before reaching up
to pull his head down to her lips. This time the urgency
came from her and he responded with a savagery that
delighted her, and when his hands pushed her shift from
her shoulders and slid on down her body, caressing her
breasts, her hips, her thighs, she slipped her own hands
inside his shirt and held him closer to her, kneading the
muscles of his back with an urgency the rest of her body
could only echo.

There was a brief hiatus when he removed the pins
from her hair so that her long dark curls tumbled to her
shoulders and beyond, so that his fingers had to brush
them aside before his questing lips could explore the
treasures they concealed.

Araminta arched her body against his, seeking his
manhood, filled with a longing to feel it leap to a
crescendo within her. Her loins burned with the longing
and he eased her gently on to the rug before the fire and
took her without further preamble, knowing it was what
she wanted, what they both desired above all things.
Araminta cried out with the pain of his first entry, and
then gave herself to the ecstasy of such unimaginable
oneness and total fulfilment. And when the ecstasy
merged into contentment, they lay together, un-
speaking, finding no need for speech, in the glow and
warmth of a subsiding fire that echoed unconsciously
their own desires. For a while, at least, contentment replaced passion, and only when the last red glow in the
hearth had faded to grey did Justinian carry his bride
to the greater warmth of the waiting bed.

It was not long after that before they felt the need to
reaffirm their long-frustrated love, but now the urgency
was gone, replaced by a deeper, more satisfying con-
summation that led at last to a sleep of dreamless
quietude from which neither of them woke until the
morning was well advanced.

With the shutters closed, it still seemed like night, and not until a discreet tap on the door heralded the housemaid with a tray of chocolate and a self-conscious pretence that there was nothing new about today's routine did the full glory of a winter morning strike them through the soon unshuttered windows. Lord Cosenham's exclamation soon had the girl drawing the curtains so that a softer light fell on the bed, and she hesitated, looking at the remains of the fire.

'Shall I relight it, my lord?' she said hesitantly. In normal circumstances someone would already have crept quietly in so that a fresh blaze and a warm room would have greeted the sleepers.

'Leave it,' he said, keeping impatience out of his voice with an effort. 'See that the fire's lit in my room. That will do for now.'

She bobbed him a curtsy. 'Yes, my lord. That's already done, my lord. Hours ago,' she added helpfully.

'Then go. Cerney will fetch you when you're needed.'

From beside him Araminta giggled. 'Poor girl. She didn't know what do to for the best. You quite frightened her, I think. I'll have a word with her later.'

Justinian leant over and kissed her lightly on the forehead. 'I thought you were asleep. Had I known you were listening, she could have lit the fire and welcome. I didn't want you disturbed.'

Araminta sat up and poured the chocolate. She smiled at him. 'I don't think anything will have the power to disturb me ever again,' she said.

'I dare say you will find you're mistaken,' he said drily.

'How long do we stay at Copenore?' she asked. 'Shall we return to London or do you intend to go to France?'

He shrugged. 'Whichever you prefer.'

'My lord, I take leave to point out to you that neither Lord Cosenham nor Jack Ranton were in the habit of letting others make up their minds for them. I don't think you will be able to sustain so great a change of character for very long.'

He smiled. 'It so happens in this instance I really have no preference. My schooner is anchored in the creek south of the house. If you really want to go to France, I have only to send a message.'

'Is it empty?'

'Of cargo? Of course it is. It doesn't sit on my own doorstep laden with contraband.'

'Why did you ever take to that enterprise?' Araminta asked.

'Boredom, I suppose. The desire to add some excitement to a dull, predictable existence. It seems futile, looking back on it. My father will be glad to see me abandon it.'

'He knew?'

'He guessed. Something he once said. No fool, my father—and, of course, it did account for the son he knew differing so greatly from the one Society encountered.'

Araminta wrinkled her nose. 'Justinian, do you *have* to adopt your foppish ways in London? It's what people have become accustomed to, but if you can devise an explanation for dropping them—or simply become less exaggerated during each successive Season—I shall feel much easier. Quite apart from any other consideration, I shall be less inclined to burst out laughing.'

'I think perhaps the efforts of an eminently sensible wife will prove to have reformed me, so prepare yourself for the compliments on your handiwork when we eventually return to the capital.'

'Eventually?'

'You may recall everyone believes you to be increasing, hence your indispositions. I think you had better miscarry fairly quickly so that you can conceive in reality. Your continued absence is therefore explained and we shall be able to enjoy the peace of Copenore for as long as it suits us.'

Araminta flung her arms round her husband and kissed him. 'I knew it!' she exclaimed triumphantly.

'You knew what?'

'That you wouldn't leave the decision to me. No wife could transform you to that extent!'

The Marchioness's subsequent behaviour left her husband in no doubt that she was entirely satisfied with this state of affairs.

GREAT SPRING READING SELECTION

ADORING SLAVE
Rosemary Gibson

AFTER THE AFFAIR
Miranda Lee

CONDITIONAL SURRENDER
Wendy Prentice

STUDY IN LOVE
Sally St. John

Don't miss out on this unique presentation of four new exciting Mills & Boon authors, carefully selected for creating the very best romantic fiction. Packed with drama and passion, these novels are guaranteed to keep you turning the pages.

Published: April 1990   Price: £5.40

*Available from Boots, Martins,
John Menzies, W.H. Smith, Woolworths
and other paperback stockists.*

MASQUERADE

Experience the thrill of

2 Masquerade
Historical
Romances

Absolutely free!

Experience the passions of bygone days in
2 gripping Masquerade Romances from
Mills & Boon — absolutely **free**! Enjoy
these tales of tempestuous love from the
illustrious past. Then, if you wish, look
forward to a regular supply of
Masquerade, delivered to your door!

TURN THE PAGE FOR DETAILS OF 2 EXTRA FREE GIFTS, AND HOW TO APPLY.

An irresistible
offer from
MILLS & BOON

FREE GIFT

Here at Mills & Boon we would love you to become a regular reader of Masquerade. And to welcome you, we'd like you to have two books, an enchanting pair of glass oyster dishes and a special MYSTERY GIFT- FREE.

Then, every two months you could look forward to receiving 4 more brand-new Masquerade romances for just £1.75 each, delivered to your door, postage and packing free. Plus our free newsletter featuring competitions, author news, and special offers!

This invitation comes with no strings attached. You can cancel or suspend your subscription at any time, and still keep your free books and gifts.

A SURPRISE MYSTERY GIFT

POST TODAY!

It's so easy. Send no money now. Simply fill in the coupon below at once and post it to-
Reader Service, FREEPOST, PO Box 236, Croydon, Surrey CR9 9EL

✂ - - - - - - - - - - - - - - - - - - - *No stamp required* - - - - - - - - - - - - - - -

YES! Please rush me my **2 Free Masquerade Romances and 2 FREE gifts !** Please also reserve me a Reader Service Subscription. If I decide to subscribe, I can look forward to receiving 4 brand new Masquerade Romances every two months, for just **£7.00** delivered direct to my door. Post and packing is **free**, and there's a free Mills & Boon Newsletter. If I choose not to subscribe I shall write to you within 10 days - I can keep the books and gifts whatever I decide. I can cancel or suspend my subscription at any time. I am over18.

EP67M

NAME _____

ADDRESS _____

_____

_____ *POSTCODE* _____

SIGNATURE _____

The right is reserved to refuse an application and change the terms of this offer. You may be mailed with other offers as a result of this application. Offer expires Dec 31st 1989 and is limited to one per household. offer applies in the UK and Eire only. Overseas send for details

mps
MAILING
PREFERENCE
SERVICE